Ex Orbis

B. C. Giles

Copyright © 2025 B. C. Giles

All rights reserved. No part of this publication may be reproduced, distributed, or transmitted in any form or by any means, including photocopying, recording, or other electronic or mechanical methods, without the prior written permission of the publisher, except in the case of brief quotations embodied in critical reviews and certain other noncommercial uses permitted by copyright law.

ISBN: 979-8-9917342-1-9
Ebook ISBN: 979-8-9917342-0-2

Any references to historical events, real people, or real places are used fictitiously. Names, characters, and places are products of the author's imagination.

Front cover image courtesy of Freepik.

Published by Mad Ostrich Press, in the United States of America.

First Printing, 2025

For Jill and the kids – I love you to the stars and back

Ex Orbis

PROLOGUE

Jeff Guzman was unconscious within seconds of booster ignition.

James watched, bemused, as Jeff's head rolled back and forth with each jerk and jolt of the capsule. James knew he shouldn't be so indifferent - the decent thing would be to show some concern for the man - but he was too fucking terrified to think.

The person next to him tried to say something reassuring. At least, James thought so. He couldn't hear a damn thing. Nothing except the roar of rockets violently expelling their contents.

Before launch, James had repeatedly been told how "routine" all of this was, and how the crew were "practically bored of it all by now." It was bullshit of course. Nothing about this was routine. The most experienced astronaut had made, what, less than ten launches in their life? For Martian trips like this one the travel times were so long - on the order of years – that no more than a few handfuls of manned launches had even occurred since the first one, decades ago. So, no, nothing about this was routine. Each and every launch was an experiment. The total trip bordered on miraculous. "Let's strap a bunch of people into a metal capsule, put that capsule on top of thousands of pounds of rocket fuel, hurl it all into the sky, and see if we can hit a moving target a few million miles away!" That wasn't routine. It was insane.

Still, James appreciated the gesture.

As the rocket's acceleration increased, the G's intensified, and James began struggling for breath. He kept his abdomen and lower body as flexed and tight as he could, but it wasn't enough. He felt his head becoming lighter, vision dimming. Soon he would be like Jeff, head rolling, mouth slack, eyes rolled back into their sockets. As his thoughts slowed, he wondered if he would soil himself while unconscious. Had Jeff? James hoped he had. He didn't want to be the only one.

Then, silence. The rattle and roar of the craft stopped just as suddenly as it had begun. The pressure lifted from his chest, and James began to catch his breath. Color slowly seeped back into his vision. He looked around. Was that it? Was it done? Were they in space?

No.

The second stage kicked in, and James's head slammed into the back of his helmet. He blacked out.

NASA Personnel Manifest

Rockwell-Fredrickson Polar Research Station – Alpha

Caroline Johnston	*Pilot/Mission Support Specialist (GSS)*
Jermaine Reed	*Pilot/Mission Support Specialist (GSS)*
James Wilmot	*Site Lead (EPMS)*
Geoffrey Guzman	*Project Engineering Lead (EPMS)*
Kate Cooper	*Lab Assistant, Biological Sciences (EPMS)*
Miguel Valdez	*Science Support Technician (EPMS)*
Elias McCarthy	*Science Support Technician (EPMS)*
Lewis Rowe	*Chemist (USGS)*
Freddie Nelson	*Geologist (USGS)*
Cecilia Myers	*Biochemist (Hansen Memorial Exo-life Search)*
Saul Parker	*Microbiologist (Hansen Memorial Exo-life Search)*
Melvin Clarke	*Mathematician (Ares LHC)*
Louis Wheeler	*Particle Physicist (Ares LHC)*
Lindsey Brooks	*Particle Physicist (Ares LHC)*
Mark Jacobs	*Theoretical Physicist (Ares LHC)*
Jay Rice	*Astronomer (Tyson Deep Field Project)*
Isabella Rios	*Astrophysicist (Tyson Deep Field Project)*
Neil Nash	*Cosmologist (Tyson Deep Field Project)*
Ira Aguilar	*Sociologist/Author (Kapoor Art Grant)*
Charlie Gibson	*Artist (Kapoor Art Grant)*
Olive Warren	*Visual Artist (Kapoor Art Grant)*
Blaine Nelson	*Materiel/Logistics Specialist (SLI)*
Steven Reese	*Facility Engineer (SLI)*
Lynette Perez	*Heavy Equipment Mechanic (SLI)*
Jim Webster	*Heavy Equipment Mechanic (SLI)*
Lucas Gordon	*Machinist (SLI)*
Colin Massey	*Welder (SLI)*
Andre Flores	*Electrician (SLI)*
Dewey Hanson	*Power Plant Technician (SLI)*
Chris Marshall	*Power Plant Technician (SLI)*
Brad Austin	*Aerospace Propulsion Systems Specialist (GSS)*
Owen Scranton	*Aerospace Propulsion Systems Specialist (GSS)*
Cameron Gill	*Life-Support Technician (GSS)*
Arnold Wong	*Life-Support Technician (GSS)*
Toby Soto	*Network Systems Analyst (GSS)*
Alvin Armstrong	*Information Technology Specialist (GSS)*
Ryan Brooks	*Chef (BLS-I)*
David Weaver	*Janitorial Lead (BLS-I)*
Connie Stone	*Registered Nurse (BLS-I)*
Carolyn Boss	*Medical Doctor (BLS-I)*

PART ONE

ONE

James stood before the North American Space Administration building and sized the place up. The building was smaller than he had expected. Not small, exactly, but smaller than in his imagination. It was six or seven stories tall, not including any sub-levels lurking beneath the surface. Considering that it was the main building for the entire Space Program, it was modest.

James walked up the steps toward the entrance. Once there, he was greeted by a guard and the familiar security protocol – items out of your pockets, stand still for the body-scanner, place your palm on the reader, look directly at the camera, etc. Once his palm and fingerprints had been read, his face and eyes scanned, his body explored for contraband, his possessions handled by strangers, and his identity confirmed on a dozen databases, he was allowed to proceed. As always after a thorough security check, James was frazzled, and he stood in the lobby with a lost expression on his face while he tightened his belt, put away his things, and tried to recover his dignity.

A man approached, handsome and in his late thirties. "Hi there! Jermaine Reed. Nice to meet you."

James looked down at the hand extended toward him. After a beat he shook away the fog and took Jermaine's hand. "Shit, yeah, sorry...James Wilmot. Nice to meet you."

Jermaine smiled. "I assume you're an astronaut candidate?" Without waiting for an answer, he continued. "I'm chief pilot on the upcoming *Vectio* launch."

James nodded. "I'm headed to the Martian south pole."

Jermaine's smile continued to beam. "Yup, that's the one! All new candidates are asked to head to room 103, just down the hall there. We'll give everyone a little more time to arrive and then we'll get started on orientation. Welcome!"

Jermaine slapped James jovially on the shoulder and moved past him. James turned to ask a question, but Jermaine was already busy ambushing another new arrival; a mousy, older woman who looked even more lost than James. He turned in the direction Jermaine had pointed to and looked for room 103. He found it a little way down the hall. The room was already crowded with people. Most were sitting at one of six large, evenly spaced conference tables. A few milled about in the back of the room, nervously making small talk and drinking coffee. James looked for an open seat. He found one next to a balding man with large, coke-bottle glasses. James guessed he was in his late forties, perhaps early fifties.

"Hi!" He said, a little too loudly. "I'm James."

The man practically jumped out of his seat. "Sorry, I seem to have drifted off there. I zone out, you know? When nobody is talking. My name is Jeff."

James immediately softened his tone. "Nice to meet you, Jeff. Sorry for making you jump."

Jeff smiled. "Oh, it's quite alright."

The two men lapsed into an uncomfortable silence while each wondered what to say next. James spoke first. "So, are you support crew or science?"

Jeff smiled wryly. "A little of both, I suppose. I'm the Project Engineer from EPMS: Extra-Planetary Mission Systems. So, I'm support crew, technically, but a lot of what I have to do will be science based."

James grinned at the serendipity of his chosen seat. "You don't say? I'm the new Site Lead from EPMS."

Jeff sat up a little. "Well, it is certainly a pleasure to meet you. A real pleasure indeed." He awkwardly re-extended his hand for a second shake.

James accepted the shake, then quickly changed the subject. "It's nice to know I'm not the only 'dirty contractor' in the room."

Jeff looked surprised. He had totally missed James's attempt at humor. "Well, you're far from it. There are all sorts of contractors on this mission. From our company and others, which we have sub-contracted. I would have thought they would have given you an introductory brief on the status of the Project at headquarters..."

James stopped Jeff before he could get too spooled up. "They did, they did. I was just...joking. Poorly."

Jeff looked upset that he had missed something. "Oh, sorry. I apologize. Am I right in assuming you weren't serious about our status as 'dirty?' Because I assure you, we are well respected among the members of the agency..."

"Nothing to apologize about. And yes, I was joking about that too. Sorry for the terrible humor so early in the morning."

Jeff's eyebrows raised. "Quite alright. No trouble."

Both men lapsed into silence again and stared at the empty podium in the front of the room.

James decided he had to do better. "So, Jeff..." he asked, "How long have you been with the company?"

Jeff looked relieved. "Seven years, I believe." He stopped talking and looked at the ceiling for a moment, thinking. "Yes. Yes, that's right. Seven years this July. How about yourself?"

James had been with the company fifteen years, but he was hesitant to share that with Jeff. Reason being, Jeff might expect him to have more to show for it. And he would have, too, if he had been in the same department for his entire tenure. But he hadn't.

James had started with EPMS as a teenager, running surveys for their housing and security division. Now that most of the world's open and undeveloped areas had been claimed for food production or housing, businesses didn't have the option of putting their more sensitive assets in empty areas. The vast urban cityscape that the world had become was constantly shifting as people sought out work, and companies wanted to make sure they weren't setting up shop in an area that was likely to become unfriendly to business anytime soon. So they sampled the population in areas they had interest in before moving, making sure the demographics were favorable, or at least controllable. Of course, none of the big wigs wanted to pour through all of that data, even when most of the analysis was done by AI, so they hired kids like James.

James spent his first few years of adulthood reading endless reports about what people's favorite foods were, and if they had any unusual political affiliations. The work was boring, but steady, which was rare enough to be precious. Eventually, the company offered him another job, physically scouting new locations they had their eye on. This new job would allow him to live in the company's private housing compound. He couldn't say yes quickly enough.

James did well in the new position. His new home was quite comfortable. The house itself didn't vary substantially from the government issued homes he and his family had lived in growing up, but the neighborhood was above and beyond his expectations. People had a purpose behind these walls - a reason to get up in the morning. They didn't sit around taking drugs or planning their next score. Children played freely – but safely - in the streets. Adults waved and said hello when they passed one another. When social events did happen, they were always clean and subdued affairs, with no one ending up falling down drunk or cursing in front of their kids. To be honest, James found them to be incredibly boring, but it was a nice change not to have to keep an eye on his surroundings.

It was at one of these parties that he met Heather. She was beautiful, the kind of woman any man would be lucky to have: petite frame, shoulder length blonde hair, incredible green eyes and an adorable button nose. Her sense of humor was amazing, and she could hold a vibrant conversation about almost any subject. And, most importantly, she smelled fantastic. James was hooked. One date led to two dates, and two dates led to ten. They were married within eight months. The company made sure they were taken care of; their home came fully furnished, with two additional rooms for any children that might come along. And come along they did: Noah and Anna, born twenty-four months apart. James loved being a father. The moment he first looked in Noah's eyes, he knew he would never be the same. The love he had for the three of them was incalculable. Life was good.

Then it all went to shit. In one quick deal between the tycoons that owned the world, James's portion of the company was sold off. More specifically, the services offered by James's division would be outsourced (in return for something of value, no doubt), and the company would close its own Demography division. All of the employees within his department were to be laid off within six months. Suddenly, this life he had built, and thought impenetrable, was in danger of slipping away.

James panicked. First, he reached out to the new company, hoping to make the transition as smooth as possible, but they had no openings. They had streamlined an already efficient process long ago, and employed half as many people as James's group. James checked for other, similar jobs within his own company. There were none. He checked for jobs different from, but related to, his own. There were none. He checked for jobs he was completely unqualified for. There were none. Finally, in desperation, he reached out to friends for help. He asked anyone he had worked with in the intervening years, even for a day, if they knew of an opening he could fill.

In the last month before his impending unemployment, one of his contacts came through. The job opportunity they offered was small, in a relatively obscure department that wasn't often on people's minds. It wasn't "sexy," and it came with pretty heavy travel requirements which would keep him away from his family for extended periods, but it was a job.

The North American Space Administration, one of the company's many government clients, needed a Site Lead for one of their Martian bases. The base was newer, located in a region that hadn't yet been thoroughly explored, and real scientific work was just beginning to ramp up. The position would require him to travel to this base and babysit a few dozen scientists and subcontractors for a couple of years. Upon his return, he could live off of the accumulated per diem from his extended work trip, while he searched for a new position within the larger Government Services division, in which the NASA position fell.

Government Services jobs were rare, and very secure. His contact was offering him a golden opportunity. James was surprised to hear that research-related Space Administration jobs even existed anymore. Other than automated mining operations, he hadn't heard of any exploration activity in his entire life, history texts notwithstanding. Apparently the research mission had continued quietly plugging along, off the radar, since the first manned missions to Mars decades ago.

James initially declined the offer. He was woefully unqualified to be an astronaut. He had no technical background and he didn't want to leave his family. However, as his contact promptly pointed out, James had managerial experience, and familiarity with the company's operations. He had been responsible for the schedule, budget and success of many a survey project, and had interacted with people from all walks of life throughout his career. These things: managing money, managing people, and troubleshooting basic problems, were the essence of the job. The rest could be taught or learned through experience. The only real difference between the new position and any other was its location.

The thing most in his favor, of course, was that practically nobody wanted the job. Travel to the big, red, dead rock of Mars had long since lost its appeal to most people. Only the diehard scientists and the sad saps, like James, who relied on Mars for their paycheck, cared about it anymore. The position was grunt work. Dues paying work. The "only way to stay in the company" kind of work. James took the job the next day.

There were some caveats of course: James had to be in good enough shape to go skyward, and he had to pass basic astronaut training. Neither the physical or training standards were what they had once been, at the outset of manned space flight, due to increased reliance on automation and the relatively routine sort of thing it had become. A sick or clueless astronaut, while bad, was no longer a mission-ender. The human presence in Space was simply too robust to be scuttled by a single individual. That didn't mean the selection and training process was easy, of course. Far from it. But it was doable for your average person.

Luckily for James, he had maintained a decent sort of shape through his first few years of being a father, so beefing up and cutting some fat in preparation for his entrance interview wasn't prohibitive. Similarly, for the training portion, James felt ready. He had always been a quick study, and he had a knack for technical things, even if his life hadn't called on him to use it too much. Because of this, he knew he was as ready as a man like him could be in the final weeks before his departure.

Readiness wasn't his problem. No, his problem was of a different sort entirely: he had to break the news to his wife.

TWO

James closed his front door behind him, trying not to trip over the dog. Their dog, Susie, was a small Pekingese-terrier mix who yipped and nipped every chance she got. She was also ugly. And painfully stupid. Despite these flaws, James loved her dearly. He crouched down and scratched between her ears. Susie's tail wagged and she bound off, eager to report his arrival to Heather.

Noah was on the couch watching TV. He looked up at his father and waved. "Hey Dad."

"Hey pal. Good day?"

"Yup! Roman got sent to the principal's office."

"Uh oh. That doesn't sound good."

"No, it was."

"Why's that?"

"Cause' I don't like Roman."

James laughed. "Well, that's very practical of you, son. Not very nice, but practical."

Noah shrugged. "Romans' a butt."

"What did he do?"

"Yelled at the teacher about something. I don't know. He's been a jerk lately, so I just stay away from him."

"You guys used to be friends, right?"

"Yeah, but not for a while."

"How come?"

"He just started being mean to everybody."

James put down his bag and sat on the couch. "Is there something going on at home?"

Noah nodded. "Yeah. I think so. He said something about his mom losing her job, and them having to move."

James shook his head sadly. Roman's mother, Marcia, hadn't made the latest cut. "Well, I want you to be nice to Roman anyway, ok?"

"But Dad..."

"Stay away from him if he's being a jerk, but give him a second chance if he comes around, that's all I'm saying. Moving can be hard. Poor kid."

Noah sighed. "Ok, Dad. I do feel bad for him."

"I'm sure you do. Its cause of that big heart your mom gave you..."

James reached over and patted Noah's chest, then tickled his tummy. Noah laughed and feigned as if he was trying to get away, but James grabbed him and pulled him into a bear hug, all while continuing to tickle. "You're so sweeeet...what a sweet boy! So full of looooove..."

Noah spoke in a staccato, between gales of laughter. "Dad...stop...jerk!" He got an arm free, then elbowed James once, softly, in the gut.

Laughing, James let him go. Noah adjusted so he wasn't in James' lap anymore, but he stayed close. It suddenly dawned on James that he wouldn't see his son again until he was thirteen years old. Tears welled up in his eyes involuntarily, and he had to blink hard to make them go away.

"Hey, pal where are your mom and sister?"

"Moms in her office and Annas upstairs."

"In her room?"

"Yup."

James stood up. "Ok, I'm going to find them. You...continue to be a slug."

Noah gave a thumbs up. "On it!"

James went upstairs to check on Anna first. He wasn't ready for the conversation with Hannah yet.

When he entered her room, Anna was on the floor, playing with her toys. Her head snapped up at the sound of her door's creaky hinges, which he kept meaning to fix but never seemed to get around to.

"Daddy!"

She ran over to him and embraced his legs. James swept her up in his arms and sat down with her on the bed.

"How is my favorite daughter?"

"Good! I painted some pictures today."

"Oh yeah? Let me see?"

She climbed down off his lap and ran over to a nearby shelf, returning with a stack of papers covered in paint.

James pretended to assess the paintings with a critical eye. "Hmmm...the shadows...the use of color and form...they are simply...magnificent!"

TWO — | 17 |

Anna giggled. "Thank you, Daddy...I made this one especially for you..."

She handed him a painting from the bottom of the stack. It was a picture of James in his work clothes, a crude smile plastered over his face. The word 'yessssssss' was drawn in red across the bottom of the page.

He pointed to the word. "What's this?"

"That's you. Because you're sooo excited to go to work."

James laughed. "Ah, I see. Man, you must think I really like my job."

"Don't you?"

"Well...I like having it, that's for sure."

"See?" she said, triumphantly, "It's you."

"Yup, you got me. You nailed it. Do I get to keep it?"

"Of course!"

"Thank you!" He set the picture aside. "Good day?"

"Yeah, it was fine." She leaned over and gave him a big kiss on the cheek. "I missed you."

He hugged her tightly and kissed her back. "I missed you, too. You know, this is one of the favorite parts of my day. When I see you."

Anna beamed. "Me too."

James ruffled the top of her head and stood. He grabbed the painting and headed for the door. "This is going on the refrigerator."

"It better!"

"I'm gonna' go find you Mom, ok?"

"Ok, love you daddy!"

He had to blink back tears again. "Love you too."

He closed Anna's door behind him and went to look for his wife.

...

He found Heather in her office, closing up shop for the day. Susie sat at her feet, alternating between panting heavily and licking herself.

"Hey honey," said James.

Heather stood and leaned in for a kiss. "Hey handsome."

James returned her kiss, but Heather could tell something was off. She drew back.

"What is it?" asked James.

"You tell me."

James sighed and sat on the couch at the back of her office. "Let's talk for a second."

Reluctantly, Heather sat and turned her office chair to face him. "What's going on Wilmot? Spill it."

He explained the situation.

By the time he was done, the kids were knocking on the office door, asking for dinner. Heather shooed them off, then sat back down with a heavy sigh. She was quiet for a long time.

"Are you gonna' say anything?"

"I'm thinking," said Heather. After a long pause, she spoke again. "It sounds like you don't have much of a choice."

"You really think so?"

Heather sighed again. "I...you...James, don't put this on me. Don't make this my decision."

James raised his hands in a gesture of peace. "I'm not, honey, I swear. I'm not trying to do that. I wouldn't."

Heather shook her head. "But yes, I can't think of another way. We both know they won't let us stay here otherwise."

James nodded grimly. "It's just...I'll be gone so fucking long." He lowered his head.

Heather scooted over to him, put her hand on the back of his neck, and pressed her forehead against his. "I love you. So much. I wish I could think of another way...but you'll be doing it for the kids. You'll be doing it for us. They'll understand."

James rested in her embrace. "God, I hope so."

...

Anna lay in bed, eyes wide. "You'll be gone HOW long?"

James squeezed her shoulder, comfortingly. "Three years, start to finish."

"But that's so long Daddy," said Anna. "We'll miss you too much."

Noah didn't say anything, but stormed from the room, lay in his bed and drew the blankets up over his head.

James sighed, unsure what to say next. This reaction was the one he had feared.

Heather chimed in, loud enough for Noah to hear her in his room across the hall. "Listen guys, Daddy and I know it won't be easy. It'll be really hard, and we'll miss each other a whole lot. But we'll call each other as much as we can. We'll send each other videos, and Daddy can tell us stories about all the adventures he has in space!"

James prodded Heather gently. "Actually, honey, we won't be able to call in real time. The delay is..."

Heather interrupted him and smiled at Anna. "What Daddy means is, our calls to each other will be more like messages we leave for each other. Like when one of us leaves a note in your lunchbox. Or when Daddy and I check our voice messages. But we will call. All the time."

"All the time?" confirmed Anna.

Heather nodded. "All the time. We swear. Right Daddy?"

James forced a smile and nodded. "Swear."

The two of them lingered in Anna's room awhile, giving her reassurances and affording Noah more time to process their news.

The truth was that Anna was too young to really understand what they were telling her. Three years to a child was an eternity. She wouldn't start to appreciate how long he'd be gone until he'd already been gone too long. It made James sick to his stomach with sadness and guilt.

After a final hug and a gentle kiss, James and Heather finished putting Anna to bed and left her room. They closed her door most of the way, but left it open a crack, the way Anna liked it.

James looked through the open doorway, across the hall at Noah, who was still buried under his covers.

"Do you want to talk to him alone?" asked Heather.

James nodded. "I probably should. I'll catch up after."

Heather nodded. "See you downstairs."

TWO - | 21 |

James crossed the threshold, closed the bedroom door behind him, and sat on the bed. "Hey pal. You want to talk?"

Noah remained silent.

"Noah...son. Please look at me so I know you're listening."

Noah's voice was muffled by his comforter. "Go away."

"I don't want to go away. I want to talk to you. Can you stick your head out for a second?"

"No. You're going to go anyway, so just go."

James sighed. "Honey, I don't want to go away. Not at all. In fact, it makes me really sad to go away."

"Then why are you going?"

"Because I have to. That's the only reason. If I don't go, my company won't pay me money anymore. And without money we can't afford anything."

Noah finally stuck his head out. "If you don't go, you're fired?"

"Yes."

"Like Roman's mom?"

"Yes."

"Can't you find another job?"

"I've looked. This is all there is."

Noah sat up. "That's not true. There are tons and tons of jobs here, on Earth, where everybody lives. Dinesh at school says people don't even need a job anymore."

"Well, technically that's true. But not all the jobs available allow us to live where we live. And if you don't have a job at all you have to live in the public housing across town."

Noah's eyes went wide. "Where Aunt Jen lives?"

"Yes. Where Aunt Jen lives."

Noah was quiet, deep in thought.

"Now, Aunt Jen's house has all the stuff she needs. It has a toilet and a bed and four walls. But not much else. And its crowded and noisy and sometimes people steal things...it's not a place I want you and your mom and sister to have to live in. And if we leave here, you have to leave your school, and all your clubs and...a lot of good things. And I don't want that for you. For any of you. That's the only reason I'm going."

He cupped Noah's chin in his hand and guided his eyes upward, to his own. "That's the only reason. You hear me? The only reason." James tried hard not to choke up. "I love you and your mom and sister so darn much...I would do anything else if I could think of it. Anything."

Tearfully, Noah reached across the bed and held James tight.

...

James slumped on to the couch, emotionally drained.

"How'd it go?" asked Heather.

"Good, I guess. He doesn't hate me anymore."

Heather nodded, and they sat in silence for a while.

"When do you have to go, again?"

"Two days from now."

"Jesus, that's soon!"

James reached over and took Heather's hand. "I know. I'm sorry. The spot was a last-minute fill-in. Agapito had to pull some strings to even get my name in the hat. And there's some training first."

Heather withdrew her hand. "You know I should be furious with you for holding on to this for so long. How could you not tell me they were automating your position?"

"Well...outsourcing, technically. Then automating."

Heather stood with her arms crossed, a sour expression on her face.

James nodded, sadly. "I know. You're right. I didn't want to worry you...or tell you before I had a solution. But I should have told you sooner. I'm sorry."

"This affects me too, you know. I didn't sign up to be a single mom for three years. Or a widow."

"Honey you aren't going to be a widow. These trips are very safe now. As for the time away...I don't have to take the job. We can hope for something else."

"We both know there isn't anything else."

James sighed. "I know. I know. Look...I'll be gone a long time...what I don't...I don't want you to be lonely. And I didn't give you much choice about this. What I don't...know about...while I'm gone..."

Heather rolled her eyes. "Fuck you, Wilmot. We both know that isn't happening. Why would you even say that?"

"I don't know. I just feel bad. I'm obviously glad you won't..."

"Well, I won't. But not because you're so great. Because I can only handle so many pains in the ass at one time."

A silence followed. She studied his expression, stoic and unchanged. She nudged him. "I'm kidding. I might miss you. A little."

James grinned, sheepishly. "Swear?"

"I guess."

Heather walked over to the center console and called up their collection of music. She selected one of their favorite slow-songs and started pulling James off the couch. "Come on, doofus. Dance with me."

James stood and took her in his arms. She laid her head against his chest, and the two of them danced in the otherwise quiet room.

"I'm going to miss the shit out of you," said Heather. "You know that?"

James held her tightly and rested his cheek on the back of her head. "I know. I'm going to miss the shit out of you, too."

The music stopped and Heather drew back for a kiss.

James leaned down and kissed her slowly, expressing through touch what words could not.

After, the two of them stood, embracing, in the living room.

"I love you," said James, "so much."

Heather smiled bravely. "I love you, too. Come back to me?"

"I will. Swear."

3

THREE

James snapped out of his reverie and forced a smile, blinking back the haze of tears that had begun to form on his eyes. "Fifteen years." He said. "I've been with the company fifteen years."

"Fifteen years, huh? That's pretty good. You beat me." Jeff paused a beat, then added, "You're just now going up, after all this time?"

James spoke with his thin smile fixed in place. "Well, you know how it is. My people just couldn't bear to let me go."

A woman with close-cropped hair and a stern expression strode to the front of the room. "Attention, everyone! We're ready to get started. Please take a seat."

James took measure of the woman as the rest of the room shuffled towards their seats. She looked to be in her late thirties or early forties. Attractive, but in a plain sort of way. A close look at her betrayed deep worry lines in her forehead, and laugh lines near her eyes. This was a woman, James decided, who knew how to have a good time, but had no time at all for bullshit. He sat up in his seat a little.

THREE

"My name is Caroline Johnston. I am the lead Mission Support Specialist for the upcoming *Vectio* intercept and transfer. If you're in this room, my assumption is that you will be joining us on our upcoming trip to Mars. If that is not true of you, you are in the wrong room, and I suggest you leave now."

After a moment's pause, Caroline continued. "I'm going to start by taking roll. We have had a few people get lost before, so it's necessary. Please bear with us, it will only take a moment, then we can get on with the orientation." Caroline smiled and looked down at the list of names on the podium in front of her. "Ok. These names aren't in any particular order. Valdez, Miguel?"

"Here."

The reply came from a handsome young man in the front row. He also had close cropped hair, and his posture was impeccable. James guessed both he and Caroline were former military.

Caroline continued to read off names. James tried to keep up, as a way of learning who everyone was, but Caroline was reading too fast. The names and the faces all started to blur together. Eventually James gave up. He allowed himself to zone out a little, waiting to hear his own name. Suddenly, he noticed that Caroline's face bore a frustrated expression.

"Wilmot, James? Are you here? Going once, going twice..."

James snapped back to reality and sat up straight in his seat again. "Here." He said, raising his hand in a quick wave. "James Wilmot, right here."

Caroline smiled wryly. "There you are Mr. Wilmot! Nice of you to join us."

James blushed. "Sorry."

"Oh, not at all. I understand. It's early." She looked down at her list. "It says here that you're the relieving Site Lead for this expedition, is that right?"

"Yes, that's right."

"Great! That's great. I guess that makes you the boss, huh? Say hello to the boss everybody."

James felt his blush increase. Every head in the room turned in his direction.

"Hi everyone! As I'm sure you are all well aware now, my name is James."

A very slight chuckle breezed through the crowd.

"It's true that I am dropping into the Site Lead billet once we arrive at our destination. Looking forward to working with all of you and doing whatever I can to support the important scientific work that's being done. Apologies for zoning out for a second there."

He turned his attention back to the front of the room, back to Caroline. "It was a long flight getting here."

"Well," said Caroline, "you ain't seen nothing yet."

Another chuckle swept through the room.

Caroline continued. "I think I speak for all of us when I say it's very nice to meet you, James. Let's move on. Wheeler, Louis?"

...

THREE

Once roll call was done, Caroline launched into an overview of the Mars mission to date, and their mission on this trip in particular. The broad strokes were that Martian exploration had slowed down somewhat from its heyday, but never ceased. The human presence on Mars remained relatively robust: fourteen research stations, five of which were continually manned, representing nine different countries and scattered all over the planet. The station they were heading to, nicknamed "Alpha Base" by some supremely unimaginative NASA bureaucrat, was the fifteenth station to be established and the sixth station primed to inherit the "continually manned" mantle, just as soon as their group arrived. Their arrival would mark the fifth year of uninterrupted operations at the facility, the minimum number required to gain the title.

Alpha Base, or, more accurately, the *Rockwell-Fredrickson Polar Research Station – Alpha*, represented the first major human presence in the Martian South Polar region, or the Planum Australe. Technically, the base was located three degrees north of the official marker for the polar region, but it was close enough for government work. The few degrees difference was actually intentional, from what James understood. It provided a relatively temperate base of operations that was within spitting distance of the more "exotic" features of the polar area...although "temperate" was a word that had to be utilized with a grain of salt when used in reference to a place like Mars.

The base was very new, by Martian standards. So new, in fact, that all previous visits to the Alpha Base site had involved setting the place up. Theirs was the first group that would be engaging in serious scientific inquiry at this location. The majority of their support personnel were already there, having shuttled over a year ago as a part of their own separate mission. James's group would be relieving half of the existing support crew, and joining the other half on the surface for a two year stay.

Two years of daily scientific operations. An unprecedented opportunity for most of the scientists gathered here. They would be able to catch up on a lifetime's worth of conjecture and theorizing in one fell swoop. It remained to be seen if any major breakthroughs would come out of the trip; the other sites hadn't had much luck, apparently. In any case, the scientists were eager to get there and get going.

That eagerness gave companies like James's a chance to make a profit. The number of resources and support staff needed to enable these scientists to do their work was not insignificant. There were dozens of contractor personnel working for five separate companies, millions of dollars of equipment and the facility itself, all of which required management. Each project also had its own schedule and budget. The powers that be had approved some money to be spent on each effort, but not a penny more. James would be responsible for all of these things: helping the scientific teams to stay on task and within their means, keeping the contract and subcontract personnel in-line, and making sure the various pieces of equipment needed to keep all of them productive and alive stayed functional. It was no small task. James certainly hoped he was up to it.

The overview of the site and their mission complete, Caroline moved on to their training plan. As she spoke, the blank surface of their desks lit up to reveal an embedded screen scrolling through a prepared presentation.

"Over the next six weeks," she said, "all of you will receive instruction in basic astronautics. In week one, we'll cover the details of our ascent/descent vehicle, the interplanetary shuttle that will take us to Mars, and the operational layout of Alpha Base. In week two, we'll begin your physical conditioning program, cover the basics of space-based emergency mitigation, and review the life-support systems we'll be using for the duration of the mission. Week two will also include a medical inspection. Please don't be concerned if you have any known medical issues. The inspection process is designed to detect and treat potential problems, not to rule candidates out. On the off chance we do identify a problem so severe that your journey cannot continue, you'll likely be so sick you wouldn't want to be anywhere but a hospital on earth anyway. Week three, we will review some of the topography and other phenomena you are likely to encounter during your stay, as well as some of the things we don't understand yet. Many of you are going on this trip just to answer those questions. Week four, we'll address some of the other issues you may each encounter during a long stay in such an isolated place, and we'll go over some coping mechanisms and techniques for encouraging pro-social behavior within yourself and others. Week five, we'll stop classroom instruction for a health-check. This will include a physical component, testing the results of your medical and fitness preparation plans, as well as a psychological component. The psychological component will include meetings with our mental health staff, to go over any final misgivings or concerns you might have before our departure, as well as a general well-being check in. You will also have the opportunity to meet with some of our leadership here at the agency, where you can provide them your feedback on the program and give them a sense of where you are in terms of mission readiness. Week six will be devoted to departure, transit, arrival and emergency egress procedures. We will depart the planet on the first day of week seven. Does anyone have any questions?"

Jeff raised his hand. "When do we sleep?"

Caroline smiled. "I'm glad you asked. Class will begin each day at oh-eight-hundred and end at seventeen hundred. That's 8am and 5pm for you civilians."

A polite chuckle slipped from the crowd.

"Lunch will be from twelve hundred to thirteen hundred every day. Physical training will take place at two separate times each day: oh-seven-hundred to oh-seven-thirty, and seventeen-thirty to eighteen-hundred. You can attend one or both of these sessions each day, but you must attend one. It's very important that we boost your physical fitness as much as possible in preparation for the rigors of spaceflight. The cafeteria and gymnasium are located in this building. Your dormitories are across the street. The doors to both buildings lock at twenty-one-hundred – that's 9 pm – each night. I can't force you to be in your dorm building before that time, but I can promise that you won't be getting inside once the doors lock. For that reason, I strongly urge you to treat this like a

THREE

9pm curfew, although you are free to do what you want. The weather isn't so bad here this time of year, so you might find the sidewalk quite comfortable."

The group gave another small chuckle.

"Once this orientation session is done, you'll be afforded an opportunity to get acquainted with the facility and your rooms. Any luggage you dropped off at the door or had sent ahead of you will be waiting for you in your rooms. You each still have your own space for now. Don't get too used to it – you'll be living in quite close quarters for some time to come. But we have to ease you into it."

Caroline paused for laughter once again. She was met with silence.

"There's information in your room about the other necessities you will require during your stay – laundry service and the like. Unless there are any other questions, I'll turn things over to your instructor. Anyone?"

Nobody took the bait.

"Ok. Kayla, over to you."

A voice rose from speakers embedded in each desk. As the voice spoke, subtitles appeared on each screen and slides began advancing.

"*Hello. My name is Kayla, your virtual instructor. In this lesson, I'll be walking you through the schematics of the craft which will take you to your final destination. Please hold all questions until the end.*"

As the classroom AI began its spiel, James settled in for a long day of learning.

FOUR

It was hot. Hotter than hot. Charlie wiped the sweat from his brow and looked around for some shade. He found a tiny sliver of darkness in the shadow of a nearby storefront and rushed to it. The wall of the storefront, only just out of the midafternoon sun, was hot on Charlie's back, and he found himself wishing the silhouette of the building was much larger.

He knew he shouldn't be there. He had been told to stop venturing off estate grounds. But he was bored. And he wanted drugs. He could have sent someone else for the drugs, but that wouldn't do anything for his boredom. He wanted to be out in the world...where the action was.

Charlie heard a pounding on the thin wall behind him. A moment later, the door of the storefront flew open, and a very angry woman marched out of it.

"Hey, asshole! You wanna' stop leaning on my wall? You're gonna' make the whole thing tip over!"

Charlie smirked and stood up straight. He spread out his hands sarcastically. "Sorry. Didn't realize your store was such a piece of shit."

"Fuck off." With that the woman turned on her heels and walked back inside, the door slamming shut behind her.

Charlie laughed, then decided he would go inside this woman's store and look at what she had to offer. He needed to get out of the sun anyway.

The door's handle was hot to the touch, but the interior of the shack itself was surprisingly cool. Charlie spied a small air conditioning unit in the corner of the room, and figured that must be why. The unit, clearly printed in pieces and cobbled together by hand, sputtered and shook as it struggled to keep the hut's temperature down. A hot breeze blew in from outside, the walls trembled, and a wave of dust and heat hit him from narrow cracks in the corners of the room, where the walls joined. He marveled that the A/C unit hadn't broken down already.

The woman stood behind the counter, watching him with a mixture of bemusement and concern. He smiled to himself over her discomfort. She would think twice before talking to him like that again.

Charlie walked the makeshift aisles of the woman's ramshackle hut, enjoying the sight and smell of her freshly made bread. The breads came in all manner of shapes, sizes and colors. Some were covered in seeds and other bits of plant material. Some looked like round balls, with brown, crusted dough on the outside. Others were long and thin, their stippled crusts closer in color to white than the usual shades of beige or brown. A medium sized orange loaf caught his eye. He leaned down to smell it and found its aroma quite enticing. He also heard a disapproving tut from the woman at the counter.

"No breathing on the merchandise, please."

Charlie assessed the woman. Her jaw was set firmly, and her hands hovered suspiciously underneath the counter, below his sight line. He considered that she might have a weapon, or a means of calling for help.

"How much are these things, anyway?" He asked.

"Five each."

Charlie nodded. "You realize I could lick each and every one of these loaves if I wanted, right? Or I could push hard on that wall over there and break your whole fucking hovel?"

The woman blanched. "I'll call the cops."

"Call em'! IF they come, they aren't gonna' do shit about it. Because I'm me and you're...you. You realize that, right?"

The woman drew back, startled at his bluntness. "I don't give a shit who you are...I need you to leave. Right now. Get the fuck outta' my store."

Charlie laughed, considered his options, then turned on his heel and headed for the door. On his way out he knocked over four tables full of bread, then slapped the A/C unit off the wall. It fell to the ground and shattered into pieces, a puff of smoke rising from its remains. The door swung closed behind him, muffling the shocked protestations of the woman inside.

It was time to find his drugs, then get the hell home. Charlie plunged into the market's maze of unlicensed lean-tos and shanty's, searching in earnest for his dealer. He slowly made his way through the labyrinth, to one of its deepest and darkest corners. His dealer's storefront was there, toward the back of its alley, away from the street.

Charlie knocked.

Zeke answered. Zeke's pockmarked face broke into a half-toothless smile. "Charlie!" He croaked, opening the door wider and ushering him in. "It's been too long!"

Charlie laughed. "Three days is too long for you?"

"It is when it comes to my favorite customer! Why don't you have a seat, take a look at the merch…"

Charlie walked toward a large, comfortable, worn leather chair in the corner. He glanced at the merchandise table to its left. Packets of various sizes lay there, waiting for eager buyers such as himself.

"I don't want anything new. Just the usual."

"The usual for the extraordinary man! Take a seat – I'll cut you a line."

Charlie held his hand up. "No, thanks. I've gotta' run."

Zeke shrugged his shoulders. "Suit yourself. How much?"

"A thousand milligrams."

"As you wish, sir! That'll be two thousand dollars."

"What? It's usually a dollar a milligram! I only brought a thousand!"

Zeke shook his head, disappointed. "Well, I tell ya', that's too bad. That's not enough."

"What? I don't understand?"

"Price has gone up, my friend. It gets harder and harder to keep up with demand. Everybody wants a taste of what

Zeke has to give. Makes the days go smooth and fast." Zeke took note of Charlie's shaking hand and the sheen of sweat on his brow. "But you know that, don't ya'? Yeah, Charlie boy knows all about that."

"Fuck it. You take standard digital?"

"You know I don't. Blockchain only. Or cash. No cancelled transactions"

"Zeke...I only brought a thousand. Let me pay you back. You know I'm good for it."

"Two thousand. Upfront."

A flash of anger shot through Charlie's chest. He did his utmost to stay calm, reminding himself that an outburst could trigger one of Zeke's associates to make an appearance, and if that happened, Charlie was fairly sure he wouldn't be leaving Zeke's store alive. "Come on, man, that's outrageous. Fifteen hundred. Half now, half later."

Zeke shook his head. "No can-do compadre. Price is the price. Take it or leave it."

"Zeke...like...I'm one of your loyal customers, man. Most loyal."

Zeke struck a conciliatory tone. "Charlie...I know you're loyal. Most loyal, like you said. But you can afford it. Now pay up and get the fuck out, or just get the fuck out."

Angrily, Charlie reached into his pocket and withdrew two thousand dollars, cash.

Zeke snatched it out of his hand, counted the bills and put them in his pocket. "Pleasure doing business with you. First bag on the table, closest to the door. Take another one and you'll be dead before you turn around."

Charlie wasted no time. He grabbed the bag and headed straight for the exit. As his foot was crossing the threshold, Zeke's voice rose from behind him.

"Hey, Charlie..."

Charlie stopped and turned around.

Zeke's smile had returned, broader than ever. "Don't ever try to hustle me again, or I'll slit your throat myself." He raised one hand and made a slight gesture – a subtle wave goodbye. "See you real soon."

Charlie rushed back into the labyrinth. He weaved his way through streets and between storefronts, eager to get home. He was angry that Zeke had raised the price again, and he was over the stench of piss and desperation prevalent amongst the poors. He was ready for tree-lined boulevards and marble. He was ready for home.

A whiff of smoke caught his attention. He stopped, looking for the source. Now that he was still, he noticed people rushing by him. Some were headed toward the smell. Most were headed the other direction. Curious, he headed toward it.

As he got closer, a dark cloud became visible, fingers of flame dancing at its base. The fire was spreading quickly, jumping between poorly constructed huts made of wood and tin. He watched as the store owners desperately tried to snuff the flames. He kept watching as it became obvious their efforts would fail.

Bored, he called for a car. His app said the car would take five minutes, and he sighed in frustration. He wondered if anything else could go wrong today.

The woman from the bread store was among the group trying to put out the fire. As Charlie stood, impatiently waiting for his ride, she noticed him. Charlie watched as she got the attention of the other store owners and pointed in his direction. Charlie looked behind him, trying to see what they were pointing at, but saw nothing.

The group began running his way.

All at once, Charlie realized they were angry. Very angry. Only then did it occur to him to wonder what had started the fire. He remembered the bread woman's A/C unit, and the puff of smoke that had risen from it before her door slammed behind him.

Charlie ran.

The car he had called pulled in front of him and the passenger door opened. He dove in, slammed the door closed, then began screaming at the AI driver to go. The car was motionless for a moment as the software processed his request.

The angry mob caught up and surrounded the car, rocking it violently and cracking windows. Thankfully, this triggered the car's security protocols, and it immediately took off. Bodies fell to the left and the right as Charlie was carried home to safety.

The rest of the trip was a blur. Charlie thought about Zeke, and how his business was a part of the ramshackle labyrinth. If Zeke's store was destroyed, and if Zeke got word that Charlie was the one who started the fire...

At last, Charlie's car stopped at the gate of his family's estate. He waited for the facial scan to finish, then the gate swung open. Automated turrets, cleverly hidden in the brick façade of the estate's perimeter wall, scanned the area for threats as the car drove through the gate.

The voice of the house AI came in over the car's speakers. *"Welcome home, Mr. Gibson."*

Charlie barely acknowledged it. "Hey. Hold all my calls and visitors."

"No need," the AI replied, *"your calls and visitors are still being held, per your last request."*

The car pulled up to the front door. Charlie grunted as he stepped out and slammed the passenger door behind him. The door to the house swung open, and the AI kept talking.

"I have already summoned the elevator for you. It will arrive in approximately fifteen seconds to take you to the fifth floor."

Charlie grunted again. He was trying to think, and this AI was annoying the fuck out of him. "Good."

"Have a wonderful day Mr. Gibson!"

The elevator ride was blissfully short. He opened his bedroom door, shut it behind him and made a beeline for the bed, shedding clothes as he went. His kit was ready, and he was practically salivating by the time he sat down on the bed and cut himself a line. He needed to get straight, then figure out how to deal with Zeke.

He had just bent over the mirror when the speakers in his room started chirping. He spoke aloud to the house AI. "What the hell? I told you to hold all my calls!"

"I know, Mr. Gibson, but your request has been overridden by someone with priority access. I apologize. Would you like full interaction or audio only?"

Charlie knew right away that it must be his mother. "Audio! Audio only! Jesus Christ."

"Very good, Mr. Gibson. Please stand by."

After a second of silence, his mother's voice filled the room. "Charlie. Are you there?"

"Yes, Mom, I'm here."

"Why won't you let me see you?"

Charlie rolled his eyes. "I'm not dressed Mom, I just got out of the shower."

His mother's response sounded more irritated than normal. "All right. Get dressed so we can talk."

Charlie looked around at his messy drug den in a panic. "We're talking now."

"Jesus Christ, Charlie! Do you think I'm a fucking idiot?"

"What? No! I just...I don't understand. We're already talking."

His mother cleared her throat, loudly. "Check your monitor, Charlie."

"Mom...I don't understand...."

His mother's voice wavered between anger and exhaustion. "Charlie...check your monitor. Now."

Being careful to avoid accidentally opening a video chat with his mother, Charlie activated the wall-length monitor in his room. "Ok. It's on. Where are you calling from, anyway?"

"Never mind that. Select the news."

Charlie did so. Footage of the fire was already all over the net. A digital recreation of the perpetrator, displayed on every feed, matched his face almost exactly.

"What do you know about this Charlie?"

"Mom...I mean...it looks like an awful tragedy. But what does it have to do with me?"

His mother's voice boomed from the speakers. "DON'T FUCKING LIE TO ME, CHARLIE! Don't fucking lie! GPS has you at those exact coordinates less than an hour ago. You were at that goddamn market again. Buying drugs."

"Wait a minute...you have me tracked?"

"Of course we do! All of your clothes are chipped. And so are you."

"You put a tracker IN me?!?"

"At your last vaccination."

Charlie stood in a rage, picking at the spot on his arm where the doctor's needle had pierced his skin. "How DARE you?"

His mother quickly cut him off. "How dare I? How dare you? You are dragging this family's name through the mud, Charlie! After the twelfth time you disappeared for more than a week, we had to start tracking you, for your own protection. And now we know exactly where you were. At an illegal market, buying drugs and starting fires! And soon everyone will know, Charlie! This isn't an isolated assault charge or some drunken coed crying rape! This is too big to cover up. Not like the other times."

Charlie rolled his eyes. "It will be fine! When you and father have your little 'dalliances,' or when one of your factories has a spill, you make it go away. Just do that."

"No, Charlie. We can't. People died. Do you hear me? People died. Because of you."

"Like your factories never killed anyone!"

"This isn't a multi-million-dollar industry hub, Charlie! This is an underground beggar's market, known for its unlicensed products and narcotics sales. Hundreds are dead, and the place is still burning. Nobody has any interest in keeping things quiet, and the common people want blood. They're going to find out it was you, and we can't keep you out of it. Do you hear me? Father has already agreed to turn you over to the police. You have officially fucked up beyond my ability to save you!"

Charlie slumped on the bed and put his head between his hands. Father had sold him out...agreed to turn him over in some backroom deal. He was going to go to jail. Because he killed the right kind of people in the wrong kind of way.

He sat bolt upright as a horrible thought occurred to him: Zeke. Everyone knew he had started the fire. Including Zeke, and all his people. Nobody could keep him safe from Zeke in Jail...

"Mother, are you still there?"

"Yes, Charlie."

"You have to help me! There must be something you can do! Anything!"

A long silence followed.

After a time, his mother spoke. "There is something. But you aren't going to like it."

5

FIVE

Falling. He was falling. James came to with a start and braced for impact with the ground. But the impact never came. He blinked rapidly several times and waited for his vision to clear. Gauntleted hands floated in front of him. His hands. It all came back, now. He was in space!

"Not bad for a first timer!" laughed the man next to him. "At least you didn't puke in your helmet!"

"How long was I out?"

The man shrugged. "Eh, couple minutes."

Jermaine's voice came in over the helmet intercom. "Let's keep the chatter down on the main channel gentlemen."

The man shrugged and turned away.

James looked around the cabin. He could tell from the looks on the other passenger's faces that he definitely wasn't the only one feeling nauseous or recovering from a sense of overwhelming terror. The launch had been more intense than they were led to believe.

Ten minutes of silence stretched into thirty. Thirty minutes stretched into an hour. Some passengers slept. Others listened attentively for any sign that their target was close. At last, the signal came.

"We're here, everyone," said Jermaine, "get ready for a bump."

When they docked James felt a small jolt as the capsule made contact with the ship, followed by a subtle shaking as the pressurized docking compartment made a firm seal. A series of whistling noises followed, then the top of the capsule opened. Disembarking the craft proceeded in an orderly fashion. The pilots went first, followed by the others. When James' turn came, he unstrapped himself and marveled as he floated upward. Pushing off of his seat, he carefully maneuvered up the ladder, toward the capsule hatch. He emerged into a large open space - the *Vectio's* hangar, located in the center of the cylindrical ship.

He followed the others toward a hole in one of two rotating sections in the wall - the rings that anchored the habitation and working modules to the rest of the ship. Each hole was the end of a "spoke" in the giant, wheel-like modules. Each "spoke" was actually a tunnel that led to the interior of the "wheels." As James moved through the tunnel, feet first, toward the outer surface of the ship, he started to feel as if he was descending, although he knew such terms had no real meaning in space. A sensation of weight returned to him about halfway down the spoke, and by the time he reached the opening on the other end, normal gravity had returned.

Caroline helped him climb down from the end of the tunnel, now the "roof" of a long hallway which curved in front of them until it was out of sight. They were in the giant wheel, spinning fast enough that their feet were stuck to the outside wall. The effect was almost indistinguishable from normal gravity, although he couldn't shake a vague sense of nausea, akin to seasickness.

Caroline read the expression on his face. "Don't worry, you'll get used to it. Welcome aboard the *Stella Vectio*. Jermaine will show you to your cabin."

James nodded and followed Jermaine down the hall, while Caroline helped the next arrival down from the ceiling.

"After we get you out of your suit," said Jermaine, "I recommend you lie down for a half hour or so, just until your body gets used to the rotation."

James nodded, trying not to be sick in his helmet.

Jermaine stopped next to an open door and gestured for James to go inside.

James stepped tentatively through the doorway, where other sickly looking travelers were gingerly shedding their spacesuits and hanging them up. He did the same. When he was done, he rejoined Jermaine in the hallway.

"Follow me to your cabin."

The cabin wasn't far. A few feet later they arrived at the doorway. Stepping inside, James saw a small open area, framed by two bunkbeds, one against each wall. The bottom bunk of the bed on the right was occupied by an unconscious scientist. James took the one on the left. He lay down, closed his eyes, and tried not to vomit. Passing out in front of the others had been bad enough.

...

A day had passed. James and the majority of the other guests spent the time eating, laying in their bunks and making quiet small talk, while the two astronauts busily readied the ship for the next six-month leg of its never-ending journey. A few guests assisted - mostly the members of the base crew, who had made this journey many times before. The rest of them did nothing but wait, which made James feel guilty, as if they should all be lending a hand. In truth, they knew so little of what to do they would be more of a hinderance then a help.

Now they were standing in line, waiting to enter one of the ship's longitudinal connecting tunnels. Each ringed habitat module was connected at multiple points with the other, the connections taking the form of long cylindrical hallways. The same physics sticking the group to the outside hull of the wheels stuck them to the outside hull of the tubes. To the observer traversing them, they were simply long tunnels the group had to go down to reach the cryo-bay, where they would all be frozen like popsicles for the rest of their journey. Mentally, however, James couldn't shake the image of the assembly crossing a narrow plank, outside of which was...nothing. No ship. Simply void.

The fact that they were easily as safe in the tunnels as they were anywhere else in the ringed modules was little comfort. Intellectually, James knew that a repulsion field extended the full length of the ship - they had covered as much in their training. The field, channeling a constant stream of recirculated particles around the craft, would redirect any micrometeorites that might stray too close to their vessel. The fact remained, though, that in the hallway, they were as physically close to empty space as they could get.

His heart beat hard as he took his turn down the narrow hallway. At one point, stuck in the middle of the hallway because the line stopped moving, James placed his hand on the wall, expecting to feel cold, or vibration, or...something. It felt no different from any other wall on the ship, and he arrived at the other side without incident.

The line eventually led to the cryo-bay, and James entered with wide eyes. He had heard many things about stasis: that the process was excruciating, that you actually died and they used your frozen tissue to clone a replacement at your destination, that you were conscious while frozen, trapped helplessly for the whole journey. It all made him nervous. The official story, as related in pre-departure training, was that the freezing process did exactly what you'd expect - it froze you. The chief difference between it and normal freezing was the chemicals they pumped into you before the process started - chemicals that would prevent your cells from breaking apart when you started to thaw. The other difference, of course, was the fact that you were made unconscious first - a blessed mercy from the excruciating pain of being frozen alive.

When his turn came, he self-consciously disrobed and stood, naked, with his hands covering his genitals, next to the pod he had been assigned.

Across the room, Caroline finished helping another person enter their pod.

James watched as the person laid back, closed their eyes, and the clear tube slowly filled with fluid. Apparently the fluid was breathable, although the body didn't know that - it would spasm and convulse once the substance was inhaled, the same as it would while drowning in anything else. Unlike normal drowning, though, eventually the spasms would calm down, and the person in the tube would still be alive. James had wondered how the delicate lungs, designed for air, were able to push the fluid in and out while the person was asleep, and he had asked as much. The instructor's answer, disconcertingly, was that they didn't. The diaphragm eventually gave up, and the person would float motionlessly in the cooled emulsion until they were awoken, months later. The fluid was so hyperoxgentated, though, that it didn't matter. It's presence in the lungs, even unmoving, was enough to keep the body alive.

"Your turn," said Caroline. She smiled gently and focused on the control panel before her, while James' blush progressed through many shades of red. Half a minute later, the pod's hatch slid open, and Caroline gestured for him to get in. "Step on up, please."

James nodded and, letting go of all dignity, swung his legs over the side of the tube and laid down. The clear material - acrylic, plexiglass, or something else - was cold and uncomfortable against his back.

"Hands at your sides, please," said Caroline.

James complied reluctantly, then listened to his own breathing bounce off of the walls of the open topped cylinder. This experience was entirely unlike he had imagined, and he was scared.

"Deep breaths, James. Your heart is beating awful hard."

James turned his head to look at Caroline, who was standing off to the side, busily tapping on buttons. "You can see my heartbeat?"

Caroline nodded. "Lots of sensors in there with you. State of the art. Now please calm down a bit or the system won't be able to start the process. It'll think you're about to have a medical emergency."

He laughed bitterly. "What if I am?"

Caroline smiled. "You're just fine. Deep breaths."

James nodded and inhaled deeply, counted to three, then exhaled. He did this a few more times, and felt his heart slow a little.

Caroline nodded to herself. "That's better." She pressed a final button, and the machine sprung to life.

A mechanical contraption he hadn't even noticed slid along a rail hidden under the lip of the tube opening. It stopped, lowered, and pressed a small black box against the crook of his right arm. A similar box slid along a rail on the other side and did the same, attaching to his left arm. Each box adjusted its shape a little to form a tight seal against his skin. Then he felt a pinch.

"Ow! What's that?"

"Just your IV line."

"IV line?" asked James, trying not to panic again.

"Yep. One gives you the secret sauce and the other removes the excess CO_2 from your blood."

James nodded. "Because we can't breathe out while we're in here."

Caroline moved so that she could look right down at James' face. "That's exactly right."

"What's in the secret sauce?"

"A little something to help you sleep. And wake up."

A wave of dizziness hit him. "The stuff that stops your cells from exploding."

Caroline chuckled. "That's the one. Now you just lay back, relax, and when you wake up, we'll be there."

James closed his eyes. Whatever this sedative was, it worked fast. "Promise you won't let me die?"

"I promise. Now get some sleep."

James was out before he could respond.

6

SIX

Oblivion gave way to a vague sense of place; of cramped discomfort and general unease. Then the cold came. Cold so cold it felt like fire. Discomfort became agony. Agony become panic – he was in a coffin sized chamber, after all. He tried to claw at the walls, but his arms wouldn't move. He tried to scream, but his lungs were filled with oxygenated fluid, so he just gagged. After twitching helplessly and silently for a few moments, he realized that all the movement in the world wouldn't get him out. He was still thawing, and he had to wait.

Time passed. It seemed like hours, but it could have been minutes. Finally, the seal popped, and the hatch of the pod opened. He was lifted from the stasis pod's anti-freeze goop. He tilted his head to the side and started throwing up. Six month's worth of cryo-goop poured out of his mouth, stomach and lungs. Fear swept through him as the metal surface beneath him adjusted itself again without warning. It formed a kind of reclining chair. The chair rose upwards until his body was completely clear of the fluid, and a heat lamp stuttered to life overhead. At some point, someone - he wasn't sure who - gave him a heat blanket, which he clung to, shivering.

Eventually, enough of him had come back to life that he was able to swing his leg to the floor. It was then that the real fun began: pins and needles coursed throughout his body as each limb came back online. If the fire of the pod was bad, this was hell. From what he had heard, the pins and needles didn't stop for a whole day sometimes. Nor did the intense nausea that was creeping up on him even now. His head hurt. It felt a little like a concussion and a hangover had a baby, then let that baby crack him in the head with a baseball bat. Ironically, according to the manual, the only real cure for all of this was sleep. The last thing he wanted to do.

After a few minutes of letting him stare at his own liquid vomit on the deck, Caroline, who had woken days earlier, strode over to him and helped him limp toward the showers.

He found a faucet and turned it on, full blast, letting the hot water soak deeply into his skin. He stood that way for some time, then reluctantly soaped down and toweled off. He hoped his cabin had extra blankets.

...

James ate, happy to be keeping food down again. It had been four days since they'd been awoken from stasis. He was sat in the dining room closest to his bunk, picking at the freeze dried and re-heated food in front of him. They were one day from Mars.

The reflection staring back at James from the table's reflective surface did not seem like his own. The eyes were haunted, and the expression vacant. He had been told it was common to look like this after stasis. To the body, the experience was traumatic; unlike anything it had known before. The feeling was similar to severe jetlag, but combined with a strange disassociation, from the self and from the external world. James hated it and hoped it would pass soon. At least the vomiting and shaking had stopped.

"You gonna' eat that or just stare at it?"

Ira Aguilar smiled and sat down, holding a steaming tray of her own re-hydrated and re-heated slop. Her expression softened into one of concern. "Are you doing OK?"

"Better." James said. "The vomiting has stopped. Now I just need to get my appetite back."

Ira nodded. "Well, it's important that you eat. We're almost there! Can you believe it?"

"No, I know, I know. It's incredible. Eighty-three-million-mile journey, almost finished."

"And then we'll set foot on Mars. Mars dude. Mars." Ira raised her eyebrows and took a big bite of her food. "I'm so excited I can't even stand it. And I'm ready to get some fresh air." She laughed to herself. "Well, you know what I mean."

James nodded. "You're ready to stretch your legs. I get it."

"How about you? Are you excited?"

James paused before answering. Excited? "I'm...prepared."

"Prepared, huh? That doesn't sound very good."

"What's wrong with being prepared? Boy scouts are prepared."

"You're a boy scout? Like an Eagle Scout?"

"Well, no, I just mean...like the expression, you know? 'Always be prepared.' 'It's good to be prepared...'"

Ira stared at him in silence, a slight grin playing at her mouth. "I don't wanna' live on Mars with a boy scout."

James wasn't sure what to say. "How am I supposed to feel if not prepared?"

Ira looked for a moment as if she might raise her voice, then thought better of it. She continued in hushed but emphatic tones.

"How about ecstatic? Enthusiastic? Longing? Yearning even! We just traveled through space for six months to ANOTHER PLANET. How many people can say they've done that?"

James stared at her in silence as he fought another wave of nausea. "Yeah, I guess. It's pretty cool."

"Pretty cool?!? I..." Ira reminded herself again to keep her voice low. "Look, James...James, right?"

James nodded.

"James...you're being kind of a bummer."

James laughed. "Tell me how you really feel."

"Hey, I'm just trying to be honest. Let me give you a piece of friendly advice: there is no faster way of isolating yourself from a team than by having a bad attitude. We're about to face a ton of dangers together. All of us. Every second, the planet will be trying to kill us. And we'll only have each other to lean on. Preparation doesn't get you through something like that. At least, not on its own. You need enthusiasm. Like, deep, scary enthusiasm. Commitment to the mission. You think everyone else on here doesn't have their own concerns? Their own discomforts? Their own fears? They do. But if we spend all our time dwelling on them, we'll get bummed out, stop working together, and die."

"I'm not asking anyone else to be...prepared."

"It doesn't work like that my man. Attitudes are contagious. You go down there all mopey, and pretty soon you'll succeed in making everyone else all mopey. Then we die."

James grunted. "Sounds a bit dramatic."

"I'm just saying that this is gonna' be a long, hard trip, with the same group of people all living on top of each other. Dealing with each other's bullshit, day in and day out. You can either help make that hard situation easier, or you can make it way harder. On everybody. When you're a gazillion miles away from home it pays not to push away the only people you have. That's all I'm saying."

James took a bite of his re-hydrated slop. "I guess I follow. Sounds like you're speaking from experience."

Ira leaned back, shrugged her shoulders and took a bite of her own food, speaking between mouthfuls. "I've had my share of trips through the suck."

"Mars? You've been here before?"

"No, no, never Mars. Research stations. Couple warzones."

"What are you, a medic?"

"Nope. Reporter."

"They sent a reporter up here?"

"Well, I'm only a reporter on this trip. Normally I'm more of a researcher."

"You're gonna' have to explain that one."

"I'm a sociologist. Graduate student, Indiana University. I go on trips to isolated, off the grid places – whether permanently or temporarily – to study how the people there are reacting to the new environment and each other. It's all part of my thesis."

"How long have you been working on your thesis?"

Ira chortled. "Bout' six years now. It's a longitudinal study."

James grinned. "I guess it will be almost a decade by the time you get home, publish and graduate."

Ira winked. "You're assuming I pass the board the first time! I might be at this into my forties!"

They both laughed. Ira ate. James poked at his food.

"You said you were here as a reporter this time. What's that about?"

"Mmm, right." Ira swallowed the last bite of her food and put her fork down. "There were no science grants available for a sociologist going to Mars. So, I applied for the art grant."

"There's an art grant to Mars?"

"Umm hmm. For three spots. Three roundtrip tickets to the red planet for two years. Me and two other guys."

"Who?"

"Dunno', really. We haven't talked much. Ones kind of a dick...not sure what he does. The other...he's a painter, I think. The skinny guy with the weird hair."

"Olive?"

"Yeah, that's right. Olive Wren. I've looked up his stuff online. Pretty decent."

"So, the powers that be were willing to give up seats that could have been filled by scientists or life-support staff...to artists?"

"Yeah. I mean, if it makes you feel better I only kinda' count. The data I collect is for my thesis, but I had to promise I'd write a book about the trip."

"I'm sorry, I didn't mean to imply..."

"What? That art was frivolous or something? Don't be sorry. It's not!"

"I was going to say sorry for implying you weren't a scientist.

Ira shrugged. "We aren't robots you know."

James gave up on his food. It tasted like crap. "Shit. Yeah, art is great. Of course." He gave a weak thumbs up.

Ira laughed. "Very convincing."

"So, what exactly is your book about?"

"About this trip. My experiences."

"So, what, you're up here spying on us?"

"Well...I wouldn't call it spying. I told you I was doing it didn't I?"

"But you're writing all of this down?"

"I don't know what parts I'll end up writing down. But I'm writing about my experiences up here, yeah."

James pushed away from the table and stood up, slowly, still unsteady on his feet. "Well, on that note, I think I'll retire from this conversation. It was...nice? To meet you."

Ira laughed. "I can't tell if you're serious."

"To be honest, right now, neither can I. I'm going to go lay down and think about it. See you later..."

"Ira."

"Ira. See you later Ira." James took a few tentative steps, then stopped and turned around. "By the way, Ira, this whole conversation was off the record."

Ira smiled. "Nope! Too late!" She pointed to her head. "It's all up here, now. This will be the opening chapter. Hell, it might be a book of its own: grumpy man goes to Mars."

James nodded. "I'd read it. Me and, like, two other people." He turned to go. "Bye."

"Bye James. Remember what I said! Enthusiasm! Yearning!"

7

SEVEN

Steven Reese stood on the command deck and watched the skies with great concern. Through his binoculars he could still see the capsule, now a tiny dot that grew ever fainter with each passing second. "Get me a telemetry update on the departure."

Blaine Nelson rolled his eyes and checked his monitor. "No change since last update. Departing capsule is on-profile and scheduled for rendezvous within the next half-hour."

Steven grunted an acknowledgement and checked his binoculars again. "Continue to update me in two-minute intervals."

"Copy that." Blaine looked directly at Steven, attempting to meet his eyes. "She's going to be fine, Steve."

Steven lowered his binoculars and looked at Blaine. Then he grunted again and looked back to the sky. "What's the status on our arrivals?"

Blaine consulted his monitor again. "Getting ready to undock. Disconnection scheduled in five minutes."

"What was the last direct communication you had with the transport?"

"Confirmation of green condition. Fifteen minutes ago."

"Ping them again."

"We're getting remote system updates. It's all coming in just fine..."

Steve cut him off. "Ping them again. We need to be sure."

Blaine swallowed his irritation. "Understood." He opened a channel to the transport. "*Stella Vectio*, this is Alpha Base. Come in please."

A few seconds passed with nothing on the line but static. Then, a voice. "Alpha Base, this is *Stella Vectio*. Ready to copy."

Blaine smiled. "Hey, is that Jermaine?"

After a half second delay, another response. "It sure is, the one and only. That Blaine?"

"It is indeed. How was your flight?"

On the other end of the line, Jermaine laughed. "So far so good. I'll be honest, I was asleep for most of it."

Blaine feigned shock. "What the hell kind of a pilot are you? Jeez!" After a pause for laughter, he continued. "We were just wanting to check on you, make sure everything is running smoothly."

"Yeah, yeah, we're all good here. On profile, standard plan. Should be all done with the switch by the end of the hour, then headed back out. Are you guys not getting our updates?"

"No, no, we are. Just crossing our T's and dotting our I's"

"Ok, fair enough. We'll reach out when the transfer is complete."

"Sounds good *Stella Vectio*. Thank you for your time. Alpha Base out."

"Out here."

Blaine turned to Steve. "Sounds like they're on track."

"I heard," he said. After a pause he added: "Thanks for checking."

Blaine nodded and Steve returned to scanning the skies.

The two men spent the next few minutes in silence. Blaine swallowed hard and fought back a lingering sense of dread. It was always like this at transfer time. At least, so he had heard. This was Blaine's first transfer at Alpha Base since his own arrival. The next transfer he would be involved in, a year from now, would be his own departure.

He had been warned by a few of the veterans that this time would be difficult. How could it not be? They had just spent a year living and working in close proximity to the same group of people every day. Now half of them were headed off world, only to be replaced by a totally new group. There were so many questions: would the new mix of people get along with each other? Would they ever hear from or see the departing residents again? Would any friendships or relationships made over the past year survive the real world?

Blaine thought it must be the last question which was bothering Steve. He had made a friendship with one of the departing group. A close one. Honestly, it was probably more than a friendship. And now he had to say goodbye. Blaine reflected on how hard that must be. He didn't mind admitting to himself that he had been jealous for a relationship of his own out here in the wilderness. But the look on Steve's face now made him grateful that he hadn't found one.

Blaine's console beeped, breaking the silence. "Good separation. Our guests are on their way down to greet us."

Steve acknowledged the news with another grunt, never taking his eyes from the expanse overhead.

Blaine stopped what he was doing and joined Steve by the window. He couldn't see anything but the yellow-red tinted sky. Both capsules were outside of the atmosphere at the moment, indecipherable to the eye. Blaine thought about pointing this out to Steve, then thought better of it. He returned to his station and followed the live updates from the console. Atmospheric entry was starting. That was easily the riskiest part, aside from landing. Blaine did not give Steve the update. Assuming the arriving capsule stayed together, he would be able to see it through his binoculars soon enough.

A few more minutes passed. Like clockwork, the console beeped, indicating successful re-entry, just as a small point of light became visible in the heavens. Steven perked up. "I've got something here, possible atmospheric entry."

"Telemetry confirms good re-entry," said Blaine. "First drag chute is deployed. Estimated landfall in ten minutes."

"Roger that. Update on the departures?"

This time Blaine made no effort to hide the irritation in his voice. "No change."

"Copy."

Blaine activated the comms channel to the hangar. "Welcoming committee, are we all set to go?"

Brad Austin, senior Aerospace Propulsion Systems Specialist and welcoming committee team lead, answered the call. "Affirmative, ready here. Standing by in the hangar until we get confirmation of landfall and a good location."

"Good deal. Connie with you?" Connie was the facility's Nurse. Her mission duties did not call for her to leave the base that often, so the welcoming committee represented a unique opportunity for her to stretch her legs. She was excited, and it showed.

"Connie here! Ready to go! We have the med bay all prepped to receive any sickness or casualty. I have my field kit packed for emergencies and triage. If anyone in the arriving group is feeling any kind of way, we have what they need to get right again in double time!"

Blaine was grateful that the comms channel was audio only, so Connie couldn't see his raised eyebrows. "All right, Connie. Awesome. Sounds good."

Blaine added the hospital to the line. "Carolyn, you got anything to add?"

Carolyn Boss, the facility's Medical Doctor, shared Blaine's sarcastic sense of humor. She knew what he was trying to do. Normally she wouldn't mind, but she liked Connie, so Blaine wasn't allowed to make fun of her. "Yes, Blaine, all set here. Just like Connie said. Ready to help as needed."

Blaine smiled at the response, sensing Carolyn's irritation. "All right, excellent. Just making double sure you're as ready as you can be."

At her workstation, Carolyn opened a private chat window to Blaine. It read, "Fuck you buddy. I'm double sure you're an asshole." The text was followed by two pictograms depicting raised middle fingers.

At his console, Blaine opened the chat window and laughed.

"Something funny?" Steve asked.

Blaine quickly composed himself. "No, no, nothing. Sorry."

Steve gave him a confused look, then went back to his binoculars.

Blaine looked out the window in the direction of Steve's gaze. The capsule was plainly visible to the naked eye now, rocketing across the sky toward its landing site. Blaine checked the console and gave a verbal report. "Touchdown in eight minutes."

Steve did not respond.

Blaine once again toggled the comms channel to the hangar. "Brad, you there?"

"Go ahead."

"This is my first transfer on this end so let me go over this one more time: you're taking three vehicles, is that right?"

Brad responded quickly. "That is accurate. Three vehicles: two rovers and one heavy lift platform. Connie and I will be in Rover One, and Owen and Jim will be in Rover Two. The lift platform will follow on autopilot."

"Copy. I'll let you know as soon as we confirm landfall."

...

SEVEN

On the whole, James found the trip to the surface far less terrifying than the trip to the ship. After everyone was strapped snugly into their seats, there wasn't any sensation of movement at all. James followed the progress of the mission via the comms channel, and he was surprised to hear that they had detached from the *Vectio*.

A few minutes into their descent, Ira locked eyes with him from across the capsule and winked. "You ready to make history Mr. Enthusiasm?"

Just for giggles, James decided to play along. "Hell yeah! Let's do this!"

Ira hooted. James didn't think that was something people actually did, but Ira did it. "That's what I'm talking about! Mr. Enthusiasm bringing the heat!" Ira laughed loudly to herself before lapsing into silence.

The other passengers made no response, either for or against her outburst.

James wondered what Ira's bravado might be hiding. Was she just as scared as him? Maybe more so?

These thoughts were interrupted by shaking as the capsule ran up against resistance from the Martian atmosphere. The air here was thin, so the resistance was far less noticeable than it would have been on Earth, but it was still enough to give the passengers a start.

James looked straight up, toward the capsule's hatch. He could see a faint glow through the windows located there. He knew that meant the capsule was absorbing tremendous heat, generated by the friction of striking a blanket of molecules while moving at thousands of miles per hour. James was slightly unnerved to remember that the bulk of that friction wasn't occurring in the area he was looking at, but was instead happening directly beneath his feet. If he could see some light at the top of the capsule, where the windows were, the bottom of it must be glowing like a candle.

James swallowed hard and decided to look at something else.

The glow subsided soon enough, and the sensation of movement lessened, although he could still feel a gentle rumble underneath his feet.

Jermaine's voice came over the comms channel from the *Vectio*, where he was overseeing the capsule's descent remotely. "Alrighty folks, you should be on the ground in about ten minutes. Releasing the first drag chute now, so get ready for a bit of a jolt."

Jermaine wasn't kidding. James went from feeling like he weighed zero pounds to hundreds in less than a second. He felt the blood drain from his head and an unpleasant, vertigo-like sensation take its place.

This process continued several times: a drag chute would be discharged and the sensation of weightlessness would return, followed by another Jarring sensation, quickly replaced with a feeling of steady weight, followed by another chute-discharge.

On the fourth cycle, the process stopped. This chute deployment felt strangely different – more permanent. The capsule was no longer traveling at a breakneck speed, although James had a hunch that it was still traveling fast.

Jermaine's voice came over the comms channel again. "Last set of chutes away. It's all easy sailing from here, ladies and gents, so sit back and enjoy the ride. Should make final landfall in five minutes."

...

Blaine perked up at the update from the telemetry console and turned to Steve. "Final chute is away. Landfall in five minutes."

"Roger that. Any idea of the final landing area?"

Blaine pressed a few buttons. "Looks more and more likely they will touchdown in sector six. North-eastern corner."

"Did you pass that on to Brad and his team?"

Blaine was already switching to the comms console. "Doing so now...Brad, you copy me?"

"Brad here, go."

"Sector six, north-east corner. Confirmation in less than five minutes."

"Copy all, standing by for confirmation."

Blaine turned once more to Steve. "Welcoming committee is all set."

Steve nodded. "Excellent. Rooms are prepared, right?"

"Yup. I spoke with Weaver this morning and he confirmed."

Steve nodded again and stood silently, staring out the windows. Curiously, he was no longer scanning the horizon and sky with his binoculars, even though he now had something to look at. Instead, he simply stared, eyes glazed over, deep in thought.

A beep from the console caught Blaine's attention. He cleared his throat. "Steve?"

"Hmm?"

"Just got confirmation that the departing capsule has matched velocity with the *Vectio*. Final docking procedure is initiated. Should be complete in the next ten minutes or so."

Steve frowned. This was the most dangerous part of the transfer, for everyone involved. "Understood."

Blaine shuddered as he thought of the implications of a botched docking procedure. If that happened, in all likelihood, the departing capsule would explode, killing everyone on board. The *Vectio* would either explode or sustain severe damage, leaving the future of its surviving crew in doubt. Residents of Alpha Base, meanwhile, would be stranded on Mars for the foreseeable future. In a best-case scenario, the *Vectio* could only manage one pick up a year, and that was assuming no interruptions in its current velocity and flight path.

At present, the *Vectio* performed a kind of "figure eight" orbit between Earth and Mars, barely slowing down enough to drop off and pick up capsules at either end of its loop. That analogy wasn't exact of course, since variations in the timing and position of orbiting planetary bodies necessitated constant minor adjustments to the craft's flight path, but it captured the essence of the *Vectio's* mission: to be a constantly rotating transport. Any interruption in that rotation, any slowdown for repairs or, God forbid, replacement, would add months or years to the transit time between Mars and Earth.

SEVEN

The craft would have to be slowed down, fixed or replaced, then sent back out into the stars. Once it finally reached the correct velocity, months would still lie ahead of it before Mars was reached. And all of that assumed the ready availability of replacement parts and/or a new space craft. If something else had to be built first...well, the math was clear: it could take a while to get picked up.

Blaine supposed it was possible that one of the other shuttles, which serviced different bases located in different spots on the Martian surface, could be redirected to pick them up. But each of those shuttles had their own orbits, and each fed into their own rotation schedules. It seemed unlikely that the folks back home would choose to fix one problem by creating several new ones. No, if the shuttle ran into any problems they would be on their own for a while.

Blaine wasn't sure if Alpha Base had adequate supplies for such a long layover. The Base was regularly re-supplied by the incoming capsules. In the event of a shuttle breakdown, those supplies would obviously become unavailable. Many of the base's resources were harvested in situ: water was recycled and oxygen reclaimed where possible. A greenhouse made some fresh fruits and vegetables. Hydrazine fuel was made locally. Plus, a sizeable spares stock existed for most equipment parts. With all of that taken into account, Alpha Base could last a while without resupply. But Blaine didn't think they could last indefinitely. Plus, people had lives. Not only would some lives be lost in a docking failure, but the people left behind on Alpha Base would spend that much more time away from loved ones. Suffice to say, a broken shuttle would be bad for everybody.

...

Just before landfall, a sudden roar filled James's ears and shook him in his seat. It was the retrorockets firing in order to provide a final cushion for their landing. The impact still shook James to the core and rattled his teeth in his head. Then, just like that, there was no movement at all. The sensation of stillness – not just stillness but weighted stillness - was surreal. After all that time in space, constantly moving in some fashion or another, they were here. They were at rest. On Mars.

Jermaine's voice came in over the comms channel again. "Well folks, you made it! We're gonna' need everybody to keep their seats for a minute here while we run some system checks and get ahold of your ride. We'll let you know when its ok to unstrap yourselves. Thanks for your patience."

Jermaine signed off from his lofty perch, and, for a moment, they were alone.

James wasn't sure what he had expected from the group at landfall. A round of applause perhaps? Cheers? Certainly not silence. Were they all stunned? Nonchalant? Or something else?

...

SEVEN

The telemetry console beeped and flashed green. Jermaine's voice rose from the speaker. "Alpha Base, this is *Stella Vectio*, over."

"Go ahead *Stella Vectio*."

"We are all good here. Departures are on board and arrivals are ready for pick-up."

"Copy that, Jermaine, thanks for the update. I'll pass it on to Steve. You take care, ok?"

"Roger, roger, will do. See you in a year or two."

"Sounds good. Alpha Base out."

Blaine paused for a moment of reflection before giving the update to Steve. That was the last time he would speak to Jermaine in at least a year. Strange.

He turned to Steve. "Good dock. They're all tucked in."

Steve breathed out heavily, in a noise that was both satisfaction and relief. "Good. Thank you, Blaine."

Blaine nodded and turned back to the console. "Welcoming committee, you have a green light. Sending the arriving capsule's coordinates to you now."

Brad's voice came through the radio quickly and strongly, his excitement clear. "Copy that. Welcoming committee is moving out."

Blaine turned to Steve. "They're on their way."

Steve nodded, once again in control. "OK then. Let's see how this goes."

...

Brad stood on top of the heavy lift platform, fully suited up but for his helmet, and yelled for his team's attention.

"Listen up! Its time. Let's follow procedure and get this done smoothly. Connie, I want you with me in Rover One. Owen, Jim, you follow in Rover Two. We should be at the site within the hour. Any questions or concerns before we head out?"

Jim Webster headed wordlessly for Rover Two.

Owen Scranton followed, but not before looking up at Brad with a wry smile.

"I guess not." Brad muttered to himself.

Connie approached him as he jumped from the platform onto the hangar floor. "Is he always in such a hurry?"

Brad understood her concern, but dismissed it. "Ahh, he's just Jim. Grumpy fuck."

Connie's eyes widened at his foul language.

"Sorry," he said, sheepishly.

Connie laughed. "Oh, please. I have boys of my own and two ex-husbands. I've heard worse."

Brad smiled. "I didn't know you have kids."

"Oh, yeah. Well, if you came by the clinic every month like you're supposed to we might have talked about it by now."

Brad kept smiling as he led the way to Rover One. "Every month? We're supposed to check in with you guys that often?"

"Indeed, indeed. Once a month, per site policy. Lots of things can go wrong with you out here you know. Bone & muscle atrophy, chronic stress, undetected injury, pressurization issues. All kinds of things. That's why you need your myostatin inhibitor shots and regular checkups."

Brad stopped in front of Rover One's passenger door and opened it for Connie. "Lots of things can go wrong with you back on Earth, too."

Connie climbed up into her seat. "I don't joke about mission fitness, Mr. I wanna' see you in that clinic after this, you hear?"

Brad laughed and closed the door behind her. "OK, yes ma 'mm."

He turned to his left and began walking around the back of the rover, toward the driver's side entrance. He affixed his helmet, climbed behind the wheel, activated the driver's console, then checked radio comms, both inside and outside his suit. "Rover Two, this is Rover One. Good copy?"

Jim's grizzled voice came back in reply, echoing in his helmet. "Yeh."

Brad removed his helmet, then asked Blaine the same question over the rover's channel.

Blaine responded. "Good copy from control."

Finally, Brad synched his suit and the rover's console, so he would be able to control the rover remotely if needed. He closed the rover's door behind him.

"Ok, we are about ready." He said aloud to no one in particular. "Dexter?"

Dexter, the station's AI, replied. *"Ready."*

"Please synchronize Loading Platform One's movements with Rover One. Continuous distance of fifteen meters."

"One moment."

From behind them, Brad could feel the enormous vehicle's engine turn over. The lights on the surface of the platform all sprang to life.

"Loading Platform One is now synchronized with Rover One. Following at a distance of fifteen meters."

"Thank you, Dex!"

The AI did not bother with a reply.

Brad cleared his throat. "Opening doors now, Control."

"Roger." Blaine replied. "Safe travels."

Brad toggled a switch on the rover's console and opened the hangar's inner airlock door.

Rover Two drove forward first, the airlock closing slowly behind them. There wouldn't be enough room for all three vehicles in the lock at once.

Brad watched through the inner airlock's windows as the outer airlock door opened and Rover Two drove a few meters away from the hangar's entrance, onto the planet's surface.

Brad waited for the outer airlock door to close and the pressure within the lock to equalize, then triggered the sequence again.

Rover One entered the lock. The heavy lift platform followed.

Brad heard a rushing sound which slowly faded away as the airlock space reached vacuum. The doors of the rover seemed to press outward, straining their seals.

All three vehicles headed northward on the Martian plane, the anticipation of meeting their new arrivals seeming to hang in the air, like cobwebs.

...

James heard a series of popping sounds, then a rush of air as the capsule hatch sprung open. The inner lining of the capsule's walls seemed to protrude inward ever so slightly as the pressure dropped to 0.087 psi – the average of the Martian surface. Their suits, too, became stiffer and more difficult to manage.

Each man and woman took turns unbuckling themselves and climbing up the ladder from the base of the capsule to the top.

At his turn, James stood stock still. He looked down at the floor and stomped once, hard, clearly feeling the impact but only hearing a dull thud. The stomp should have made a loud metallic clang, but here, nobody seemed to notice. He realized that the vibrations had traveled through his suit to his ears, and nobody else had heard a thing.

Shaking his head in wonder, he walked to the base of the ladder and looked straight up through the hole at the top. He could see the sky. It was darker than he had expected. Almost, he imagined, what an earthen sky must look like during a sandstorm.

He took his turn up the ladder slowly, ensuring that each booted step and gauntleted handhold was sure before proceeding. Up he went, hand over hand, boot-step after boot-step. When he reached the top, he was greeted by a vista that took his breath away. The sky, butterscotch yellow with hints of pink, extended in a glorious dome in all directions. He could clearly sense the planet's curvature in this place, so unimpeded by buildings and other structures was his view of the horizon. He wasn't sure he had ever seen a sky so large. At some points far in the distance he could see mountainous formations, red-hued rocks in familiar but alien shapes. At other points he saw only a line, where the sky and ground seemed to meet as it curved away from them. He had never been in a place so expansive, or felt so small.

This must have been what the American pioneers of old felt like when they looked out on the great plains, he thought. A literal world of possibility awaited them – but were they too small for the job? What a delightful and terrifying thought to ponder.

James swung his legs clumsily over the side of the hatch and started down the ladder on the other side, still silent and awestruck by their new environs.

As he stepped off the lander and onto the Martian surface for the first time, he was surprised at the firmness of the ground. He had expected a soft sand. It was sand all right, or, at least, finely ground particulates of rock that were like sand. But they had been compressed by forces older than human thought into a sort of hard clay. It felt like walking on a dry lakebed. In their immediate vicinity there were rocks, ground, people, lander and nothing else.

James joined the cluster of suited bodies huddled together to the left of the capsule. He thought it was funny how the instinct to cluster for warmth and safety persisted, even when their warmth was already provided for.

Ira stepped forward and pointed away from the group, toward the horizon.

SEVEN

James followed the direction of her gaze, and saw their ride – a grouping of amorphous shapes lumbering towards them, a cloud of dust kicked up in their wake.

The landing party's radios crackled. "Alright folks. I'm broadcasting on open comm. Can you all hear me? Thumbs up if you can hear me."

Everyone gave a thumbs up.

"OK good. Hello, everyone! Let me be the first to welcome you to Mars! My name is Brad Austin. I'm the lead Aerospace Propulsion Specialist at Alpha Base. We are your ride. Hold tight and we'll be there with you shortly."

Nobody said anything, but James could feel the group's tension ease somewhat. Here was proof that they had not been stranded. Soon they would be safely aboard a vehicle and headed toward their new home.

As they got closer, James was able to make out the shape of the vehicles coming their way in greater detail. It looked as if there were three of them: two smaller, car-like vehicles and one enormous, flat monstrosity with giant treads. It was the last vehicle that had been kicking up all the dust. It had a shape in the middle of an otherwise flat deck. James was able to make it out as a folded-up crane. He figured it must be some kind of rolling sled for the capsule itself.

The vehicles finally arrived and rolled to a stop. The group waited while the dust cloud that had followed them briefly engulfed the area, dimming the already preternaturally dark sky by a few more degrees. When the dust cleared, James saw that his landing party's nearly pristine white suits were now covered in a thin layer of red clay. He would have called it dust but it seemed to stick to whatever surface it landed on, like a thin talc you just couldn't brush all the way off, no matter how hard you tried.

The doors to the first car-like vehicle opened and two suited figures got out. The taller of the two suited figures strode over, faced the crowd, and spoke over an open channel. "Once again, my name is Brad and I'll be your tour guide today."

Brad paused as the comms line filled with nervous laughter.

He gestured to the smaller figure at his side. "This is Connie Stone, our registered nurse. She's here to help any of you that might be feeling woozy or any other kind of way after your trip down. If you need her assistance, please let Connie or myself know and we'll take you aboard Rover One for a quick checkup before we get going. Now, having said that, does anyone feel like they need urgent medical attention?"

The channel was silent.

"Ok, very good. If that changes at any time, let one of us know right away. In the second rover behind me, you have Owen Scranton and Jim Webster. Owen is going to help me load the capsule behind you onto our giant mobile loading platform here, while Jim and Connie help get you each settled into one of the rovers. It's very nice to meet you all and I'm sure we'll have an opportunity to get to know each other better in the coming months. Before I turn things over to Connie, is it correct that our new Site Lead is in this group?"

James awkwardly raised his hand. He felt each helmeted head turn imperceptibly in his direction. "Right here."

Brad smiled and waved. "OK, very good. I'll have a quick word with you, sir. Connie, take it away."

Brad clicked off the open comm line and Connie's voice replaced his, barking directions at the group and herding them into two lines.

Brad approached James and extended his hand. As they shook, a private comms invitation popped up in his HUD and James accepted. Connie's voice faded into the background.

"Brad Austin. Very nice to meet you."

"James Wilmot. Likewise."

"Once we arrive at the base, I'd like the opportunity to introduce you to the staff while the others get settled in their rooms."

James nodded. "Of course, absolutely. It would be great to meet the team."

Brad seemed pleased with his reaction. "Ok, great. Why don't you ride with me in Rover One and I can brief you on a few items of interest on the way there?"

"Sounds great."

"Excellent! Again, sure is nice to meet you, Boss-man!"

James guffawed. "Oh, please, just James is fine."

"Ok, James, see you aboard."

"See you then."

The private comms line clicked off and Connie's voice came in at full volume once again. "...follow me to Rover One and Jim to Rover Two."

James fell into step behind the group headed toward Rover One. As they got closer, James realized that each rover was larger than it had looked from far away, in the shadow of the moving crane. They were more akin to armored personnel carriers than cars.

The group paused at the entrance of Rover One.

Connie made some practiced motions near the door and a light on a panel to its side went from red to green. Then she turned and faced the group.

"Ok, everyone, eyes on me! Each of the rovers has an airlock, capable of fitting two people at a time. When you embark on a rover under normal circumstances, you're going to open the exterior door, step inside, close it, wait for the airlock to cycle, then open the interior door. For this particular ride, Brad and his team have gone ahead and depressurized the whole interior, to make loading easier. What that means is, do not remove your helmet once seated. You will die. There is a sign on the hull above the interior door, which will turn green once the cabin is pressurized. After everyone is loaded and that panel turns green, you may remove your helmets if you wish. Be advised, however, that this dust on our suits is basically asbestos. A little won't kill you as long as you don't have any respiratory issues, but it is irritating to the eyes and throat, and it probably isn't any good for you in the long run. Personally, I'll be keeping my helmet on until we get where we're going and have been properly hosed down. Everybody clear?"

A chorus of acknowledgements filled the open line.

"Good deal. Once on board, go ahead and file in all the way to the back until each seat is taken." With that, Connie turned around, made another motion, and the rover's door slid open.

The group took turns filing into the rover. Each person paused at the door, grabbing the handhold to the left of the entrance and hauling their body up into the cab. James was at the back of the line. Once James was seated, Connie closed the inner airlock door, stepped outside and closed the exterior airlock door as well.

For a time, there was nothing. Then, James became aware of a gentle hissing sound, coming to him as if from far away. The sound grew louder, then became accompanied by pinging and snapping noises. The cabin was pressurizing. Still, James kept his helmet on, as Connie had recommended. The others did the same.

They waited for what seemed an interminable amount of time. James supposed they were loading the capsule onto the mobile platform. He strained to see the platform's claw in action, but, although he could see into the driver's cabin and through the cabin's windshield, they were not turned in the right direction.

Still more time passed, and James grew restless. He was relieved when Jeff spoke up. "Does it usually take this long?"

Brad's voice came over the line. "Sorry folks, we're doing the best we can. Gotta make sure we don't leave any scratches, as this capsule is gonna' be someone's ride home in the near future. Won't be much longer, I promise. Also, let me remind you, this is the open comm line. Private chats can be initiated with more than one person if you need."

James cringed internally for Jeff. Jeff seemed unfazed.

Finally, Brad and Connie returned to Rover One. James saw them open the hatch, then watched as they stood in the airlock and waited for it to cycle. The interior airlock door opened, and Brad took the driver's seat. Connie sat by his side.

Brad removed his helmet. He set it down on the console between him and Connie and started talking. James and the others couldn't hear much more than muffled warbling through their helmets.

When nobody answered him, Brad finally looked up and noticed that everyone but him was still fully suited. He turned to the dash and spoke some commands, then pressed a few buttons. His voice snapped into focus over their helmet radios. "Can you guys hear me now?"

Ira responded. "Yeah, we have you."

Connie interjected. "They couldn't hear you because they had their helmets on."

Brad seemed confused. "Yeah...I know."

"Well why don't you have yours on?" Connie asked.

"I prefer to drive without it..."

"It's terrible for your lungs. This stuff is toxic." She gestured toward the red and orange stains on everyone's suits.

Brad smiled. "Well, you're not wrong. And I don't blame any of you for keeping your helmets on. But when you've been here a while...let's just say I'm pretty sure that if I'm going to get cancer, I've already got it."

Connie's reply was stern. "There is a decontamination protocol that these new arrivals will soon be learning. The protocol exists for a reason. You should make sure they have seen how it works."

SEVEN

Brad sighed and looked at the faces in the cabin, clearly irritated by this exchange and embarrassed that it was happening in public. He flicked a toggle on the dash, and his voice disappeared from the radio. Then, he re-donned his helmet and pressurized the seal. "Can everyone hear me, ok?"

Ira responded in the affirmative again.

"Good." Said Brad.

The ride to Alpha Base proceeded in silence. Any communications between rovers One and Two must have taken place over a private line, because James never heard them. All he heard was the lurch and rumble of the rover as its hardened wheels crunched over the rough desert terrain.

EIGHT

Alpha Base started as a silver-white speck on the horizon, barely visible through the rover's windshield. As they trundled along on the open terrain, the speck grew bigger and began to take on a shape. The central hangar was the station's dominant feature. It stood, tens of meters high, a lone skyscraper on the desolate plains around it. The rest of the station, basically a series of metal boxes on stilts that were connected by tubes, lay diminutively beneath it. A greenhouse facility lay several yards to the left of the station. It looked to be at least half as large as the station itself – perhaps bigger. The only other equipment he could see was a bank of solar panels and a generator for the perimeter radiation shield. The whole installation, from greenhouse to hangar, appeared inexpressibly tiny in the vast expanse surrounding it. The entirety of the base's footprint on the planet was visible to James and the others in this moment. The next closest human habitation was thousands of miles away, at a different base. It was a startling reminder of just how alone they were. In all the ways that mattered, the crew here were all each other had.

As they drew ever closer, all he could see was a tiny sliver of the metal box nearest the hangar, then only the hangar itself. The hangar's enormous door began to move upwards. As it finished opening, James could see a second door behind the first one. The intervening space, James assumed, was a very large airlock.

Rover One drove into the airlock, followed by the dutiful platform.

Brad's voice came over the open line. "We can only fit two of the three vehicles in here at a time. Rover Two, you guys will join us in a moment."

With that, James noticed a shadow falling over the rover's inhabitants as the hangar door slowly slid closed. Once it was shut all the way, they sat in silence until James heard a rushing sound. The airlock was filling with air so fast he could hear it through the walls of the rover. That he could hear it at all meant it must nearly be full.

The cycle completed and Brad drove forward into the main hangar bay. There, three technicians wearing clean suits and respirators ushered them into an area surrounded by plastic curtains.

The rover came to a stop, and Brad's voice filled their helmet speakers. "Alrighty. Everyone sit tight while the decon crew processes us."

James watched through a porthole as the technicians sprayed the rover down with water. Thick chunks of Martian clay and machine oil fell to the ground and mixed together into a slushy puddle. That puddle lingered a while, its top layer shimmering in the light, before joining a river of sandy water making its way to a drain in the floor.

The rover's lock cycled, a small gust of air moving through the cabin as the outer and inner doors were opened.

James and the others followed Brad and Connie as they disembarked the rover and moved clockwise toward the rear of the vehicle. There, they each took turns standing with their arms and legs held out to the sides as pressure washers cleaned their suits of dust.

James looked behind him as he waited his turn and saw one of the techs attaching a large plastic sleeve to the frame of the rover's open outer hatch. The sleeve extended away from the rover, eventually forming a clear plastic duct. A loud noise came from somewhere beyond the curtains enclosing them, and a cloud of dust from the rover's interior began collecting in the sleeve before being whisked away.

When his turn came, he stood with legs and arms akimbo. The water from the washer struck him with unexpected force, and he stumbled backwards before catching himself and leaning into the spray.

Once his turn was over, he joined the line of people forming on the other side of the plastic curtains. There, his compatriots were removing their helmets and taking grateful breaths, free of their suit's claustrophobic insides.

James reached up and broke the seal around his neck. Hangar air rushed into his helmet, and he was met with an acrid smell, like rusty metal mixed with compost.

He craned his neck backward, taking in a view he hadn't had access to before. The roof of the structure was higher than he had thought. Two metal walkways led from the floor of the hangar, where they were now, to a catwalk that lined the hangar's walls. The catwalk formed an aerial perimeter of sorts, from which every square foot of the hangar's floor could be seen at once from above. The catwalk lining the back wall led to a door on the left, behind which he assumed they would find the rest of the base.

The last of his companions joined them from the other side of the curtain, along with the rest of the crew from the second rover.

Brad spoke up. "OK, all, decontamination is complete. Please hang up your suits on the wall over there, then follow me."

After they were all unsuited, Brad led the party up the closest flight of stairs and along the rear catwalk. The group paused as Brad unsealed the door at the top and it flew open, a gust of air flowing past their heads.

"As you can see," he said, "the tunnel connecting the rest of the base to the hangar is kept at a slightly positive pressure. It helps keep the dust out."

Brad went through the door first, followed by the others.

James turned around, took one last glance at the hangar, then crossed the threshold into Alpha base.

...

James watched the others make their way through the base's cylindrical corridors in search of their rooms and instantly regretted agreeing to a tour. He was tired, more tired than he had realized, and all he wanted to do now was curl up in a ball, collect himself, and sleep. He supposed it was his job, though, as the new boss, to make a good first impression. He swallowed his disappointment and forced a smile onto his face, while Brad briskly led the way to the control center.

Upon entering the center, he was struck by the beautiful panorama revealed through its main window. The structure of the base was on raised support beams. Consequently, the control center was located at about the midline of the hangar's height, and overlooked the vehicle staging area below. The Martian plain spread out from the staging area as far as the eye could see, with canyons and small mountains visible at the very edge of the horizon. The hazy, caramel sky filled the rest of the view, and for a moment James had his breath taken away all over again. The sun hung in the air, white hot but dim, while unfamiliar shapes cast barely perceptible shadows in the sky. James wondered to himself if they were one of Mars' twin moons or artificial satellites, placed in the heavens by humans.

"Nice to meet you."

James snapped out of his reverie and registered the hand thrust out to meet his. It belonged to Steven Reese, the Facility Engineer. Reese ruled the roost whenever someone from James's company wasn't on site, and he was the direct manager of over a quarter of the support staff. His company, Solar Logistics Incorporated, was arguably the most important segment of the contract team, as the facility and its equipment would begin to waste away without their hard work. He wasn't a man you wanted to get on the wrong side of.

"It's very nice to meet you, as well," James said, shaking Steve's hand vigorously – maybe a little too vigorously. "Apologies for spacing out, I'm still trying to get a handle on this view..."

Steve turned and looked at it, then grunted. "Well, you'll get used to it quick. Has Brad shown you much of the place?"

"No, this is our first stop."

"Well, let me get you acquainted then."

Steve turned to his left and gestured to a man busily interacting with the control center's command console. "This is Blaine Nelson. He's more or less my right-hand man. He can tell you where anything on this base is and how much we have of it."

Blaine spun around and pushed his glasses up on his nose. "Nice to meet you, Mr. Wilmot. We've been looking forward to your arrival."

"Likewise, Blaine. I've been looking forward to getting here."

Blaine smiled politely and went back to his work.

Steve took him to the next waiting hand.

"This is Alvin Armstrong, our IT specialist, and Arnold Wong, our SATCOM engineer. They're with General Space Systems, and no matter how many times we ask they won't send anyone else."

The line was delivered so dryly that James had to turn toward Steve and verify that it was a joke. Steve's smile confirmed that it was.

Alvin and Arnold shook his hand, all smiles and greetings.

"That's it for the control center," said Steve, "You'll have to take a walk to meet the others, I'm afraid."

James shook Steve's hand again, with what he hoped was the right amount of enthusiasm this time. "No problem at all. It was great to meet you. Thanks for the quick introductions."

Steve smiled. "You bet. We'll be seeing you. We'll be seeing you plenty."

James wasn't sure how to take that. He laughed along, politely, and let Brad usher him out of the control room.

Brad led him down a sloped hallway that connected the control module and hangar portions of the base to the other modules, which were closer to the ground. "There are a few maintenance folks that you haven't met yet. They're mostly working in the hangar or outside, so we'll have to catch up with them later – maybe at meal time."

James was secretly relieved. "No problem."

"Meanwhile, there are other folks we can say hi to. And speaking of mealtimes, the cafeteria is right through here..."

Brad took a sharp left, and they entered a large module, roughly the size of a one-story office building back home.

James was presently surprised. Not only did the module feel spacious and fresh, but there were plants all around, and pictures hanging on the walls. Some of the pictures were hand-drawn art or paintings. Others were photographs. All of them depicted the majesty of nature on Earth or Mars. The vast majority were scenes of lush vegetation or wildlife from various places on the globe – places that, truth be told, hardly existed anymore - but that nonetheless gave the viewer a sense of freedom and calm. The impression was of a place that had been consciously designed as an oasis in the midst of a desert, which James supposed is exactly what it was.

The open floor plan of the module had been sub-divided into several smaller regions. James and Brad found themselves in the central lounge area. To the right, a small dancefloor and a bar gave way to an area populated by what looked like several exercise machines and a couple of children's sandboxes. An interactive video screen dominated the wall nearest the door they had entered through. The wall on the other side featured another entrance, then glass panels, from which the exterior of the base could be seen.

The panels extended to the right-most wall, providing an uninterrupted view of the outside. They had a sheen to them which James recognized as a liquid crystal layer, meaning they could be polarized or even used to display an image, albeit a poor quality one. He supposed that made sense. After enough time here, a person might want to look toward the window and see something other than inhospitable desert.

To their left, a dining facility of some kind awaited. Brad led the way through the door leading into the facility.

James noted that this door, like the two main entrances, was embedded into a real wall, which was part of the facility itself. All of the other walls in the open space of the module behind them were flimsy and artificial, moving or collapsing as required. This also made sense to James, as having movable and collapsible walls made the space that much more versatile. It was a true multi-purpose room.

The dining facility was surprisingly spacious. It took up the left quarter of the recreation/dining module and included a kitchen area hidden behind another permanent wall. He saw everything you would expect in a standard cafeteria back home: a central salad bar, trays, railings to slide the trays on, glass partitions between the patrons and the food preparation areas, service windows. James didn't know what he had expected. Maybe a room full of freeze-dried food, or food in the form of heatable cubes, or tubes of paste. But this was a place in which you could have a full meal, or at least a reasonable facsimile of one.

A middle-aged and mildly heavyset man strode over to James and extended his hand, a smile lighting up his features. "A pleasure to meet you, sir! Names' Ryan. Ryan Brooks."

James returned the shake and the smile. "James Wilmot. Heck of a facility you've got here."

"Oh, yeah. It's nice to work in the one area people like to come to. This whole space is designed to feel like home, you know? People are usually in a pretty good mood when I see em', at least after breakfast. Everyone has a hard time in the morning. Check this out..."

Ryan led the way into the kitchen.

James was not met by the sight of people slaving over a grill, as he had expected, but by a series of mechanical arms hanging from the ceiling. There were areas that he assumed were for cooking food, but they weren't grills in the traditional sense. The cooking surfaces jutted out in all kinds of shapes and at odd angles, optimized for use by the robot arms above them instead of human hands.

"Yeah, with this set-up right here I can make a lot of meals that feel pretty close to home. And for a lot of people."

Ryan moved further into the kitchen, toward a console embedded in the wall. "You see, I put the recipe in here...ingredients, quantities, mix, cooking time...and the arms do the rest. Frees me up to prep the dining room, double check inventory...perform a taste test or two..."

James smiled. "Well, you have to make sure the food is coming out right."

"That I do! That I do. And if you ever come by before supper, I'll be sure to give you a chance to perform a quality check of your own!"

Ryan winked and jocularly nudged James on the shoulder, laughing. "In all seriousness though, it can be a challenge to keep things fresh in here. Fresh to experience, that is. Limited ingredients that only get renewed every couple of years. Mostly the same, even then, year after year. Low quantities in the last few weeks before a re-supply. But it's important to do it right. Seems silly, but mealtimes can be so important for morale."

James shook his head. "Doesn't seem silly to me at all. I totally get it. I imagine it's the little things after a while."

Ryan pointed at James in satisfaction. "Exactly. Exactly that. The little things."

James extended his hand in farewell. "It was nice to meet you, Ryan."

"Well same here, Mr. Wilmot! I meant what I said. Come back any time and get a free preview. Just got a re-supply so we'll be having lots of fresh and new items on the menu."

"Alright, I will. And it's James."

Brad led the way out of the kitchen while Ryan busied himself at his console.

The pleasant surprise of discovering Alpha Base's more entertaining side was quickly waning. James felt his feet dragging and his eyes drooping.

Brad must have sensed this. "I'll let you check out the rest of the rec area by yourself another time. I know you're eager to get settled. You should be – it's been a hell of a day. Let's just head down to meet the life-support and med staff real quick, then I'll show you to your room."

"Oh, sure thing, no rush," James lied. In truth, he was grateful.

They moved on, re-entering the cylindrical hall and heading deeper into the facility. On their way, they passed a man who was headed in the other direction. Brad stopped him.

"James, I'd like you to meet Mr. David Weaver. David heads up our sustainability and custodial staff. David, this is James Wilmot, the new Site Lead."

David took James's hand. He had a strong grip. "Nice to meet you, James. If you see the rest of my staff, careful not to step on em'."

James looked at David, confused.

David laughed. "They're bots, Mr. Wilmot. Bots. I keep em' programmed right and running. Kinda oversee things. Brad here is too kind."

James looked past David, and sure enough, there was the bot he has been working on when they walked up. It was a surprisingly boxy thing for something with such smooth edges, white and black in color, about knee high. It headed busily down the hall and turned a corner, out of sight.

"Well, that's one of the most important jobs here. Without them we'd be..."

David interrupted him. "Knee deep in shit." He laughed again, hard. "Hell, I'm just glad I don't have to be the one who shovels it. It was nice to meet you, sir."

James moved aside so David could walk past. "And you as well!" he called after him.

Brad and James resumed their walk.

"He really is doing some pretty important work," said Brad. "Technical, too. The bots themselves are complicated enough, but he has to run the recycler. Without him, we'd be shut down in a week."

James nodded. "I have no doubt. Exactly how much do we recycle here?"

"As much as we can. Something like eighty percent of everything, I believe. Water is caught, filtered and re-used. Useful bacteria and nutrients are extracted from solid waste and used for fertilizer in the green house. Physical objects are either broken down to their constituents and 3-D printed into something else, or re-purposed whole. Basically, everything that happens on earth naturally, we have to re-create here. And we still only get it mostly right. Earth is totally self-contained."

Before James could respond, they arrived at the next stop - a full medical suite. James took in the white walls and soft ambient lighting. He also noticed what appeared to be a surgical area, a pill dispensing machine, and a predominance of robotic apparatus.

A woman noticed the two men enter, stopped whatever she was working on, and headed in their direction. "I'm Dr. Boss."

James shook her hand while Brad introduced them to each other. Her first name was Carolyn.

Carolyn seemed delighted to learn exactly who he was. "It is wonderful to meet you, James. When you get an opportunity, after you've settled in, I would love to bend your ear about a few things."

"Certainly, it would be my pleasure."

"Great! Well, as you can see here, we have it all. The other rooms in this module contain an MRI scanner, an X-ray machine...we even have an infection biohazard area, believe it or not. On the off chance one of you digs up something really nasty out there."

James nodded. "Well, that's good news! I wouldn't want to be up here without a good medical center."

"Of course," said Carolyn. "Connie and I are mostly up here as emergency backup anyway. Many of the functions are automated, as you can see. You have met Connie, right?"

Brad interjected. "He met her at the landing site."

"Of course. Well, between her and myself, we've got you covered.

"That is good to know," said James.

Brad spoke up. "Carolyn, James has had a long day and wants to get settled just as soon as he can. I'm gonna' finish up the tour and let him get some shuteye."

Carolyn nodded understandingly and shook James's hand. "We'll talk more when you've had a chance to rest."

James returned her grasp, thanked her, and followed Brad out of the room. The two men turned right as they left the medical module and continued down the hall.

"Sorry I had to cut her off. Once Carolyn gets going, you'll be there for a while."

James laughed. "No worries. You weren't lying. I am tired."

"I know. Almost done."

They passed a few other modules; the doors of which Brad did not stop to open. Eventually they came to the end of the hall, where another umbilical-like tunnel served as a bridge from one major component of the site to another. As they crossed, James noticed that this tunnel was somewhat transparent, affording the walker a muddied view of the world outside.

The tunnel ended at another door, this time wide open. They walked through it into a noisy, hot, and crowded place. The sounds of industrial machinery filled James' ears, and he realized why the designers had thought to keep this part of the facility separate from the rest.

A stairway to the right of the entrance led the men down to the floor of the module.

James looked up at the towering pieces of machinery surrounding them, like trees in a forest.

"Who goes there!"

EIGHT

The voice came from behind them, giving James a start. He spun around in surprise, only to find himself face down on the floor, having put too much torque into the turn.

Brad was quick to help him back up. "You ok?"

James grunted an affirmative reply and struggled to his feet.

"It's normal with big movements like that. Takes a while to get used to the reduced gravity. Don't worry, it's like a growth spurt as a kid – you'll relearn the physics in no time."

James appreciated Brad's optimism, even as he massaged his bruised knees.

He turned in the direction of the voice that had made him jump. "Who's there?"

A shadowy figure spoke to them from between the machinery columns. "Asked you first!"

James struggled to suppress his irritation and extended his hand in greeting. "I'm James. James Wilmot. I just arrived and Brad here is getting me acquainted."

"He's our new Site Lead," Brad added.

The figure moved into the dim light of the industrial module, blinking hard and squinting as if the smallest assault of photons was too much. "New Site Lead?"

"That's right," said James.

The figure suddenly stood tall and raced toward them.

James flinched and braced himself for an impact that never came. Instead, he opened his eyes to find a man in front of him with an outstretched hand of his own. James took the hand, and it began pumping rapidly.

EIGHT

"Nice to meet you!" The man shouted, as if James wasn't a mere foot away. "I'm Dewey. Dewey Hanson. This here is Cameron."

James spun in the direction of Dewey's gaze. Sure enough, another man had emerged from the shadows.

"Cameron Gill."

James greeted him as well. "Nice to meet you, Cameron. Didn't see you there."

Cameron gave no reply.

Dewy spoke for him. "You'll have to forgive me and Cameron. We don't get out much."

Brad extrapolated further. "Dewey and Cameron are responsible for monitoring the life support and power machinery of this facility. At least during the day. If something goes wrong with either of those systems, despite all the redundancies built into them, we could all be dead in minutes. So, Dewey and Cameron can't leave their posts while they're on duty. Ever. They do twelve hours down here at a time, before they get relieved by their night shift counterparts. Twelve hours a day in this noisy cave, every day, for over a year...you tend to develop...quirks."

Dewey smiled. "We're just mushrooms down here. Growing in the dark."

James wasn't sure how to respond.

The four men stood together, silent except for the background hums and whirs of the monolithic equipment around them. The silence stretched on, well past the point of comfort. Finally, Brad broke it. "James has to get moving. He's had a long journey. Thank you, Dewey. Cameron."

The two strange men nodded at Brad and retreated back into the darkness.

Brad and James hurried up the stairs and out of the module, back into the connecting tube.

Brad looked apologetically at James as they walked. "Sorry. You never know how those two are going to be."

James said nothing in return, simply nodding. Exhaustion crashed over his body in waves. His eyes felt dry, and forming even the simplest of sentences was becoming challenging.

Brad led the way down the twists and turns of Alpha Base's corridors. James barely paid any attention to where they were going. He just followed Brad's footsteps.

Finally, they came to a hallway which jutted out ninety degrees from the main corridor. In this hallway there were three doors. Brad strode to the furthest door and opened it. He gestured for James to go inside.

"This is your room. Your baggage will join you as soon as it's been offloaded."

James extended a hand. "Thank you, Brad, for everything. The tour was...informative."

Brad nodded and smiled thinly. "You bet. I'll send someone to get you at the beginning of our next work cycle. A single sol here equates roughly to a single day on Earth, so you should have about sixteen hours from now to rest up and get adjusted. We'll leave your luggage outside. Don't worry, nobody will touch it."

James nodded again. "Got it. Thanks."

The door closed and James heard Brad's footsteps diminish in volume, then disappear as he walked away.

James was suddenly seized by a wild urge for freedom, and for rest. He desperately stripped off all his clothes, tore back the comforter on the bed and flopped down on the sheets. He closed his eyes and slept harder than he had in years.

NINE

Routine set in quickly. James woke on his thirtieth day at the site, rolled out of bed and headed to the showers. It wasn't until he had stood under the tepid water for a full minute that he realized his sense of awe was gone. It no longer felt strange to wake up here, millions of miles from home, inches away from asphyxia. It was just another day at the office.

He finished brushing his teeth and stepped back into his room. As the bathroom door closed behind him, he threw his towel on the bed, kicked off his shower shoes, and rifled, naked, through the pile of dirty clothes on the floor. Finding an outfit that wasn't too smelly or wrinkled, James threw it on and headed toward the cafeteria for breakfast.

He arrived to find a smattering of familiar faces, and an otherwise empty room. He quickly joined the line and made his selections. The robotic arms behind the counter moved in a flurry, and his food was plated and delivered a moment later, eggs still steaming. He found an open spot and sat, alone, to eat.

A few faces acknowledged his presence with a good morning nod or grunt. Most just stared into space and worked on their food.

He took great satisfaction in the meal, disproportionate to the quality of the food, which was good but not great. Something about the process of eating, the ritual, soothed and fulfilled him. To his regret, he finished eating quickly, despite his best efforts to prolong the experience. He had learned to make as much of each moment of the day as possible: it helped to fill the hours. Once finished, he threw away his plate, stowed his tray, and took a right down the hallway, toward his office.

He rounded the corner and strode in. "Good morning, everyone!"

The office module was broken into four sections connected by a narrow hallway. James had his own office, as did Jeff, who was located next to him. The other two offices, directly across from James and Jeff, belonged to Steven Reese and the science team, respectively. The lead scientists from each team shared the science space, rotating in and out throughout the day to check schedules and archive files before heading back out to their true worksites. Steven was a fixture in his office during work hours, only ever leaving his seat to confer briefly with Blaine Nelson, who, along with the IT staff, spent his days manning the command desk in the next module over.

True to form, Steven was in his office at that very moment, staring intently at his workstation and ignoring James's greeting.

Luckily, Jeff was present and more than willing to pick up the slack. "Good morning, James. Do you have to use the bathroom?"

"Uhm...why do you ask?"

"The south latrine is backed up. Janitorial is having a look at it, but best to use the north one for now, or head to your room."

"Got it. Thank you, Jeff."

Jeff nodded, turned, and headed quickly back to his desk.

James shook his head and chuckled to himself while he logged in to his workstation for the day.

The experiments they had come here to perform were going well. The astronomy team hadn't been able to do any real work yet, since the main astronomical event they were here to observe wouldn't start for another thirty days or so. Still, they had been able to get all of their instruments set up, and they seemed happy. They spent their days calibrating telescopes, running practice tests, and, at night, taking in the unique view of the sky that Mars had to offer.

The site survey duo was quiet, as they had been since their arrival. As far as James was concerned, no news was good news.

The life scientists, like the astronomers, had some time to wait yet, before they could get started on their explorations in earnest. Their big plan was to take advantage of the spring thaw. During that time the area surrounding Alpha Base, particularly to its south, was known for widespread geyser activity. Underground reservoirs of water, warmed by the sun, melted and built-up significant pressure until they burst through to the surface. The scientists would be hard pressed to find a better way of collecting fresh deep-water samples to scour for microscopic lifeforms. Considering that they had yet to even enter Mars's winter, however, the team had a while to wait. In the meantime, they kept themselves busy with shallow ground samples and endless reviews of the base's biological archives.

The physics team was where the trouble would come, if there was to be trouble. James had been hearing repeatedly from Miguel Valdez, the science support technician assigned to the physics team. Apparently, the set-up of their equipment had been more difficult than anticipated, and a schedule delay was looming if they ran into many more problems.

The physics experiment, then, would be the necessary focus of James's activities today. First, James had to familiarize himself more thoroughly with the goals of the project. The initial briefing had gone over his head. Then, once he had the basics figured out, he would need to dive into the problems the team had already faced and determine what their concerns were going forward.

Once he was logged in, James began searching the database for the physics project briefing. He figured he would go over it once more, slowly, before making a trip down to the lab and asking some follow up questions...carefully disguised as operational questions, of course, so as not to let on that he had almost no clue what they were up to. Then, once that conversation had concluded, he figured an EVA to the worksite was in order. Going outside made him nervous, and he had avoided it for the past month. However, not only was it necessary at this point, but his boredom had reached a level where his fear was no longer prohibitive.

It only took two read-throughs for James to realize that he had a problem. He still had absolutely no idea what the physics project was about, save that they were trying to build a particle accelerator on mars.

"Well...shit," he said, taking a sip from the bottle of water he had stashed at his desk. "What now?"

He supposed that the honorable thing to do would be to man-up and admit to his team that he couldn't follow the briefing; that it went over his head and left him as confused as a first grader performing brain surgery. The other option, of course, was to fake it til' he made it. James decided to fake it. After all, he didn't need to know the ins and outs of each experiment in order to make sure everything leading up to them was getting done on time and for the right cost. At least, he hoped not.

James stood up and stepped outside of his office. He turned left, toward the command desk. He wanted to say good morning to Blaine and make sure there weren't any major issues with the base facilities before he started moving around.

Steven saw him and called out just as he reached the hallway door. "Wilmot! Can I help you with something?"

James stopped abruptly and turned toward Steven, who now sat bolt upright in his chair with his legs taught, as if ready to pounce.

"Just...going to say good morning to Blaine. See how things are going."

Steven frowned. "Blaine is Logistics. That falls under my area."

"I know...I just thought I'd say hello."

"If you have a concern, you know you can just ask me, yes?"

James tried to strike a conciliatory tone. "Oh, I know. No concern. Just curious. Do you mind if I go in to talk to Blaine? If you have a problem with it, we can discuss..."

Steven blinked rapidly and dismissed James with a wave of his hand. "No. No problem."

James was still hesitant. "Are you sure?"

Steven didn't answer. He had already returned his gaze to the monitor before him.

James took a deep breath, held it, and continued on his way.

He opened the command module's hatch and stepped from the umbilical connecting hallway to find Blaine busy at his console.

Blaine's hands interacted with buttons both real and virtual, alternating rapidly from the command desk console to the air above it and back again. He looked like a conductor overseeing a silent symphony. With a final flourish, Blaine stood stock still and regarded a spot in the window ahead of him. He looked satisfied, nodded, and sat back in his seat.

James gently cleared his throat. "Blaine?"

Blaine started in his chair and turned around. "James! I didn't hear you come in."

"Sorry, didn't mean to startle you."

"Not at all, I was just lost in thought. Please, take a seat." Blaine motioned at the chair next to him.

James sat down. "So, what are you up to?"

"I," said Blaine, "am making sure the solar panels are all aligned correctly." He pointed to the right-hand corner of the command center's window, which doubled as a screen when needed. "See that live feed there? That is our solar array. Supplements the reactor and provides most of the power for the greenhouse – at least during the summer. Now, look at the bottom of the picture. See the fourth panel down? How it looks different from the others?"

James nodded.

"That's because it has reached the end of its life. It's actually one of the older units on the base – in continuous operation since the beginning. Every cell in that panel has expended its charging ability. That's why it's not in alignment with the others. Each panel uses its own power to adjust its orientation to the sun throughout the day, get the most light."

"So, what are you going to do with it?"

"We are going to replace it."

Blaine pressed still more buttons, and a new image popped up. A suited figure was dragging a new-looking solar panel onto a flatbed. The flatbed was connected to a rover.

"That," said Blaine, "is our friendly neighborhood electrician. He is about to hook that solar panel up to the grid, then dispose of the old one."

James looked at the image closely. He realized that he wasn't looking at a video feed, but a zoomed in image of something right in front of them. "Can you get rid of the inset?"

Blaine nodded. "Sure."

The image receded into the background of the window, leaving only the true view from the command desk in its place.

James leaned forward, looking for the real version of the suited figure. He found him after a moment, a tiny speck compared to the mid-sized figure he had been just seconds before. "Can he hear us?" James asked.

"If you want him to."

Blaine pressed yet more buttons, and a graphic indicating an open comm link appeared under the real-life image of the figure.

James scanned the console for the mute button, found it, pressed it, then turned to Blaine. "What's his name?"

"That's Andre. Have you not met Andre?"

James shook his head no. "Haven't had the pleasure."

Blaine guffawed and un-muted the comm link. "Andre, how we doin'?"

A voice came in through the room's speakers. "Good here. Just about ready to go."

"I have someone with me who'd like to have a word."

The voice sounded surprised. "Oh?"

"Oh indeed. James Wilmot, Andre Flores. Andre Flores, meet James Wilmot, Site Lead of this here station."

Andre's voice sounded tense, caught off guard. "Pleasure to meet you, Mr. Wilmot."

James was quick to respond. "Oh, the pleasure is all mine. Great to talk to you, Andre. And please, call me James."

"Roger that, sir, James it is."

"All right. Well don't let me keep you, you're a busy man. Keep doing what you're doing."

Andre grunted with effort as he finished securing the panel to the rover's flatbed. "Sounds good. Out here."

Blaine leaned forward. "Out here Andre, thanks." He snapped off the comm link and leaned back in his chair. "So, after Andre hauls that panel over to the array and hooks it up, I'll tweak it from here to make sure its properly connected and calibrated. Meanwhile, Andre will drag the old panel back to base and disposition to scrap."

"Disposition to scrap?"

Blaine smiled. "Technical term. Means 'throw it in the garbage'."

James nodded. "Everything else ok?"

"Indeed! So far, so good. Pretty quiet morning." Blaine knocked on his own forehead. "Knock on wood, of course."

James returned the gesture with a soft smile and stood. "Is Andre going to be out there a while?"

"Probably a few hours. Why?"

"I think I'll pay him a visit. I'm heading out there to check on some of the experiments anyway."

Blaine raised his eyebrows, then pursed his lips and nodded in approval. "Cool. Give me a holler before you head over if you want, and I'll confirm if he's still working."

James offered a weak wave and turned to head out. "Will do. Thanks Blaine."

Blaine returned the gesture and spun back around to the command console.

NINE

James closed the command module door behind him and walked back down the umbilical toward his office.

Returning to his chair, James was halfway through logging back into his computer when he spied Mark Jacobs in the adjacent science office, busily looking for something. Deciding that his remaining paperwork could wait, James cancelled his login request and walked over to Mark.

He rapped gently on the cheap metal of the science office's doorframe. "Hey, Mark! How are things this morning?"

Mark, distracted, didn't respond, but continued frantically scanning the office with his eyes.

James tried again. "Mark?"

Mark dragged his eyes toward James just long enough to register his identity, then went back to searching. "Yes, hello James. Good morning." He sounded deeply distracted. Beside himself, even.

"Looking for something?"

Mark gave James his full attention now, his face a masque of concern. "Yes. I cannot find my copy of the schedule."

"Project specific?"

"Yes. The project specific schedule."

James was taken aback by Mark's tone but tried not to show it. The poor man seemed genuinely distressed. "Have you tried the central database? A fresh copy is posted daily…"

Mark cut him off, clearly struggling not to be rude. "I prefer a paper copy."

James nodded, resigned to the quirks of his staff. "Can I print you a new one?"

Mark looked on the verge of an outburst now – whether it was rage or tears, James couldn't say. He spoke quietly, into his chest. "The one I have includes personalized notes."

"Ok. Ok, well, we can certainly take a good look for it. Is it possible you left it back in the lab?"

The outburst came. "I already looked there!"

Mark rose to his feet and stalked past James, out the hallway and to the left.

James followed. "Mark! Hey man, I'm sure we'll find it..."

Mark said nothing. Instead, he continued down the hallway, past the cafeteria, straight to the science lab. He turned left again, and the lab door closed behind him.

James scrambled to catch up. He opened the lab door and stepped inside.

Mark was still moving about frantically, but the rest of the staff continued on as if nothing was happening. Clearly, nobody else was taking the loss of Mark's hand notated schedule as seriously as Mark was.

James stepped deeper inside the lab, dodging metal tables and various other large instruments hanging down from the walls or freely rolling within the enclosure. When he reached Mark, he saw that his energetic pace had slowed somewhat, and he was staring intently at a pile of documents while thumbing through them rapidly. Finally, he stood straight up, pulling a paper from the stack and holding it up to the light. James watched as Mark's whole body shuddered with relief and the tension rolled out of his shoulders.

He sighed deeply and turned to James with a sheepish expression on his face, now as calm as a lamb. "Found it."

James nodded. "So you did. You ok?"

Mark took another deep breath. "Yes. Yes, I am. I apologize. I just...it's important to me that I not misplace this."

James continued to nod, trying his best not to appear judgmental. "Of course, no sweat. I get it. We all have our ways of keeping things straight."

Mark nodded appreciatively.

"So..," James began, trying to break the tension between them, "what are you guys working on?"

Mark smiled, grateful for the topic change. "This is the physics project."

James smiled back, trying to be patient. "I know that. I mean what are you guys working on today? What step of the project are you on?"

Mark's grin widened. "Well why didn't you say so? Melvin!"

A voice spoke up from behind James. "Yes, Mark?"

James turned around. An older, small statured, bespectacled man sat in the far back corner of the module, where he had been writing in a notepad. The notepad he held was tattered and dirty, the cover bound in leather and the pages embossed with gold leaf. James wasn't sure he had ever seen a leather-bound journal like that in person. He thought that it must be an antique.

Mark spoke. "James, Melvin Clarke is a mathematician and co-lead of this project. He helped me come up with the idea. Melvin, James would like to know what everyone is working on."

With that, Mark turned on his heel and strode over to one of the many work benches in the science module, where he busied himself talking to another of the scientists on the physics team.

"Don't mind him," said Melvin, "he gets like this when he's nervous. Big day, today, after all."

James turned to face Melvin and sought a chair to sit down in.

Melvin saw what he was doing and pulled a chair from a nearby empty workstation. "Here you go," he said, rolling the chair in James's direction.

James caught it and took a seat. "Thanks. So why is today such a big day?"

Melvin nodded and snapped his notepad shut. "Starting at the basics, I see."

James was defensive. "Well, I mean, that is what I was trying to tell Mark..."

Melvin held up his hand. "Hey, I get it. There's a lot going on with this effort and unless you've been following it closely from the beginning, it can be hard to piece together."

James felt relieved. Finally, someone who seemed to understand where he was coming from. "A little," he said wryly.

Melvin sat back and placed his hands in his lap. "The reason today is a big deal is because today we put the third and fourth segments of the accelerator together."

"Why does that matter?"

"Because the third and fourth segments include sensitive parts we don't have any spares for. Same with the eighth and ninth segments, the thirteenth and fourteenth, and so on. If someone makes a mistake...we came out here for nothing."

"Which parts don't have spares? I thought we included the standard loadout...

Melvin held up his hand. "We did. 'No spares' is a bit hyperbolic. We have a few. But not enough to replace more than three of the junctions, if they break. And we have a lot of sections to go yet."

James nodded. "What's so sensitive about these parts? What do they do?"

"It's the laser arrays. That keep the particles moving, each one building on the momentum of the last. If we lose even one array, we can't reach the kinds of speeds we need."

James nodded again. "Well, who though it would be a good idea to set the standard loadout at such a low number for these parts? Being that they're so sensitive?"

"Well, that would be you, I imagine."

James's face twitched in horror.

Melvin corrected himself. "Well maybe it wasn't you, specifically. I don't know how these things work at your company. Maybe they don't bring you in until after loadouts have been discussed? All I know is, it was EPMS that made the decision."

James regretted asking the question.

Melvin continued. "In any case, things are going well at the moment. Lindsey is out there now with your men Elias and Miguel, putting the ring together. So far so good."

James nodded for a third time. "Well, I'm glad for that. I assure you I had nothing to do with the loadout specs before we left. It's like you said, I came along later. I know a lot of those decisions have to do with weight and optimizing the overall science package..."

Melvin interrupted. "Sure, sure. I'm sure lots of things go into it. Things none of us know about." He shrugged. "We just have to be careful, is all."

James gestured to Melvin's journal. "How long have you had that thing?"

Melvin laughed. "Oh, this? I order them special. I like the feel of writing things by hand. Helps me think."

"I didn't know you could still have things like that made."

"You can. For enough money you can have just about anything made!"

"They're expensive?"

Melvin pursed his lips and nodded. "Oh, yeah. Try finding natural leather for binding these days. You know how wasteful even a single cow is? Much easier to grow the meat in a dish...but then you don't get the skin."

"And the leather is really important?"

Melvin smiled. "I think so. My grandmother had an old leather-bound book when I was growing up. A couple of them, actually. A religious book and a notebook, like this one. I guess it left an impression."

James nodded, understanding. "What are you writing in there?"

Melvin grabbed the book and rifled the pages. "Ah, not so much writing as scribbling. Doing math."

"Math?"

"Yeah. I like to work on proofs while everyone else sets up the project. I don't have much to contribute in that regard, so scribbling in this notebook makes me feel like I'm doing something."

James laughed good naturedly. "You working on any problems in particular?"

Melvin sat up in his seat, excited to have a genuine inquiry about his work. "I've just been re-running the numbers that got us here, making sure they're right. Assuming I'm correct, the experiment we're going to run during this trip, in the unique environment of Mars, is going to yield evidence of new particles we didn't even know existed before. We may even have to rethink some of our most basic assumptions about the universe."

"And?"

"And what?"

"Do the numbers check out?"

Melvin laughed. "So far, yeah, they do."

James laughed with him. "Well, that's good. Bad time to find out you carried the wrong one somewhere."

"Indeed."

"So, Melvin, do you think it would be ok for me to go and observe Lindsey and the guys? See how they're doing?

Melvin hesitated.

"I just like to see how things are coming together. Makes things feel more real for me. Like I have my fingers on the pulse of things."

"Well, yeah," said Melvin, "I don't see why not."

NINE

...

James hadn't been suited up since landing, and he had forgotten how uncomfortable it was. He and Melvin walked like men carrying weights over a trampoline. Each step on its own was lighter than expected, requiring less force than an earthbound step would, but the overall mass of their bodies – their limbs and equipment – remained the same. As a result, they stumbled over the simplest rock or pothole, and walking uphill on a grade of less than five degrees required a comical amount of overcompensation – like they were headed directly into a strong wind.

James, breathing hard, turned to look at Melvin as they crested the small rise a few yards from the base. Melvin said nothing, but immediately began laughing.

James laughed with him. "You think we still look new at this?"

Melvin's laugh subsided into a chuckle. "Maybe a little."

Lindsey, Elias & Miguel were working at the bottom of the gentle slope. From a distance, James couldn't tell who was who: their suits hid all identifiable information. They were just three humanoid figures. As the men got closer, their visor HUDs picked up on the signal emanating from the trio's comm-links, and their identity information popped up in little boxes over each of their heads.

James selected Lindsey's box and initiated a conversation. "Hi there!"

Lindsey turned to look at him and waved. "Hi," she responded.

"Sorry to bother you...we just wanted to see how things are going!"

The other two figures turned around as well. All three stood, expressionless, their helmets reflecting the dim light of the plain all around them.

Melvin chimed in. "Good morning, Lindsey!"

"Good morning, Melvin! How are you doing today?"

"I'm fine, thank you. Just fine. James and I thought we would pay you a visit!"

"What a lovely idea," she said, "we always welcome a little more company."

Finally within arm's reach, James extended a hand.

Lindsey eyed it warily for a split second before returning the handshake. "To what do we owe the pleasure?"

"I know we didn't get much opportunity to socialize before heading to another planet together," said James, "but I wanted to come out here and really get to know what you're doing. See it first-hand. That way I can be in the best position to assist you and your project with whatever you need."

Lindsey nodded. "Okay. What would you like to know?"

He pointed to the pipe the trio had been busy bolting to a heavy looking metal base. "Is this the accelerator itself?"

Lindsey nodded in approval. "That it is."

James noted the relative isolation of the pipe. The strip the crew was working on extended no more than a few meters in either direction, and James could scarcely notice a curve. "It looks like you guys have a ways to go, yet."

He pivoted to the two other people on scene. "Hi, by the way. How are you guys doing?"

NINE - | 121 |

Miguel and Elias perked up. Miguel's comm link flickered to life. "We're good, sir. How are you, Mr. Wilmot?"

James corrected them. "James, please. And I'm well. I appreciate how diligently you've been supporting the physics team since our arrival."

Both men nodded. This time, Elias spoke. "It really is our pleasure, sir...uh, James. The science they're doing here is going to change how we see the world."

"So I hear. Lindsey, what's next?"

"Well...we have to finish assembling the accelerator. After that we can begin our experiments."

James nodded. "Sure, of course. I understand you aren't done building yet. I guess I meant...how much longer do you expect the build to take? And is everything going ok?"

Lindsey gestured at Miguel & Elias. "These gentlemen will have to weigh in on the timeline..."

Miguel interjected. "It will be at least a few more months before the ring is completed. Then we have to assemble the rest of the components...perform functional tests...the main experiments will probably take place in six months or so. And that's assuming we don't run into any issues along the way..."

James finished his sentence for him. "Which we will." He laughed. "There are always issues."

It was Lindsey's turn to interject. "As far as explaining the experiments themselves, that might take a bit more time than we have here..."

"I'll arrange a sit-down meeting between James and I later this week," said Melvin. "We'll chat and if he still has questions the two of us will seek you out."

Lindsey nodded. "Sounds good."

"Ok," said James, "I think I have a better idea of where things are. Lindsey, Miguel, Elias, I really appreciate you guys taking the time to speak with me. I'll let you get back to it."

Lindsey extended her hand. "Appreciate you coming out and showing an interest."

James grasped Lindsey's hand and shook it. "Absolutely. And remember, if you come up against any logistical issues that I can help with, don't hesitate to reach out."

"We won't. Take care."

"Thanks, you too."

James waved and began disengaging from the group.

Melvin followed him. "Thanks, Linds. See you guys inside."

Lindsey waved. "Of course, Melvin. We'll see you then."

James waited until they were a few yards away before making sure their comm links were closed and establishing a new link with Melvin. "I think that went pretty well?"

"Absolutely," responded Melvin.

James expected more, but Melvin went quiet.

James disconnected their comm link and the two men continued forward in silence. James noticed that their gaits were steadier now – they had grown used to walking in their suits. In the distance, he saw Andre's figure near the solar panels.

He turned to Melvin. "Hey, I wanted to go and check in on Andre. You mind?"

Melvin looked in the direction of James's gaze and shook his head no. "You go ahead. I'm gonna' head on in."

For the first time, James realized Melvin sounded out of breath. He frowned with concern. "Are you ok?"

Melvin laughed and waved his hand dismissively. "Oh, yes, I'm fine. Just not used to these suits. They're a bit stuffy inside, don't you think?"

James nodded. "I certainly do. You think you can make it back to the airlock ok?"

"Yes, yes, I'm fine. You go on and do what you have to and I'll see you inside later."

"Ok, sounds good Melvin. Thank you for introducing me to Lindsey. I think your endorsement paid off."

Melvin laughed again. "Well, for whatever that's worth. Glad to be of help. See you inside."

"See ya'."

James watched as the older man headed back to the safety of the base. Once he was satisfied Melvin was going to make it ok, James turned back toward Andre. The walk over was plodding and difficult. Small areas of uneven ground seemed to rise up to meet his boots at the last minute, causing several minor stumbles. Time dragged on, and James started to worry that Andre would finish his work long before James got to him. Luckily, despite the seemingly interminable length of James's journey, Andre was still standing at the panels when he arrived.

"Andre! Andre, hi!"

Andre startled at the sudden greeting and turned around. He was in the last stages of loading the now defunct panel onto the back of his rover. "Mr. Wilmot. Surprised to see you out here."

James smiled. "I said I was going to try and stop by. I wanted to see what you're up to."

"Right," said Andre. "So you did."

James strode past Andre and pointed at the Solar Panels. "So, which one is the new one?"

Andre smiled, tickled by the new Boss's naïve enthusiasm. "That one there."

James found the panel Andre was pointing at. It did look newer. "So how long did it take you to get it positioned right?"

"Not as long as you'd think. Blaine's pretty good at his job."

James remembered Blaine, looking at them from the control center. He turned toward the center window and waved.

Blaine made a quick comm connection. "Hi there James. How's the view out there?

"Great! How do we look?"

"Like Spacemen!" Blaine declared joyfully, before closing the comm connection.

James turned back to Andre. "So, what now?"

Andre finished tightening the last strap on the dead panel. It was now firmly secured to the flatbed. "Now we take this back to the hangar. Say, how did you get out here? You walk?

"I did."

"It's not an easy walk."

James laughed. "Tell me about it."

Andre pivoted toward the rover. "Come on, I'll give you a ride back to base."

James followed. "Sounds good to me. Thanks."

With that, the men boarded, the rover doors closed, and the duo headed toward the hangar, a cloud of dust in their wake.

10

TEN

Brad breathed a heavy sigh of relief as he sat down at the cafeteria table. All around him, his colleagues were gathered for today's dinner: a grey meat that might once have been ham, paired with a side of peas and rehydrated potatoes. The kitchen was clearly getting rid of the previous year's supplies. Still, it was pretty good for space grub.

He pushed the peas around a little and said his last thought out loud.

"Keep telling yourself that," said Owen, smiling and sitting down to his own smorgasbord of borderline expired food.

Brad smiled back, shook his head and dug in, feeling out of words for the day. The work had been more difficult than usual this shift, and he was glad to be done with it. Brad and Owen had been working with Jim and Lynette to get the second crew capsule fully mission capable again. Something was wrong with the damn thing's power distribution assembly, and the retro rockets hadn't fired as hard as they should have during landing. The difference would have been nearly imperceptible to the crew and passengers – this time – but the landing chassis had bent in several places, and the next crew might not be so lucky. Both repairs had generated more ass pain for Brad and his crew than he cared for, and Andre hadn't been much help.

Andre hadn't been much help at all the last few weeks, and Brad suspected he was distracted by something. More appropriately, someone. It was a little soon for hook-up season on Alpha Base – that didn't typically happen until about six months into a new group's tour, when people had grown really bored and really comfortable with one another, but he couldn't think of what else it might be. There wasn't much more that could serve as a worthy distraction on this desolate rock...unless maybe he had a new favorite show or something. In any case, it was annoying. Getting Crew Capsule Two back up and running was going to take that much longer without an electrician's expertise.

Brad surveyed the room and took in the faces, some new, some old. He noticed a few he might like to get to know better himself.

"Look over here," said Owen, nodding in the direction of the cafeteria's entrance in-between mouthfuls.

Brad looked and saw a group from the front office entering. It looked like an old man from the science team was among their number, as well as the new boss, who had come over on the latest capsule.

"What do you think of him?" Owen asked.

Brad shrugged. "Who, the new boss? He's ok, I guess. Seems like he's still getting adjusted."

In truth, Brad had liked the previous Site Lead from EPMS very much, so it was a little disappointing to see this new face among their number. Plus, the new guy seemed like a bit of a try-hard, always working to prove how involved and interested he was. He'd be better off relaxing in his office while the rest of them got down to business, as most of the Leads before him had done. After all, this wasn't their first rodeo. This base had been running just fine before his arrival and it would keep running just fine after he left. Still, he'd learn. Brad laughed to himself. They'd break his spirit yet.

Owen noticed his subtle chuckle. "What's so funny?"

"I don't know, man, I don't know. Was just thinking how he still seems so...excited."

Owen laughed. "Yeah, that'll go away."

Lynette arrived at their table, food tray in hand, as she had done every day for a year. "You boys got any room?"

Owen gestured at an empty seat. "Sorry, all full."

Lynette sat and started eating. "Fuck you, buddy. So, what's new?"

Owen gestured at the tables populated by science team members. "You hadn't noticed?"

"Ahh, you guys are discussing the new arrivals," she said. "Plenty to talk about there, it seems."

Owen laughed. "Brad sure seems to think so."

Brad raised his eyebrows and sat up a little. "What's that supposed to mean?"

"I see you looking around."

"Because you told me to..." Brad replied.

"No, no," said Owen, "before that. You've been gazing around the room since we sat down. I'm amazed the new girls haven't blown a rape whistle or something."

Brad rolled his eyes while Lynette looked at him expectantly. "I was just taking everyone in," he said, "we're going to be living with these people for a while, you know? Gotta' make friends."

Lynette snorted. "Friends."

"Yes, friends," said Brad, shoveling another piece of shriveled meat into his mouth, "and don't you smarmy fucks go around saying anything different. I don't need the new people scared to talk to me."

Owen and Lynette chuckled and stared down at their plates.

Brad joined them and the three friends ate in silence. The silence was the comfortable kind that can't be faked, only earned over time.

Eventually, Lynette spoke. "Something tells me you aren't the only one who's been looking to meet new friends lately."

Brad proceeded cautiously. "Who do you mean?"

Lynette rolled her eyes. "Oh, come on. You know exactly who I mean. Where the hell has Andre been lately?"

Brad didn't say anything, just looked down at his food.

Owen spoke. "It is a good question."

Brad sighed. "I know, I know. I was thinking about that while I was 'looking around' at the new folks. Which one did he choose?"

TEN

The three friends paused their meals to survey the room again. Any one of the myriad faces surrounding them could be the person Andre had chosen to while away his hours with.

"Definitely some pretty girls here," said Lynette. "He does like girls, right?"

"I'm pretty sure..." Brad replied.

Owen returned to his food. "It's a good bet," he said, a hint of sadness in his voice. "Most guys do."

An awkward moment passed. Brad knew it was difficult for his friend, a guy who liked guys, in this small group stranded a million miles from home. Finding a partner you wanted to share time with on Alpha Base was tough enough when everyone was on one team or the other, let alone a different league.

He clapped Owen gently on the shoulder. "Hey, man, you never know...Mr. Right could be somewhere in this room as we speak."

Owen chortled. "I'd settle for Mr. Right Now."

Brad and Lynette laughed.

"Well, Mr. Right Now, next week, next year, whatever," said Brad, "he could be here. You never know."

Owen finished his food, scraping the last few bites off the plate as he talked. "You never know."

...

Katie's eyes darted excitedly from one seatmate to the next. Rarely could she remember having such stimulating conversation over dinner. Most of her peers back home could care less about last week's news, let alone scientific theory, and her conversations during university had been so...academic. This was real scientific inquiry, happening in real time on another planet. She was elated and could hardly believe her luck, surrounded as she was by some of the brightest minds she had ever had the privilege of meeting.

"So, Ms. Cooper, where did you say you studied again?"

Katie startled from her reverie and quickly tried to identify her questioner. It was Saul Parker, Microbiologist from the Hansen Memorial Exo-Life Search.

"Please, call me Katie," she said.

Her cheeks glowed red as she rattled off the name of her institution. It was a smaller Midwestern school, of no particular renown. She had been lucky to land this job.

Saul was generous and acted as if he had heard of her alumnus. "Ah, ok, ok. Great. Are you planning on returning for graduate study?"

"Absolutely," said Katie. "My intention is to apply to a top tier university as soon as this trip is over. I figure this expedition will help my chances of getting accepted."

"A good plan," said Cecilia Myers, the unofficial head of the search project. "I think it would help a great deal."

"Agreed," said Saul. "You'll be a shoe in."

Katie smiled. "Well, anything I can do to raise my profile; I'll give it a try."

"Anything, huh?" Said Charlie Gibson, one of the art grant recipients. He didn't speak much, but when he did it was typically to say something unpleasant. He glowered at her now, gauging her reaction to his comment.

TEN

Katie met his gaze and stared back. "Within reason."

Charlie said nothing, just smirked and went back to eating.

Saul spoke again. "I went to school in San Diego. I'm close with the provost there. If you'd like I can put in a good word for you."

"Absolutely!" she exclaimed. "I would be so grateful."

"My pleasure," said Saul, "just keep me updated when you get closer to applying if that is still a place you're considering."

Katie beamed. "I will!"

"So," said Cecilia, "when do you all expect to begin our collection work?"

While the table attacked the new topic, Katie's attention drifted toward Cecilia. She found the older woman quite intimidating. After all, Cecilia was a renowned scientist who would be credited as a co-author on any papers the team wrote and a co-discoverer of any wonders they found. Katie, on the other hand, was just a pee-on who aspired to the success Cecilia already had.

It didn't help that Cecilia was also quite beautiful. Katie saw the way males over-responded to the smallest engagement from her, and it was incredibly frustrating. The last thing she needed was a woman stealing the encouragement and wisdom of her male co-workers all year, sabotaging the opportunities that Katie had worked so hard to cultivate, with pretty eyes and a nice pair of tits.

Cecilia, perhaps sensing what Katie was feeling, gently re-engaged her in the conversation. "Katie, what are your feelings on this question?"

"What question?" said Katie, embarrassed. "I'm sorry, my head was somewhere else."

Cecilia smiled kindly. "Not to worry. We were wondering aloud when we all expect to get our first positive results."

"Ah, I see," said Katie. "I honestly don't think we'll see anything groundbreaking until the geysers open again in the spring."

Cecilia's eyes widened. "Really? Not for so long? Why?"

Before Katie could answer, Saul jumped in. "That's not until halfway through the trip..."

Katie quickly clarified. "Yes, I know, it isn't for a whole year, which is unfortunate. But if you think about it, the geysers are the main thing that distinguishes this effort from all the others that came before it. Any surface microbes we find will almost certainly represent contamination of the topsoil by Earth life, as recorded in previous expeditions. It's the deep stuff – the life that might be lurking in underground reservoirs – that will be new. And that depth will also confirm that the life is really Martian. Assuming there's any life to find..."

Katie lapsed into silence and waited to see how the group would respond.

Cecilia spoke first. "I tend to agree. That is the most likely outcome. Although I hope we get lucky much sooner than that!"

Katie smiled in relief. Perhaps, she thought, her fears about Cecilia were unfounded.

Saul raised a glass. "Here's to getting lucky sooner than later!"

Katie laughed out loud as she joined Cecilia and Charlie in the toast.

She continued to ignore Charlie's leering glare as she sipped from her cup and waited to see where the conversation would go next.

A voice shattered the table's momentary silence. "Excuse me, I have a question…"

Katie looked up to see where the voice had come from, as did Charlie and the others. All eyes pivoted to the table nearest to theirs, at which two men were seated. Both looked to be in their late thirties. Both were reasonably handsome. One of the men stood and introduced himself.

"I'm not sure if you all remember me from training. I know I've forgotten half the names here…things were rushed. My name is Lewis."

Lewis began shaking hands with everyone at the table. As he did so, he gestured to his seatmate. "That there is Freddie. We're with the USGS."

Half of the table nodded in understanding. The other half looked confused.

Katie was in the latter half. "USGS?" she asked.

Lewis flashed her a cheeky grin, obviously happy to explain what he did for a living. "United States Geological Survey. We're here to map the place."

"Ahh, I see," said Katie, extending her hand. "Nice to meet you."

Lewis' hand was rough, and his grip was firm. He continued to smile while staring directly into Katie's eyes. "Likewise," he said.

Katie felt her cheeks fill with blood and she looked away to remove an invisible piece of lint on her sleeve. "So," she said, "what was your question?"

Lewis grabbed an empty chair, spun it around and sat down, his legs straddling either side. "I was wondering what you all will do if you don't find any life at all?"

Katie looked confused. "Why wouldn't we?"

"All sorts of reasons," Lewis responded. "We've never studied these geysers up close before. Who's to say the orbital probes that detected plumes of water and organic compounds didn't detect a once a decade anomaly? Maybe the plumes will be empty for a while. Maybe they'll never be home to life again. Maybe they never were."

Katie smiled ruefully. "That's a lot of maybes."

"True enough. But that's science. We're all about maybes. No sure things."

Cecilia interjected. "And that's why we have to check. And if we don't find anything this year, we'll check again next year."

"And if you check all of the geysers? Find nothing?"

Cecilia smiled. "Then we check elsewhere. Until we've turned over every rock."

Lewis smiled. He turned back to Freddie and gestured for him to come over.

Reluctantly, Freddie did so, a glass for each of them in his hands.

Lewis took his glass and raised it in a toast. "To turning over every rock!"

The group toasted again.

TEN

Freddie rolled his eyes as he drank. Katie got the impression this was not the first time he had been dragged into a social situation by Lewis.

Lewis turned to Cecilia and cracked a quiet joke. Katie couldn't hear the joke or Cecilia's answer, but she laughed, so that was a good sign for Lewis.

The table moved on in their conversation. Lewis had successfully ingratiated himself with her seatmates and was now interacting with the others as if he had always been sat with them. Katie had to hand it to him: the guy was smooth.

His friend, Freddie, continued to stand awkwardly next to the table without sitting. Katie got his attention, pulled up an empty chair and gestured for him to sit down.

"Thanks," he said, sitting slowly with a pained expression on his face.

"So, you're with the USGS too?"

"Yeah," he said. "Geologist."

"How long have you been doing that?"

Freddie took another sip of his drink and smiled. "My whole adult life."

Katie nodded. "You like it?"

Freddie shrugged. "Pays the bills." After an uncomfortable pause, he spoke again. "What I really like is mountain climbing."

Katie perked up. "Mountain climbing? Really?"

"Yeah. The whole geology thing started as an excuse to take a drive to the mountains. All I had to do was dig for a couple of hours and I could climb for the rest of the day. Hell, sometimes I had to climb in order to dig."

"Sounds sweet," she replied.

Freddie nodded. "It was, for a while. Still is sometimes. But it gets harder and harder to avoid the back of a desk as your career..." he held up his fingers in air quotes. "Progresses."

Katie laughed. "I'm starting to understand what brought you all the way out here. Not many mountains nearby though."

"Nope," said Freddie, "but there are some craters. A particularly big one, in fact."

"Oh, yeah...uh...smiddy? Smith?"

Freddie smirked. "Schmidt. Hoping to get a chance to see it up close."

"Well, I hope you do get the chance," said Katie. "Does your friend do this to you often?"

Freddie gestured dismissively to Lewis, still busy charming the rest of the table. "Who, him? Eh, he's harmless. I have met a handful of new faces with him though, yes."

Katie's gaze lingered on Lewis. "I'm sure."

...

Cecilia chatted with the men at the table, trying her best to feign interest. The new gentlemen who had joined them - a loud and gregarious "Lewis" along with his quieter friend – had made this significantly more difficult. Truthfully, she just wanted to go back to the sleeping quarters.

She looked across the table at Katie, who had engaged the quieter friend in conversation. Impressively, she'd gotten him talking. Cecilia understood – Katie was a cute little thing, very disarming and sincere. In this friend's position she would have opened up too.

Cecilia returned to taking turns staring vacantly into Lewis', Saul's and Charlie's eyes as they attempted to impress her. She smiled and nodded while thinking fondly of bed and plotting her escape.

...

Charlie watched the others at the table with a sneer. Those little sluts, Katie and Cecilia, batted their eyes and licked their lips at the idiot cucks gathered around him and they bought it – the stupid fucks bought it. These whores were no different than any other, dancing their pussies around like so much fish bait just to get what they wanted, then shutting things down as soon as they got theirs. His male seatmates were barking up the wrong tree, wasting their time.

Charlie regarded Saul, this Lewis guy, and his friend, Frankie or Fuckface or something. They'd see soon enough. Charlie had already made the mistake of probing the Katie girl to see if she was down to fuck, and he'd run into the predictable icy wall. Total waste of time.

But whatever, fuck em'. These idiots deserved it. Watching them show off like they were so much fucking better than everyone else made Charlie sick. Fucking peasants weren't shit.

As for that cunt Cecilia, bitch had been barking orders at everyone all day like she was some kind of goddamn Queen of Sheba or some shit. Well, fuck that decrepit bitch. Cunt hadn't seen a dick since the last century, and who could blame the men of yesteryear? I mean, who would want that? Gross.

...

Ira reached the table with her tray of food and stood in confusion. Her dining partners had disappeared. She looked around the dining room, trying to find where they might have gone. She didn't have to look far. Lewis and Freddie were only one table over, chatting up some of the scientists. A couple of the people at the table were very pretty women, so she didn't have to speculate about why the boys had made the switch.

She smirked, shook her head and turned away. Her interview with the Geological team would have to wait. Her eyes scanned the room. Maybe she could sit with the IT team? No, she decided. She could only sit through so many arguments about pop culture sci-fi. The worker types, perhaps? Three of them, a Brad and two others she couldn't remember, were gathered not too far away. They seemed friendly, and their conversation was clearly jovial. It would be a great opportunity for Ira to learn more about what the crew types did on the Base. There were so many, always busy, and she hadn't been introduced to most of them. But no, the vibe seemed clickish. She didn't have the energy to try and break through that social barrier tonight.

Her eyes settled on the only table left with people at it, where James sat with his geeky engineer friend and one other. They would have to do. She strode over confidently and took a seat without asking. James seemed surprised to see her but didn't voice an objection. The other two men simply ignored her.

"Ira," said James, "how are you this evening?"

"Well, I'm just great, James, thank you for asking. How about yourself? Still hate this place?"

James sputtered and choked on his food. He swallowed hard, clearing the blockage in his throat. "I...I never said I hate this place..." he stammered.

Ira took a bite of her dinner and spoke through a full mouth. "Well, sure, not hate exactly. I'm paraphrasing. Dislike. Dread. Find repugnant and depressing. Just...you know...'boo Mars'."

James guffawed. "Yeah, I don't...not sure how you got that impression. It's not accurate. I'm actually very excited about what we're doing here."

The older man to James' left spoke. "I think it's fairly normal to have some reservations about coming here, no matter how excited you are about the work. I know I had them. It's not an easy thing to travel this far from home, leaving your loved ones behind."

The other man, to James' right - his engineer, nodded. "I agree completely. It's normal to be scared. No need to be embarrassed."

James set down his knife and fork and folded his hands on the table. "I'm not embarrassed. I have nothing to be embarrassed about. I didn't say those things."

The three people at the table stared at him incredulously.

"I mean...I had concerns before leaving, certainly. As Melvin said, it's quite a thing to leave your family for so long..."

As James paused, Ira thought she saw a gleam of emotion in his eyes. The emotion was hard to qualify. Was it simple sadness? Guilt? Regret?

Then James continued. "But I would hardly say those things equal hate or dislike or whatever else you said." He laughed. "Just normal pre-flight jitters."

Melvin and the engineer smiled politely and went back to their meals.

Ira shrugged and did the same. "Ok. Glad you're good."

James nodded in affirmation and returned to his meal. "I am, thank you." He chewed a moment, then spoke again. "How about you, Ira? What brings you to our table this evening?"

Ira nodded in the direction of the empty table behind her. "Got ditched by my old seatmates."

"I see," said James. "And where are they now?"

Ira spoke through a mouthful of food. "Over with the science geeks." She stopped chewing and glanced furtively at Melvin before adding "Sorry...life-science geeks."

Melvin laughed good naturedly. "I've always said those biologists and doctors are giving us mathematicians and physicists a bad name. We'd be rolling in women and wine if not for them."

Ira smiled at Melvin, mouth once again full. "Totally."

...

Cecilia stood, and the table stopped talking. She held up her hands and gestured for them to keep speaking. "Don't everyone stop on my account," she said, laughing, "I'm headed off to bed. It's been a big day and I'm afraid I've hit my limit."

Saul was the first to reply. "Nothing to apologize for. Have a great night, Cecilia. Sleep well."

The rest of the table echoed Saul's sentiment. Cecilia waved, thanking everyone, and left the dining room.

Katie turned to Freddie. "She's right, it is getting late. We should probably wrap this up soon."

Before Freddie could respond, Lewis interjected. "But not yet." He smiled slyly and locked his gaze on to Katie's before adding, in a quiet but firm tone, "Don't leave us so soon."

Katie blushed and remained in her seat.

...

Toby turned to Alvin and asked for the salt.

Alvin passed it without looking, and the two men chewed their food in silence.

"What the fuck are you looking at?" said a new voice.

Toby looked up to see Chris Marshall, the nighttime powerplant tech, sitting across from Alvin with an expression of contempt.

Alvin didn't respond.

Chris tried again. "I said: what the fuck are you looking at?"

Chris spoke up. "Well, we aren't at home, are we? For Christ's sake man, you aren't even connected to the server."

Alvin looked incredulous. "Uh...yes I am." He laughed to himself and took a forkful of food.

"On Earth?" said Chris. "You are currently connected to the server on Earth?"

"Well, no, of course not," said Alvin. I have a private server that I've programmed all the anicreatures into..."

"Well then why the fuck does it matter what time it is? It's your fucking server!"

"I replicated an Earth day...I'm going for an experience here, Chris!"

Toby interjected. "Boys, boys. We're getting a little loud here. Take a breath."

Alvin lowered his volume but continued. "What are you so wrapped around the axle about anyway? Since when do you care so much about when and where I game?"

Chris smiled. "Do you know what I was asking you about? Before you started staring into space like an imbecile?"

Alvin's brow furrowed. "What?"

Chris smacked the table in triumph. "I asked what you thought about my sister's surgery. Of course, you would know that if you were paying attention. She's fine by the way – expected to make a full recovery." Chris sat back, folded his arms, and looked with satisfaction to each of the others at the table, as if his case was proven.

After a moment's silence, Alvin spoke again. "Shit, Chris...sorry. Glad she's ok."

At this point Alvin blinked and seemed to wake from a trance. He made a gesture in the air and turned his attention to Chris. "What'd you say, man?"

Chris shook his head and returned to his meal. "Jesus Christ, Armstrong."

Alvin looked around the table, confused. "What?"

"He wanted to know what you were looking at," said Toby, "but we all already know."

"You guys want to know what I'm looking at? I'll show you." Alvin gestured wildly in the air and pointed triumphantly at the center of the table. He didn't seem to realize he was the only one currently wearing an AR device, and it appeared to the rest of them that he was unreasonably excited about empty space.

Toby sighed, exchanged a glance with Chris and dug his AR specs out of his pocket. He put them on and linked to Alvin's device, which was publicly broadcasting its display. As he did so, a strange alien form materialized in the center of the table. The slug-like creature slithered slowly across the table, leaving an ethereal trail of goo in its wake. "Really?" said Toby. "At the table?"

"Hey," said Alvin, "these are peak hours. You catch all the best ones at dinner time."

Toby removed his specs and put them back in his pocket. "We've talked about this, man. This is our breakfast time. We don't play games at breakfast. Too early. We're gonna' be looking at screens all day."

"So," Alvin objected, "the only time we disconnect back home is when we go to sleep."

Alvin's apology seemed to have taken the wind out of the argument.

Toby slowly picked up his fork and returned to his meal, watchful and ready to jump in if the fight started again.

"Which one was it, anyway?" asked Chris.

"Slugizar," said Toby, "Two-hundred hit points."

"Well, shit," said Chris, "in that case, I'm sorry. Those are super rare."

Alvin looked at Chris, confused and skeptical.

"I'm serious!" said Chris. "What the fuck are you waiting for? You can't let it get away! Totally made all that up about my sister by the way. I don't even have one."

The tension was cut. Toby and the others at the table chuckled and shook their heads.

"You're an asshole," said Alvin.

"So are you," replied Chris, "you god damn junkie."

Alvin laughed and returned to his game.

Connie, who had been silent up to this point, put her food down and stared at the three men. Then she picked up her fork and resumed eating, shaking her head and muttering. "You boys are very strange."

...

Colin Massey couldn't believe what was happening. Red in the face, heart pounding, he turned to the man seated closest to him and shared a look of solidarity before turning once again to face his foe. In his hand, shaking, he held the tool he would use to take revenge on his enemy. Beads of sweat broke out on his forehead and began dripping down his face as he sat, frozen, contemplating his next move.

"So," asked Steve, "you gonna' sit here looking at it all night or are you gonna' eat it?"

Blaine burst out laughing. "He warned you, Irish!"

The two men wiped tears from their eyes and continued to bellow, while Colin took a sip of water and regarded the spice-filled pile of meat and rice he had promised to finish "without any trouble."

"Fuck you, you goddamn yanks," he said in-between gulps, "you knew this shite was hotter than fire."

Steven slapped Colin on the back. "You knew damn well it was too spicy for your meat and potatoes ass. Lesson learned. And by the way, Blaine's from Canada."

Colin pushed the hot meal away from him. "Yer' all fuckin' yanks to me. If I gotta' get on a plane ta' see ya', yer' a fuckin' yank."

Blaine furrowed his brow. "That...doesn't even make any sense. You can get to all sorts of places in a plane..."

Colin gulped desperately only to find his cup dry. "Whatever, you cunt. I need water, Jeezus..."

He could hear the duo laughing as he left to get another meal and a fresh cup of water. When he returned, the conversation had, thankfully, moved on. He sat and tucked into his newest selection: ham and mashed potatoes. At least, that's what the sign said. Colin wasn't sure the grey meat before him was ham...but at least it didn't burn his mouth while he ate it.

"So, you really think it's gonna' come to that?" asked Blaine. His expression was one of concern.

Steven sighed heavily and leaned in. "It's possible. I hate to say it, but it's possible. The suits back home are all spineless bureaucrats, and this guy they sent us..." He glanced towards the new Site Lead's table. "Clueless. I don't have a lot of hope things are going to turn out well."

"How would that even work?" asked Blaine, "Has it ever been done before?"

"How would what work?" asked Colin.

Steve looked uncomfortable answering. He gestured for Colin to keep his voice down. "Nothing's official...but we may be looking at a gap between contracts. We're having trouble coming to an agreement between all the parties. Again, nothing's official. And I'd appreciate it if you'd both keep this knowledge to yourselves."

Colin thought for a moment. "So, if we can't come to an agreement...what then?"

"We stop work," said Blaine.

"Like a strike?" whispered Colin.

"Yes, kinda'. Except management will be on board. At least, our management will."

"But wait," said Colin, "It's not like they can just send us home. What are we gonna' do if we're not working? Are we still gonna' get paid?"

Steven interrupted. "Ok, that's enough. We shouldn't be talking about this. Let's just hope nothing comes of it."

...

TEN

Cecilia walked down the outer corridor, rooms on either side of her. She wondered who was already in bed. Not every person on the base had been present in the dining room during dinner. She knew the astronomy team was working this evening, and a few of the crew had night duty. That left a handful of people who were neither working or eating, or who preferred to eat alone in the privacy of their rooms. The idea of running into unexpected stragglers made her nervous.

As if on cue, a door down the hallway swung open, and a woman stepped out. Cecilia slowed her walk, hoping that this person would pass her and leave before she reached the end of the hallway. Unfortunately, the woman lingered in her doorway, talking to someone.

To buy time, Cecilia stopped and crouched down, as if to tie her shoe. It wasn't until she had reached the floor that she remembered her current shoes were slip-ons. She cursed under her breath and looked up to see if the woman had noticed her error.

It was then that the woman, who she could now identify as Carolyn Boss, the ship's Doctor, leaned in and kissed another person in the doorway. The kiss lingered, as did the pair's eyes, as the unknown person placed a hand on her cheek before stepping backward and gently closing the door.

Cecilia looked down and fumbled with her shoe as Carolyn pivoted from the door and started walking in her direction.

When she saw Cecilia, Carolyn stopped dead in her tracks.

Cecilia, feigning ignorance, made a show of finishing 'tying her shoes' and stood up. She tried to act casually. "Hi, Doc."

Carolyn blushed and stammered. "Cecilia...I didn't see you there. I was just returning something I borrowed from Lucas."

So that was who Carolyn has been talking to – Lucas Gordon, one of the crew. The base's Machinist if Cecilia wasn't mistaken. Cecilia tried to make her lack of concern for Carolyn and Lucas's visit clear through her body language. "Great. That was nice of him to let you borrow...whatever it was."

Carolyn smiled, nodded, and looked awkwardly at her feet. "Yeah. Well, I'm gonna' head out, get some dinner before the cafeteria closes."

Cecilia stepped aside so Carolyn could squeeze past.

Carolyn started walking down the hallway, then stopped and turned around. "Cecilia..."

"Yes?"

"Isn't your room on the other side of the base? Near mine?"

Cecilia smiled gently. "So it is. I'm also borrowing from a friend."

Relief washed over Carolyn's face. "I see. Well, have a wonderful night."

"I will. You too."

Carolyn gave a little wave, then walked the rest of the way down the hall and out of sight.

Cecilia wrapped gently on her friend's door.

TEN

Andre opened it and broke into a wide grin. "Took you long enough. Come in."

ELEVEN

Of all the difficulties James had encountered in space, this was the hardest. He wasn't entirely sure what to do. There was a real possibility that the denizens of Alpha Base were about to perform space's first labor strike.

The situation was thus: the contract between his company, EPMS, and SLI, the logistics company which provided the base's infrastructure support, was coming to an end. Normally, this would result in an effortless renewal – a purely theoretical paperwork transaction that merely cemented the ongoing, uninterrupted relationship between the two companies. Work on-site at Alpha Base would continue without missing a beat, as it had for years, and the ultimate customer, NASA - as well as all the scientists they sponsored - would be none the wiser. This year, though, had seen a change in labor rates at SLI, motivated by inflation and other changes in the market. EPMS, the prime contractor in the arrangement with NASA, did not agree with SLI's newly proposed rates, seeing them as too expensive. If the two companies couldn't come to an agreement before the current contract was over, EPMS

- and James - would be left without a logistics organization to run Alpha Base.

To make matters worse, one of the two other subcontractors on the base – General Space Systems – had a non-disclosure and exclusive teaming agreement with SLI. If SLI dropped out, GSS would too. Considering the vital role that pilots, aerospace propulsion techs, communications techs and other GSS employees played in getting people to and from Mars, this was a showstopper.

Not to mention, all of them were plainly stranded out here for another year, the soonest the *Vectio* would be back to get them. Any replacement personnel or companies would need to be phased in over time, not swapped out overnight. The realities of space travel prevented that from happening.

So, no brainer, right? Without SLI and GSS on board, EPMS couldn't keep their people alive, couldn't get new people on site, and couldn't support the science they had been contracted to support. Their own contract was in jeopardy, as was the physical safety and wellbeing of their personnel. EPMS should have no choice but to cave. But, for some reason, they still hadn't.

Now the deadline was creeping up and James was starting to get scared. He'd known the current period of performance was coming to an end when he accepted the job, but he'd had no reason to think that this time would be different. Why was an agreement taking so long? Why had all the parties so willingly tiptoed up to the brink?

James knew there was likely some gamesmanship at play. After all, SLI was also stuck without a viable alternative for keeping their people safe, and they stood to lose a fortune in revenue. GSS, too, would likely be applying lots of pressure on SLI to simply cave already, as GSS had no problem with their current arrangement, and they wouldn't want to lose out on business due to someone else's dispute. In the long run, James could see the situation costing SLI their exclusive relationship with GSS, which they would surely want to avoid.

Maybe that was the thinking of the EPMS brass...that SLI simply had more to lose and would be the first to blink. No matter the reason, the whole thing put James in an intolerable, unenviable position. He had to keep dozens of people, already isolated and under some of the worst stress imaginable, calm and functioning despite the rising specter of a missing paycheck. And he had to do it while reassuring all the other contractors and scientists on the base that everything was alright and they had nothing to be concerned about. "Nope, nothing to see here! Nothing at all. Pay no attention to the man with a gun in the corner...he's not important."

James leaned over in his seat and tried not to throw up. He had started his day in a wonderful mood. Heather and the kids had put on a full thirty-minute skit in their latest videomessage, reenacting what they thought his daily routine must be. It had been hilarious...and disconcertingly accurate. The cafeteria had a delicious lunch lined up – one of his favorite dishes – and he had enjoyed a solid workout this morning, something that got rarer the older he got. It was going to be a great day. Then he booted up his workstation and got the terrifying news: Negotiations ongoing.

He had to do something to try and fix things before they broke for good. He closed his door and opened a blank message addressed to his superiors back home. He typed furiously, highlighting and italicizing such passages as "*urgent need*" and "*overwhelming impact to critical life-support functions.*" He hit send and sat back in his chair, somewhat relieved to have done something, but still full of angst over the unknown.

He stood and re-opened his office door. Factoring in the light delay to and from Earth, the time it would take for his message to find the right person, and the time it would take that person to compose a reply, he had at least a few hours before receiving a response. He stood in his doorway, thinking, then gingerly approached Steven's office.

"Hi, Steven. You got a second?"

Steven looked up from his console. He sighed and gestured at an empty guest chair he kept tucked away behind his door. "Sit down."

James closed the office door and took a seat.

The two men stared at each other in the cramped space, the silence between them thick, like fog.

Steven spoke first. "Well?"

James cleared his throat. "What can we do to stop this?"

"Stop what?"

James smiled ruefully. "I think you know. We can't let a disagreement over paperwork a million miles away interfere with the work we're doing here."

Steven chuckled, folded his hands and looked down at his chest. "Paperwork." He put his feet up on the desk, leaned back and looked James right in the eyes. "What you call 'paperwork' my people call 'a paycheck.' I'm not sure if you knew this, Mr. Wilmot, but we're not actually out here for the fun of it. We have families back home, and we're here at the ass end of nowhere to make sure they're well supported. If you take our paychecks away, we will absolutely not be letting our work interfere with solving your disagreement."

"Steve," said James, "I think you know I know that. Nobody is suggesting that anyone go without pay…"

"But you want us to work without a contract?"

"Well…no…not necessarily…I just want to find a way to keep operations going."

"And I'm telling you, we won't keep operations going without a valid contract."

James stopped talking and regarded Steven carefully. He recognized that it would be best to tread lightly. Steven had no time for semantics or splitting hairs. He tried a different tack.

"What I'm trying to say is that our companies are haggling over a price. In the meantime, though, all of us are still out here, trying to survive, trying to make the trip worthwhile. I believe…I am confident that our respective employers will settle on a final number. In the meantime, though, we have to keep everyone working. Not only for our safety and survival, but for the science we came out here to support. If we stop work for any appreciable length of time, we'll miss many critical deadlines, some of which our schedules won't be able to recover from…"

"Right," said Steven, "that's the point. If you want to stay on schedule, close the deal with us."

James held up his hands. "Yes, yes, I get that. But what I'm saying is that after, once we've made a deal, we want to have enough of the base left standing - and enough of the projects left running – to come back to. Without that, there is no deal, nobody gets paid, and we came out here for nothing."

Steven thought a moment. "Sounds like a great reason to get us on contract. And for my people to get paid."

"Steve, you're gonna' get paid. None of us actually see any money while we're out here, right? It's an imaginary fund collecting in an imaginary safe that becomes real when we collect at the end of the trip. If those funds 'stop collecting' for a few months while our companies haggle, what difference does it make as long as your money is in the bank once you get home? We'll back pay you guys for any lost wages during negotiation."

Steven frowned. "Well, James, if that is how your pay from the prime works, they're even stingier than I thought. We get paid as we go."

James tried to hide his surprise. He and Heather had been forced to take a high-interest loan from EPMS until he got paid at the end of the trip. "Well...do you really think SLI would stop paying you guys during negotiations? They'll front the money, right? To avoid interruption of services?"

"I can't comment on that. You'll have to ask your contracts people to talk to mine. All I can say for sure is that neither SLI or my people are obligated to work for free. If you want to avoid delays, if you want our services, agree to our terms. Have your execs sign the contract. We work for money backed by legal certainty, not verbal promises."

James sighed and responded sincerely. "You're right, of course. And I told my leadership as much. I've strongly encouraged them to sign as soon as possible. We need you guys."

Steven seemed disarmed by this admission. He took his feet off the desk and sat up in his chair. "I'm glad to hear that."

James nodded. "We really do. The work you guys do out here is top notch. It doesn't go unseen."

"Did you tell your bosses that, too?"

"I did, actually."

"Well...good. It was you guys that changed the terms, you know. Rate adjustments have been in there since the beginning. We're just looking to get fairly compensated. Same way we have been for years..."

"I know," said James, "and between you and me, I have no idea why we're contesting it this time. Some big wig probably got the idea he could save a few bucks without knowing what he was really suggesting. We just have to hope reason prevails."

James paused, then continued. "We aren't our companies, you know? They go back and forth, they haggle, but in the meantime, we're out here. I'm just trying to keep this place running."

Steven nodded. "I know. You're just following orders. I have my orders too."

Silence hung once again between the two men as they settled into a detente. A silence that was broken by a swift rapping on the door.

Miguel opened the door gingerly, without waiting for a response. "Mr. Wilmot? I'm very sorry to bother you, but Dr. Rowe needs to see you right away. He has an emergency."

James sat up in his chair. "Is everyone ok?"

"A scientific emergency," Miguel clarified.

James nodded and stood. He turned to Steven. "I'll be back later so we can finish this discussion."

Steven shrugged. "If you think there's a point."

James left the room without another word. He followed Miguel down the hall toward the labs.

"That didn't look like a fun conversation," said Miguel. "Everything alright Mr. Wilmot?"

"Everything's fine. And call me James. So, what's the problem with Dr. Rowe?"

Miguel looked at James with a rueful smile. "I'll let him tell you himself. He's got some very strong opinions."

James sighed. "I'm sure he does."

The two men entered the lab module, where the science teams busily poured over their respective data samples.

Rowe was toward the back of the room. He stood, leaning on the wall, arms folded in front of him. "The man with the plan! Hopefully you have some answers."

James stopped in front of Rowe with Miguel behind him. "I'll try my best. What seems to be the problem?"

"I'll show you."

With that, Rowe brushed past James and Miguel and headed down the hall, back the way they had just come.

James shook his head and followed.

They passed all of the other modules and came to the hangar umbilical. As the door to the hangar opened, James was hit with a wall of acrid dust. His eyes stung and his nostrils flared. All the HEPA filtering in the world couldn't seem to get rid of the chalky red powder from outside. Whenever one of the airlocks was opened, clouds of it followed. James only hoped enough of it had been removed from the air that their cancers would come on slowly, killing them in old age.

Rowe stopped at a pile of boxes near the bottom of the stairs. "What does this look like to you?"

James ventured a guess. "Cargo containers?"

"Nope," said Rowe, "this is a crime scene." He pointed to one of the boxes, which lay empty. "Where the hell is my laser rangefinder?"

James hesitated. "I...don't rightly know, Lewis. I assume it's supposed to be here?"

Rowe pointed at James in sarcastic triumph. "Right you are! And yet...nothing!"

James turned to Miguel. "Do you have any idea where the rangefinder is?"

Miguel shook his head. "No sir. I came down here to fetch it for some pre-mission testing and found an empty box. Then Dr. Rowe had me go and get you."

James nodded and regarded the empty box for a second, then started looking around the hangar. His eyes met those of a technician a few feet away. The tech quickly busied himself with whatever he was working on, but it was too late – James had him in his sights. "Hey, Scranton, is it?"

Owen's shoulders slumped and he looked up, forcing a smile on his face. "Yep, that's me. Owen Scranton."

James closed the distance between them. "Owen, that's right. Good to see you." He pointed at the empty box behind him. "Did you happen to see who took this piece of equipment?"

Owen had seen who took it, but he was reluctant to get involved in a dispute between scientists. "Well...you know...I'm pretty busy here and there are a lot of folks coming and going, so...I don't always catch who took what..."

James sensed Owen's hesitation. "We're not asking you to get in the middle of anything. I just hoped maybe you could save me a trip to look at the cameras."

Owen took a breath and ran his fingers through his hair. James was bluffing, he knew that. The cameras in the hangar had plenty of blind spots, and where they were standing may very well be one of them. On the other hand, if the theft had been caught on camera, and Owen was clearly in visual range of the incident, then he would have made an enemy in James – the man who paid the bills. Faced with a lose-lose scenario, Owen took the less damaging path. "You know...I'm pretty sure it was one of the physics people. A Wheeler something?"

"You sure?" asked James. "What did he do with it?"

"I didn't see that," replied Owen. "I just saw him grab it."

James nodded. "Where are they now?"

"The physics people? Outside, working on their machine."

James thanked Owen, turned on his heel and stalked toward the stairs.

"Where are you going?" asked Rowe.

"For a walk," said James. "I'll be back in a bit."

...

ELEVEN

Suited up, James trudged across the Martian landscape. Wheeler and his team were visible in the distance, gathered around a section of their accelerator and having some kind of discussion.

James waited until he was within a few yards of the group and hailed Wheeler.

Wheeler and the others turned around.

"James," exclaimed Wheeler, "to what do we owe the pleasure?"

"Hey Louis," James replied, "sorry to interrupt but we have a minor problem."

"Oh... it couldn't be handled over comms?"

"Unfortunately, no. I figured it was probably best to handle it face to face."

Behind the glass of his visor, Louis Wheeler frowned. "What's up?"

James pointed at the rangefinder, clearly situated on top of the section of accelerator pipe behind them. "Is that yours?"

Louis adopted an expression of confused goodwill. "Yes, we got it from the hangar. We are responsible for it and we'll return it as soon as we're done. Won't let anything happen to it, I promise!"

"That's great, but is it yours?"

"I don't follow..."

James cleared his throat. "What I mean is, was the rangefinder part of your approved equipment package? Was it included on the bill of materials and packing list for your project?"

Behind Louis, the other physicists looked down at the ground and folded their arms. Louis continued to play dumb. "Honestly, James, I'm not sure. Look, we only needed to make sure this section of pipe was level. We're bringing it right back."

"I understand. The thing is, the survey guys were looking for it. They planned to use it today as well."

"Can't they wait until we're done?"

"Apparently not. They seem pretty adamant about using it today."

Louis was suddenly angry. "Well, that's ridiculous. We have a legitimate use for this piece of equipment, and we've got a schedule to keep to!"

James held up his hands in a bid for peace. "I totally understand your position. The issue is that the survey guys have a schedule for their project as well. And this piece of equipment is assigned to them. Its theirs. Bought and paid for."

"They can't share? I thought this whole place was predicated on resource sharing?"

"To an extent, sure," said James. "But these guys have a schedule too and they went out of their way to designate this part as a critical item for their project. With that said, I'm sure we can talk to them and arrange some kind of resource sharing deal, but for now the part is theirs and they need it."

Louis shook his head in frustration. "Well, that's...fine, whatever. Take it."

He turned his back and stormed away, muttering under his breath. The others followed.

James watched as the three of them opened the airlock of the rover they were using, mounted up, and drove away to – he assumed - inspect another section of the pipe. The rangefinder remained where it was.

James approached the rangefinder and gingerly lifted it off the pipe. The unit was heavier than expected, even in the lower gravity. James held it in his arms and began making his way back to the open-top buggy he had driven to the worksite. As he huffed and puffed over a small rise, he regretted not parking closer. He hadn't wanted to appear overly aggressive by cruising right up to the physics team in a cloud of dust. "Lot of good that did me," he thought, as he mounted the buggy and drove the short distance back to the hangar.

...

Hours later, James sat with a sigh. His day had been spent chasing after busy scientists, firing off angry emails, and generally stomping out metaphorical fires. It was far more activity than he had expected to do when he woke up that morning, and he was tired to the bone. Solving his own problems in a given day was tiring enough – solving other people's left him a husk.

Melvin flashed him a kind smile. "You look done."

James smiled back. "Done?"

"Done for the day," replied Melvin, "ready to pack it in."

"Almost. But first I actually wanted to check in with you."

Melvin nodded. "I can imagine. Word's out. Wheeler stopped by earlier today."

James looked around the now empty lab, verifying that he and Melvin were the only two still there. "And what do you think?"

"I think we can make it work."

James was relieved. "Really? You'll talk to Louis?"

"Let me worry about Louis," said Melvin, "he can be stubborn but he's not a monster, or an idiot. He'll see the sense in it."

James nodded and stood. He offered his hand to Melvin. "Thank you."

Melvin took it and shook gently. "You're quite welcome. Now, go get some dinner and some sleep. This will all still be here in the morning. I hear they're serving meatloaf."

James feigned excitement. "Meatloaf? You don't say?"

Melvin chuckled and turned back to his workstation. "Good night, James."

"Good night."

James saw himself out, and the lab door slid closed behind him. He stood alone in the connection corridor and looked in either direction. After a moment's thought, he headed purposefully back toward his office. He had one more task to complete before ending his day.

As soon as he re-entered the office module he glanced tentatively over at Steven's office. To his great relief, Steven was still there.

He rapped on the door frame and took one step inside. "Got a second?"

Steven looked up, surprised and irritated. He blinked rapidly, processing this unexpected intrusion, then gestured at the empty space before his desk. "Please."

"I have a proposition."

"Oh?"

"I've been messaging back and forth with the brass all day. I think they understand the gravity of our situation, and I fully expect them to cave. But, just in case they don't, I've also spoken to the heads of each project and an independent contracts specialist back home. If EPMS refuses to award SLI, each scientific team is prepared to redirect their grant money to an account of our choosing. Your team will resign their posts, as will I, if necessary. Everyone will then be re-hired, directly by the scientists. It's totally legal for them to re-direct the money and hire who they want. There are other legal issues, of course, such as ownership of the facility and most of the equipment, but who's gonna' stop us from using it? Maybe they'll sue me later...I don't know. Either way, we keep the science going and everyone gets paid."

Steven stared at him in shock for several moments. When he spoke again, there was a newfound respect in his voice. "Why would you take that kind of risk?"

"Well, I don't actually expect it to happen. My company is smarter than that. I might not have a job when I get back, but...we all know this is temp work anyway. And if it does happen...I don't know...maybe I'll take up a collection for my legal fees."

Steven smiled. James smiled. The two men stared at each other.

Finally, James spoke. "We good?"

Steven hesitated, searching for the right words. "Well...assuming what you're saying is true...I think we can work with that."

James stood. "It's true. Good night, Steve."

James was up and out the door before Steven could respond.

Nonetheless, Steven spoke aloud to an empty office, wonder evident in his voice. "Good night."

PART TWO

TWELVE

Charlie rushed down the hall, trying to look casual. His target was the medical module and all the delightful narcotics therein. Winter was finally here, and his colleagues were falling over themselves with delight: hanging decorations, preparing festivities, generally causing a hubbub. It was exhausting.

He'd never needed an excuse to get high, and he didn't understand why they did. Just do your damn drugs – be they alcohol or whatever – in peace and leave everyone else out of it. Alas, they did not share his opinion, and they were busily readying for the bacchanal to come. This worked to his advantage. His own supply was running low, and he had no intention of seeing the night through sober.

He reached the end of the corridor and took a few steps into the clinic. He gazed at the rows and rows of medicines behind their clear, locked, cabinet doors. He then dragged his attention to the various mechanical arms and medical tools, trying to appear less fixated on the drugs than he was. He reached out to touch one of the mechanical arms, studying its joints and rivets.

Connie noticed him. "Oh...Charlie. I'm just closing up shop. What's up?"

Charlie put his hands behind his back. "Hey, Connie. It's the same as always. Damn back is spasming."

Connie nodded. "So, you'll need a muscle relaxer?"

"Well, it's not just the spasms. I mean, yeah, a muscle relaxer is fine, but it hurts in the spine even when the muscles are relaxed. I need something for that pain, too."

Connie began walking from station to station in the module, turning off various devices and checking the locks on the cabinet doors. "I can offer you a cannabinoid derived pain reducer. Most people find it really helps with discomfort and swelling."

"This is more of a nerve pain."

Connie nodded. "It will help with that too."

"Got anything with THC?"

"I do. We have a couple of full-blown cannabis analogues, but I only like to give those out if the pain is really bad."

Charlie tried to conceal his frustration. "Well, it is, really bad. I think the cannabis would be great, but I'm not even sure that's gonna' do the trick."

Connie paused at an open cabinet. "And what will do the trick, Charlie?"

"Well, those pills the Doc gave me the last couple of times really worked."

"The opioids?"

"Yeah, yeah, those. If I could get some of those, I think I'd be all set."

Connie stopped what she was doing and turned around to face Charlie directly. Her eyes regarded him with sympathy. "Charlie...I think we both know that isn't going to solve the real problem."

Charlie feigned ignorance. "What do you mean?"

Connie shook her head. "I can't give you any more opiate based pain medication. I do have a limited supply of drugs intended to mitigate withdrawal symptoms that I can offer you, if that's what you need, but they're not meant as a replacement, just something to ease the transition."

"Transition to what?"

"Getting clean."

Charlie's blood boiled. Who the fuck did this bitch think she was? When he spoke again, his voice was thick with repressed rage. "I'm sorry, I don't follow."

Connie placed a hand on his shoulder. "Charlie, addiction is nothing to be ashamed of. These meds are powerful, and they can sneak up on the best of us. I've had plenty of family and friends who had difficulty stopping when it was time. But we have medication to help."

Charlie's body stiffened under Connie's touch. "I don't...have an addiction...I have back pain. I just need something for my back."

Connie removed her hand. "Charlie, having a problem isn't a failing, but refusing to get help is."

Charlie smiled a joyless smile. "Don't be like this Connie. Come on..." He laughed forcefully. "I'm not a fuckin' junkie!

Ok...you caught me. My back is fine. But its wintertime! Party, party, right? Just give me a couple of pills. Nobody's gonna' know..."

Connie set her jaw. "Charlie...no."

Charlie exploded with rage. He pushed Connie back into the open cabinet and leaned forward into her face. Seething, he spoke through gritted teeth. "Do you have any fucking idea who you're talking to? Give. Me. My god damn medicine!" Charlie leered at Connie with malintent. "Maybe you can be my medicine, huh? Make me feel all better? What do you think?"

An interminable moment passed. Connie braced for violence...

A new voice entered the fray. "I...Is everything all right here?"

Charlie quickly let go of Connie and turned around to greet the newcomer. It was Andre. "Hey man, what's up?"

Connie was in Andre's arms now. He looked up at Charlie in confusion and down at Connie, who was trembling. "What the fuck is going on here?"

Charlie leaned back on the open cabinet then put up his hands. "You know what, I just got a little over excited. Sorry if I startled you, Connie. I'm gonna' just head back to my room and see if I can sleep this pain off." He started moving toward the door.

Connie separated herself from Andre and dragged the two of them out of the way, giving Charlie a clear path to the exit.

TWELVE

Charlie stopped mid-way to the door and addressed Connie again. "I really am sorry if I scared you. I just get crazy with this pain, you know?"

Connie eyed him coldly. "Just go."

Charlie nodded and left, hurrying back to his room. He tried once again to act casually as he fingered the pill bottles he had pocketed from the unlocked cabinet. His only hope was that they were the right kind.

...

James hummed a tune to himself as he powered down his workstation for the night. The long-awaited winter season was here at last, and in contrast to the increasing gloom outside, James was filled with cheer. Things were looking up. The strike hadn't gone ahead, and his company ended up accepting the terms and rates of every subcontractor on the base. Nobody was fired, and everyone was still getting paid. The whole ordeal seemed to have earned James some street-cred with the staff, and the icy reception he had received since his arrival was finally starting to thaw.

In a surprising twist, his company hadn't retaliated against him, or even hinted that retaliation was coming. Perhaps they realized that his only other choice was to be the first Site Lead in the history of Mars to have his crew go on strike. Such a development would be the death of his professional reputation, regardless of the circumstances behind it.

Perhaps. More likely, they were afraid of him. If James had even half the loyalty from the scientists and crew that his bold move suggested he did, he could poach all of their business, steal their equipment, and it would be years before they could do anything about it. He probably had a severance package and a swift kick out the door waiting for him at home, but, so be it. Given lemons, he'd made lemonade.

He left his office and headed toward the control room. Blaine was there, manning the console as always.

"Packing up?"

Blaine turned around at the sound of his voice. "Indeed! Shutting her down for the big party."

James leaned against the door frame. "This is your second one, right?"

"That's right," Blaine said, cheerfully, "and last! In five and a half months, I'll be headed home."

James smiled. "Well, that's gotta' feel good."

Blaine completed putting the control console in stand-by mode and stood up. "Abso-frigging-lutely. I get to go home and spend some of this money I've built up."

James laughed. "Oh, man! Don't spend it all or you'll have to come back!"

Blaine tapped his nose. "Now you're getting it. I fully expect to be back here in two year's time, desperately trying to recoup my outrageous losses."

The two men walked back into the office area, toward the main hallway.

"Will I see you at the party?" asked Blaine.

"You know, I think I'm gonna' skip it. At least most of it. I might duck my head in if I get a chance."

"Why? Other plans?"

"Yes, actually. Neil offered to take Ira and I on a tour of the observatory."

Blaine nodded approvingly. "Nice! Have you been outside at night yet?"

"No, not yet."

"You're gonna' love it. Absolutely magical."

Blaine stopped at a brachial hallway, which led to his room. "This is me. Gotta freshen up for the festivities. Have fun out there, ok?"

James waved. "I will, you too."

He stood still for a moment after Blaine's door closed behind him, unsure what to do next. He was usually so busy, running from task to task, that it felt strange to have a moment of peace. A moment of free time. He took a deep breath, then continued down the hall. He would walk past the rec module then cut over to the other side, through the med labs and amenities module, to get to his room. It was a good idea for him to freshen up as well.

...

"You have to say something."

Connie shook her head. "It's not worth it, Andre. He just got angry, that's all."

Andre frowned. "It looked like he was about to get a lot more than angry. It looked like he was about to hit you...or worse."

Connie sighed. "Andre...you don't know that. You don't know Charlie. He can be a bit of a hot head, but he's harmless. Just let it go."

Andre's frown deepened. "Let it go? Connie, that man was about to assault you! He's a danger to everyone on this base."

"Privacy laws are strict for a reason."

Andre was flabbergasted. "Privacy laws? What are you...Connie, you can't tell me there's no way to report someone if they're showing signs of drug-seeking behavior on a research base..."

"There is a way. And I will if needed."

Andre shook his head in disbelief. "It's needed!" He paused. "Connie, what's really going on? Has he done this before?"

Connie refused to make eye contact. "Andre...that's not...no, nothing like this has happened before. Look...we're stuck in a small space, with a lot of time left. Let's not make it harder than it has to be. Just let it go. I'll be fine, I promise. I can handle Charlie."

...

James stood next to Ira and finished checking the seal on his gloves. It was strange to be in the hangar so late at night. The two of them stood in one of the only pools of light available, the quiet of the place both oppressive and magical, like anything could happen.

Long ago, during his undergraduate studies, he had read of a concept in comparative religion called "spiritual timeliness" or something like that...he couldn't remember exactly. The gist of it was that some environments were extra conducive to spiritual experiences, by dint of their unique qualities: be it certain acoustics, or certain lighting, or a certain temperature...humans were extra likely to perceive those places as filled with cosmic significance...with unquantifiable energy. James had experienced the phenomenon himself: a hard to define crackle in the air while watching a sunrise, or preceding a big storm.

He felt that crackle now, standing in this big hangar all alone with Ira. He knew, without saying it, that this night would stick in his mind for the rest of his life.

Ira turned to him, helmet on, visor up. "All set?"

James nodded and grabbed his helmet. "Yeah, just gotta' put this on."

"Let me help you." Ira stepped towards him and took the helmet from his hands. James stood still as she gently lowered the helmet over his head, her face close enough that he felt her breath on his cheeks.

The seal clicked, and Ira let her hands fall to her sides, a curious smile on her face. James wasn't sure how much time had passed when Ira delicately cleared her throat. "Ready?"

James nodded again and returned her smile. "Ready."

"Good. Let's go."

Ira took his gloved hand in hers and led him toward the airlock.

TWELVE — | 177 |

...

The inky darkness of the outside was disorienting. The sunsets had been coming sooner and sooner these last few months, and now the sun was barely in the sky each day before returning to its hiding place behind the horizon. He blinked as his eyes started to adjust, then the world lit up around him. The wall of night became a murky grey as his HUD's low-light filter activated. The enhanced visuals felt as artificial as they were, and he was tempted to turn them off. Seeing this well at night made him feel like he was playing a video game. Still, he knew they wouldn't get very far without being able to see.

A buggy was parked just outside the hangar, waiting for them. James took a few steps toward it and noticed a difference in the texture of the ground. He looked down and saw a thin layer of colorless powder where hardened clay had been but a few days before. He kneeled and plunged his gloved hand in the muck, letting it run between his fingers.

He looked up at Ira. "What is this stuff?"

She smiled behind her visor. "Turn off your filter and use your light."

He did as instructed, activating the small lights embedded on the sides of his helmet. The world popped to life in true color, and he squinted at the brilliant white substance in his hands.

"Is this..."

"Snow," said Ira, "mostly CO_2. Some water."

"I'll be damned," said James, "Martian snow. If it's dry ice, why isn't it evaporating?"

"It does. Just much slower than on Earth. I swear, don't you pay attention to any of the briefings?"

He chuckled and rose to his feet. "I focused on the stuff that would stop me from getting killed. Kinda forgot the rest. Where's it coming from, anyway?"

Ira pointed at the sky.

James looked up, turned off his lights and reactivated his HUD. "What am I looking at?"

Ira touched his shoulder and directed his gaze. "Right there. Moving slow."

James looked and saw a wispy, gauze-like cloud hovering lazily over the base. He looked longer and more clouds became visible, scattered threads of cotton loitering silently above.

"If we're lucky," said Ira, "we might get some snowfall tonight."

James shook his head in wonder. "Ain't that somethin'?"

"Wait til' we get to the telescope. That'll blow your mind. Come on!"

The two of them boarded the buggy and drove out into the night. A comfortable silence settled on them as the buggy bumped and rolled over the uneven terrain. Before long, Nash and Rice were visible in the distance, tiny humanoid figures surrounded by emptiness.

The telescope, large compared to the two men, looked small compared to the landscape. James fought an irrational, primal panic as the extent of their loneliness struck him anew. They were, the four of them, at this moment, the most exposed of the most exposed. Totally cut off from the rest of humanity. Should something go wrong here, nobody would be able to help them until it was far too late.

He shook his head and cleared such thoughts from his mind. Thinking that way would make him crazy. He had learned early on that the difference between a good day and a bad day on Mars lay almost totally in the mind. If you dwelt on the existential threat that every minute of every day in this place posed to your existence, you were sure to have a bad time. The trick was simply to tell yourself it was all normal, that everything was fine, until you believed it. Then this place became like any other place: repetitive, boring & mundane, with the occasional flash of terror or sublime beauty, depending on the week.

The buggy stopped and the two of them got out. The telescope, Nash and Rice were steps away. A four-way comm link was opened.

"Hey guys," said Rice, waving, "what brings nice people like you to this neck of the woods?"

"Hi Jay," said Ira, a smile coloring her voice, "we heard there was trouble around, thought we'd take a look."

Jay laughed. "Well, that's for sure." He turned to Nash. "You good here?"

"Yup, all good," said Nash. "Thanks for helping me set up."

"My pleasure."

Jay waved at James in greeting as he mounted his own buggy. "Have fun, but don't spend all night out here. You don't want to miss the party."

James waved back and gestured at his air tank. "Don't worry, we have a built-in stopping point."

"True enough. See you guys inside."

"Sounds good. Be careful driving back."

Jay waved to the group one more time and drove away into the night.

It was against policy for a person to be outside of the habitat on their own during darkness, and Jay's drive made James nervous. It was a short trek, however, and he knew Jay was eager to get back. No point in making him stay just to watch the three of them stargaze. Jay had been told to stay on comms until he got back to base. He would be fine.

Ira walked over to Nash. "Hi Neil."

Neil smiled behind his visor. "Hi Ira. Hey James."

James smiled and waved. "Neil. Thanks so much for meeting us out here."

Neil made a dismissive gesture. "Ah, no problem. Ira has been so enthusiastic in her support of our work the last few months...it's the least I could do. We're grateful that she'll be shining a spotlight on us...a whole chapter in her book is more than we could ask!"

James turned to Ira with a smirk. "A whole chapter, huh?"

Ira shrugged.

Neil interjected. "And you, too, Mr. Wilmot, of course. We're happy to show you what we're up to. We couldn't do any of this without you behind us."

It was James' turn to make a dismissive gesture. "Sure, sure. Always happy to back you guys up. And you're right about Ira...she's something else."

Neil paused a moment and smiled. "Yes, she is."

Neil turned and made his way over to the telescope, indicating that they should follow. "Now, the first thing I'm going to ask you to do is to turn off your night filter. It'll be hard to see, at first, but we've gotta' give your eyes some time to adjust."

James did as instructed. The world was suddenly pitch black again. He struggled not to lose his balance without a visual reference, and he ended up leaning on the base of the telescope to stop from falling over. Ira must have been having the same struggle, as no sooner had James righted himself before she fell into his arms for support.

"Sorry," she said, struggling to stand up straight, "I got dizzy."

James made sure she was steady on her feet before laughing awkwardly and letting her go. "I know, me too," he said.

"Once you're both adjusted," said Neil, "we'll take a look at our first star."

...

Jay bounced in his seat as he pushed his buggy to the operating limit. It was foolhardy to drive this quickly over rough terrain in reduced gravity; the handling was shit. But he didn't care. He'd driven over worse land on his family's ranch back home, and he couldn't wait to get back to base and cut loose.

His tires chewed up the freshly laid snow – really more like a frost in most places – as he drove, forming a slight mist all around him. He drove without his vehicle lights on, since the low light filter on his HUD worked well enough using star light and the occasional glimmer from Phobos or Deimos as they made their erratic journey through the southern sky.

The figure took him by surprise when he saw it. It popped into his peripheral vision as an unmistakable human shape, and he swerved far more than he should have. When he hit his breaks a moment later, the buggy, predictably, tumbled over on its side, and Jay went ass over teakettle across the rocks and dunes.

When, at last, he had come to a stop, he laid motionless in a panic, listening for alarm bells. None came. The relief that his suit was unharmed was short lived, as the terror of finding the unknown and unexpected while alone in the wild soon replaced it.

He jumped to his feet and ran back toward the buggy. Thankfully, it had come to a stop right side up. Aside from a few scratches, it seemed undamaged. Jay re-boarded, started the machine and drove cautiously back toward the anomaly.

His HUD showed no other personnel active in the area, save for his three colleagues at the telescope. He was tempted to turn on his vehicle lights, but he didn't want to draw any attention to himself. Not only would doing so alert any would be intruders, but James, Ira and Neil would know that something was wrong. He'd be happy to take the news of his reckless driving and subsequent accident with him to the grave.

He found the spot where he had swerved in short order. There was no sign of anything alive, let alone anything human. Then, he spotted something on the ground: a shape of some kind. He dismounted the buggy and approached the shape slowly, senses alert to anything else out of the ordinary. He kneeled in the dirt and snow and grasped the black, snake like object in his hands.

It was a cable. A piece of tubing and a few scattered nuts and bolts. Innocuous enough, but what was it doing here? He looked around again but saw nothing resembling a human figure. His eyes must have been playing tricks on him. Perhaps the cabling and bolts were from his buggy, and the damage was more extensive than he had realized.

He stood up to return to his vehicle when he saw the unmistakable print of a boot on the ground. He froze and felt ice water flow through his veins. Was there someone else out here with him? He spun again, starting to panic. An alarm in his suit indicated that his heart rate and blood pressure were spiking. He took deep breaths and did his best to remain calm, to think through the problem. There was no one else out here. They were as alone as they could possibly be. James and Ira must have hit a bump or something on their way out to the telescope, and this cabling and these footprints were left by them after they got out to investigate.

He laughed to himself and felt his body relax. He was glad to know that he wasn't the only person to run into trouble at this particular spot, or to have his eyes play tricks on him. He knelt down again to retrieve the debris and walked back toward his buggy. He would have to make fun of James and Ira later, then tell them the story of how they had scared him half to death.

He started the buggy and began driving back toward the base, slower this time. A few feet into his drive he thought better of telling James and Ira. After all, why would he have seen the debris in the dark if he hadn't been dismounted from his vehicle and inspecting the dirt? And why would he be dismounted unless something had gone wrong on his drive back to base? No, better to let sleeping dogs lie. He laughed to himself again and pressed the buggy's accelerator to the floor, eager to close the last few meters of distance between him and the party that was about to begin.

...

The three of them stood quietly together in the darkness, occasionally cracking a joke and giggling to break the tension. The setting was surprisingly intimate, and James was reminded of slumber parties he had attended during his teenage years, when the conversation turned private, intense, and sometimes silly as soon as the lights were dimmed.

Once their eyes had completed their adjustments, all conversation stopped. The night sky above them was the most expansive and breathtaking thing that James had ever seen. The light pollution on earth was more or less constant, so the view of the stars he had now was completely unprecedented. The other two, who had made many trips outside at night since arriving, seemed to sense his awe, and they respected it by standing silently with him under the starlit canopy, allowing him to take it all in.

His mind returned to the faraway religious studies class, and a line he had learned there from the Abrahamic Bible. Something about children being as numerous as the stars in the sky. The significance of that line had never really hit James until now. The number of stars overhead was truly countless – a million points of light set against the backdrop of a million more.

Ira nudged him gently with her elbow and spoke softly on a comms line just to him. "Told ya'."

When James took his turn to look through the telescope, maneuvering his head into position over the helmet sized view piece, he was no less impressed. The relative lack of atmospheric diffraction yielded images so crisp and clear, it was a marvel to him that they were seeing them with almost nothing but their eyes. Such clarity would normally require enhancement by a computer, but here it had been achieved with only the barest of magnifications.

"Bear in mind," said Neil, "that the weather is favorable right now. If we get more clouds later on, or if some dust kicks up, image quality really goes down. But you two picked a good night to go stargazing."

James said nothing, but smiled and looked through the telescope once more.

Hours passed, then the time caught up to them. An alarm chimed gently in each of their suits, letting them know it was time to head back. Tempted as he was to ignore it, James knew the sound would only get louder and louder as their air ran thinner and thinner. Like it or not, the greatest show on Mars was over.

The two of them thanked Neil for the guided tour of the heavens, then waited as he shut down the telescope for the evening. The three explorers drove back to base in shared silence, having just experienced something they knew they would never be able to fully express in words.

As the hangar door drew near, Ira got his attention once again, and put her palm out flat in front of him. "Look," she said, "snow."

Sure enough, a single white flake fell on her palm, followed by another, then another. James looked up to see that the sky was full of snowflakes, a slow-motion shower of white specks falling down all around them. "Wow," said James, "just...wow."

...

Neil dropped them off and headed right for the party, which was now in full swing. James, however, was tired, and he never knew how to act at parties with colleagues – especially colleagues he had some nominal authority over. Too stiff, and he was seen as a buzzkill. Too loose, and he lost respect. For that reason, he decided to head back to his room and get some rest.

Ira offered to accompany him to his door.

When they arrived there, James did not immediately enter. Instead, he paused at his doorway and turned around to wish Ira a good night. "Thank you for setting that up. That was much more fun than I expected."

Ira walked toward him, stopping about an arms-length away. "Thank you for joining us. I'm glad you got to see it."

The warmth in her voice caught James off guard. He became aware of a tension between them that he hadn't noticed before. Standing in the hallway before his bedroom door, everyone else at the party, he felt very alone. Alone with Ira.

She stepped closer. "I'm glad I got to see it with you."

James smiled and nodded in agreement, unsure of what to do next. Ira stared at him in silent anticipation, and James stared back. She was beautiful. He had always noticed but had never stopped to appreciate it until now. She was close enough that James could smell her scent, a mix of perfume and the natural smell of her skin. She took one more, small step forward, and now their foreheads were touching.

James felt his heart pounding in his chest. His thoughts were frozen, and the moment expanded until it was almost all he knew. Almost. As her hot breath grazed his lips, James paused one last time, taking a moment to consider what might have been, then turned his head, placed a gentle kiss on Ira's cheek, and embraced her in a hug.

When, at last, they separated, Ira's face was flushed red.

James placed a hand on her shoulder and gave what he hoped was a comforting pat. His own expression was crestfallen, and he hated to see Ira in discomfort. "Listen," he said, "I'm going to send my wife a message and then hit the hay. I'm beat."

Looking at the floor, Ira nodded. "Of course. Thanks again for a great night." With that, she looked up, forced a smile, and walked away.

James sighed deeply before unlocking his door and plopping down on the bed. He took his AR specs off the nightstand and called up an image of his wife, which hung, suspended and invisible to everyone but him, over his prone figure.

"I miss you so much," he said, before turning off his lights and laying silently in the dark.

13

THIRTEEN

Freddie sipped his drink, tipped his head back and sighed. The sun was warm on his face. The ocean crashed in the background and seagulls passed overhead. The sand beneath him felt gritty but reassuring. He curled his feet and felt particulates build up between the webbing of his toes. He sighed again. He was home.

He turned to his left and saw a family in the distance. Two children were playing in the waves, while their parents looked on with sublime expressions. A woman jogged in front of him, barefoot in the sand. She was pretty, and Freddie felt the urge to call out, to connect, to say hello. Suddenly a wave of sadness washed over him. The illusion was broken. There was no point in calling out. She couldn't hear.

He removed his headphones and goggles and looked around with a mix of resignation and bemusement. The winter party was in full swing. A movie was playing on the central screen – one of hundreds running back-to-back, all with a space theme. The first dozen were, of course, set on Mars. Music played over the speakers, while his crewmates lounged and talked and laughed. The dance floor had been cleared of tables and chairs. Snacks were available in the kitchen, and the bar was open, providing a full selection of subtly watered-down alcoholic beverages.

Freddie stood up in the box he was in and brushed the sand off his butt and legs. He stowed his VR goggles and headphones, turned off the heat lamp above him, and killed power to the oscillating fan before him. He picked up his cocktail and headed toward the bar for a refill.

...

Katie laughed and took a sip of her second drink. The only alcohol she had been near in months was for lab use only, and her head swam. She had to slow down. She placed her cocktail back on the soggy napkin she had lifted it from and got Ryan's attention. "Hey barkeep!"

Ryan smiled and sidled over. "Madame?"

"A glass of your finest water please."

Ryan nodded. "Coming right up. Sparkling or still for the lady?"

"Sparkling...with a cucumber on the side."

"I don't have cucumbers here, although there might be some in the freezer. Can I interest the lady in a slice of orange or lemon?"

"Lemon should do nicely."

Ryan placed the glass of soda water on the bar in front of Katie and made a show of gently placing the slice of lemon on the rim.

Katie laughed. "Thanks Ryan."

"My pleasure. Holler if you need anything else."

Katie turned her head back toward the conversation on her right, where several of her colleagues were arguing about nonsense.

Colin pounded the bar, took another shot, then gestured at Ryan for a refill while continuing the argument. Between his slurred speech and his thick Irish brogue, he was barely understandable. "All I'm sayin'," he said "is that pineapple has no biznes' bein' on pizza. It's a fuckin' tropical fruit for chrissake.'"

Steve, Colin's primary adversary in this debate, happily egged him on. "And why is that, exactly?"

"Why? You have to fuckin' ask why a tropical fruit don't belong on an Italian dish? It's a goddamn abomination, that's why!"

Steve and the other men gathered at the bar roared with laughter. Katie joined in. She was about to suggest a debate topic of her own when she felt a gentle tap on her left shoulder.

"Hi," said Freddie, gesturing at Ryan for a refill, "been' a while since I've seen you around."

"Hello," said Katie, taking a sip from her water. "It's Frankie, right?"

"Freddie."

"Sure, Freddie. Sorry."

"No worries."

They lapsed into awkward silence.

Katie decided to throw the guy a bone. "So, what have you been up to, Freddie?"

He smiled. "Not a whole lot, Katie, let me tell ya'. Not a whole lot. Visited the beach today."

Katie glanced past him at the VR stations in the background. "Oh yeah? How was that?"

Freddie shrugged. "You know how it is. Fun for a while, but then sand...gets everywhere!"

Katie laughed. "I'll have to take your word for it. I've never been to the beach."

"Never? Not even once?"

"Nope. I'm a Midwestern girl. Nothing but corn as far as the eye can see. We've got a few lakes, but they aren't safe to swim in."

Freddie nodded, understanding. "You've never even tried out the VR booth?"

Katie scrunched her nose and shook her head, no. "I don't want my first time to be fake, you know?"

Freddie nodded again, then sipped his drink and laughed.

"What?" asked Katie.

"I was just thinking," said Freddie, "how funny it is that you will have gone to space, then to another planet, before visiting the beach."

Katie shrugged her shoulders and laughed. "Maybe I'll visit when I get home. To celebrate." She thought a moment, then added a small concession. "I guess it is a little strange..."

"A little," said Freddie.

"Well, maybe I'm a little strange."

"That's ok. I like strange."

THIRTEEN — | 193 |

The two of them stared at each other in silence. The moment seemed to stretch on forever. Then Katie burst out laughing.

"What?"

"Katie spoke between tears. "You like strange?"

Freddie blushed bright red. "I was hoping you were gonna' let that slide."

"Nope! No mercy here, buddy!" She dabbed her eyes with the napkin under her drink. "Oh, shit that's funny."

Freddie said nothing and looked crestfallen.

"Hey," said Katie, nudging him and winking. "Don't feel bad. I mean...who doesn't like a little strange once in a while?"

Freddie perked up and lifted his glass. "I'll drink to that."

Katie moved to lift her own glass, but her motion was interrupted by the sudden appearance of a blurry figure. The phantasm placed its hands aggressively on Freddie and Katie's shoulders.

Freddie leaned back to get a better view of the interloper. Once his eyes focused, Lewis came into view, smiling his charming, bullshit smile.

"What are we toasting party people?"

Katie was already blushing. "Freddie and I were just...talking about strange."

Freddie sat, hunched over at the bar as Lewis spoke.

"Strange, huh?" said Lewis.

"Yeah, you know," said Katie, "strange people. Strange...places. Strange...hobbies"

Lewis eyed her with over-exaggerated skepticism. "Right. Strange people. And...hobbies. What counts as a strange hobby?"

Katie broke eye contact and took a big swig of her mocktail. "I dunno'. Collecting things or something."

Lewis leaned in close and spoke directly into Katie's ear.

Katie laughed.

Lewis slipped into the open spot next to her and added another softly spoken comment, which was followed by another laugh.

Freddie sighed and finished his own drink, slamming his now empty glass on the table. He looked around at the room of self-interested, indifferent partiers, then stepped away from the bar and back toward the VR stations.

Gratefully, he noted that the continuous-current pool was open. He made a beeline for it, stripping off most of his clothes as he did so. He suddenly felt like going swimming.

...

Cecilia lay in bed with Andre, their bodies nestled closely together. Tonight, she was the little spoon, and she rested comfortably while Andre played with her curls, slowly straightening one out, letting it go, then repeating the process, until her whole head had been examined, stretched out, and allowed to spring back into place.

Cecilia was happy to do nothing during this examination. She stared dreamily at the ceiling and listened to her own breathing. When, at last, she spoke, there was a feeling of brashness, like she had broken something sacred.

"I was married once."

Andre didn't break his rhythm. "Yeah?"

"Yeah. He passed away a few years ago."

"I'm sorry," said Andre. After a pause, he added, "I had no idea you were married."

"I was," said Cecilia. "Twenty-five years. He was the love of my life."

"Is that why you're here?"

"I suppose. Partly. I go where the work goes...but, yeah. I guess I could have let someone else run the experiments, read about them later."

"I guess so," said Andre. "People usually have their reasons. For coming here."

"What's yours?"

Andre smiled. "Money."

Cecilia chuckled. "That's a reason."

The two lapsed into silence again.

This time, Andre broke the sacred veil. "You miss him?"

"Terribly. Every time I close my eyes. And every time I try to close them. I always think of him. And other things. It's worse at night, don't you think?"

"What is?"

"Everything. Loneliness. Fears. Worries. Regrets. All the things a busy day helps keep at bay. At night, they're all I'm left with."

Andre stopped his playing and gave her a gentle kiss on the head. "Not all."

Cecilia turned to look in Andre's eyes. She placed her free hand on his cheek, pressed her lips against his, then smiled. "No, not all."

...

Lynette entered the central module and her spirits immediately lifted. The booming music and swirling, synchronized light display made the ordinarily drab meeting hall feel like a trendy nightclub. This celebration was long overdue.

She moved slowly toward the center of the room, past a few brave souls who were already venturing out on the dance floor. As she walked, she picked up a hint of her own scent, and was glad to find it clean and refreshing. She had taken her first shower in days for this moment, and, if her reflection in the window was to be believed, her close-cropped hair looked glossier than she remembered it could. She felt like a new woman, and she hoped it showed.

As she weaved her way between the partiers, her gaze drifted toward the bar. The jocular talk and backslapping there looked pleasant enough, but not what she was in the mood for. The lounge area, where groups were leaning forward to whisper-yell conspiratorially in each other's ears, was easily the busiest area of the party, and she headed in that direction. A terrible, B-rated space movie played silently on the central screen, and Lynette chuckled to herself as she noticed people elbowing each other and laughing at the most egregious moments.

Lynette found a seat. A woman she didn't recognize approached her.

"Mind if I sit down?"

Lynette looked up at the woman in confusion. "What?"

The woman repeated herself, half yelling. "Do you mind if I sit here?"

Lynette understood this time. "Not at all," she said, smiling and patting the seat next to her. "Be my guest!"

"It's Lynette, right?"

"Yeah! And you're..."

"Isabella."

Lynette took her outstretched hand. "Isabella. Nice to meet you. You're one of the science people, right?"

Isabella smiled. "Guilty as charged. How long have you been working crew?"

"This is my second tour. At this station. Did one before it up north."

"North Polar?"

Lynette shook her head. "Not that far. Hephaestus Fossae. You know a lot about Mars."

Isabella shrugged. "I do my homework before taking a new job."

Lynette smiled and winked. "Smart." She turned her head and surveyed the room while sipping from her drink.

Isabella pressed on. "So, what exactly do you do?"

"Heavy Equipment Mechanic. All that stuff outside that lifts or rolls or what have you. I fix it."

"Wow," said Isabella, flipping her hair back and crossing her legs.

THIRTEEN

Lynette shot Isabella a funny look, unsure what to make of her body language. "What do you do?"

"Astrophysics. I'm an Astrophysicist."

Lynette nodded. "Cool."

"Do you work a lot on earth?"

"Some," said Lynette, "most of the work is out here, these days. Less competition."

Isabella nodded. "I understand. It can be like that in science sometimes. Saturated. Like all the best ideas have been taken, or there are just too many voices. Hard to get a word in edgewise. To get noticed."

Lynette's brow wrinkled slightly. "Yeah. Kind of like that."

"So, tell me, what do you do to blow off steam around here?"

Lynette laughed. "You're pretty much looking at it. When I'm not working, I'm probably here."

"Sounds boring," said Isabella. "Don't you wish you could spice it up?"

Lynette shrugged. "I guess. Not much else to do, though!"

Isabella smiled coyly. "I can think of some things."

Lynette stared at her, uncomprehending.

Isabella laid it all on the table. "Look, I'm just gonna' be straight up with you. I think you're hot. Like, really hot. I'm bored as hell here, and lonely. If you're into it, I'd love to take you back to my room."

Lynette took a deep breath. She looked around awkwardly, then leaned in to give her response. "Look, I'm really flattered. Really. But I'm...already with someone."

Isabella's eyebrows raised in surprise. "Oh...I had no idea. There's so few of us I just thought...what's her name?"

"His name is Alvin. He works in IT."

Isabella was taken aback. Her cheeks flushed red. "I'm so sorry. I just assumed..."

Lynette put her hand up. "Don't sweat it, really. It happens all the time. I get it."

"Shit," said Isabella, "I'm embarrassed."

"Don't be, please," said Lynette, "It's no big deal. If I liked chicks, I totally would."

Isabella looked down at her hands, unsure what to say. "Thanks."

"For real, you're a beautiful girl."

At that moment Jay, Brad, Alvin and Owen arrived, a bundle of excited energy. Lynette rose to greet them. "Where have you fuckers been?"

Alvin reached Lynette first, embracing her and laying a kiss on her cheek. "Sorry we're late, babe." He nodded subtly toward the others. "Had to get everyone rounded up."

Brad found an open space on the couch and flopped down. "Oh, please Alvin. We were ready ten minutes ago. You were the one busy fuckin' around with that stupid game."

Alvin turned to Brad, aghast. "I was not playing; I was getting Owen."

Owen also sat, then turned to Brad. "He showed up at my room like, a minute before you guys."

"See!" exclaimed Brad. "Gamer boy here is the reason we're late."

Jay joined the pile on. "I told you, Armstrong. We're all over you and that game. You've got a girlfriend now – which I still can't believe – and she should be taking up all of your time."

Lynette slapped Jay's leg. "Alright, alright, lay off. We all have our ways of blowing off steam. If my boyfriend would rather hunt for imaginary animals than pleasure me, that's neither here nor there..."

Brad, Owen and Jay erupted into peals of laughter.

Lynette continued. "Besides, don't tell me Brad and his hair weren't part of the problem. Is that three different colognes I smell on you? Or just two?"

Brad chuckled. "It's one, one very good one, thank you very much. Brought it up special, just for tonight."

Lynette raised her eyebrows. "Feeling confident, are we."

Brad nodded. "We are indeed." He turned to Isabella, who hadn't moved from her place on the couch. "Speaking of which, hello, I'm Brad and it is a pleasure to make your acquaintance."

Jay, Owen and Alvin laughed.

Isabella said nothing.

Lynette spoke up. "Brad, this is Isabella. Isabella, ignore him. He's..."

"Incorrigible," interrupted Brad. "I'm incorrigible. But seriously, it's nice to meet you, Isabella. I've seen you around. Bio team, right?"

Isabella finally spoke. "No... Astro." She turned to Lynette. "I think I'm going to go. You guys have a fun evening."

THIRTEEN

"Nah, don't," said Lynette, "we're just hanging out, shooting the shit. We'd love to have you join us, get to know you more."

Isabella stood. "That's a very kind offer, but I think I'm going to get a nightcap and call it early. It was nice to meet you guys."

"But..." Lynette trailed off as Isabella walked away.

"What's her deal?" asked Brad. "Jay? What'd I do?"

Jay shrugged. "She's always been kind of quiet."

Lynette shook her head. "I dunno' man. Best just to leave her be." With that, she sat at the edge of the couch and patted her lap, gesturing for Alvin to come and sit with her.

Alvin rolled his eyes. "Seriously, dude?"

Brad laughed. "Whatever, man. You're still getting laid tonight."

Lynette gave Brad the finger. Alvin shrugged and sat on her lap.

Jay found a spot next to Owen.

Now that they were all seated, Lynette noticed that someone was missing. "Hey, where's Jim?"

"Beats me," said Brad. "We knocked on his door on the way over here. No answer."

Owen stood up. "He was probably taking a shower or something. I'm getting a drink. You guys want anything?"

They all did, of course.

Once the group had finished giving Owen their drink orders, Brad spoke. "Jay was the real reason we were late."

"That true, Jay?" asked Lynette.

Jay shrugged. "Yeah. I ran into a little trouble on the way back from the telescope. Rolled the buggy."

"Jesus! What happened?"

"It was just rough terrain and me not paying attention, that's all. Nothing big. Buggy wasn't even banged up."

"That's what we get for letting you science boys out after dark unsupervised," said Brad, "you're a hazard to yourselves and everyone around you."

Jay made a show of rolling his eyes. "Says the 'roughneck' with the advanced degree. What was it again? Poetry?"

"Philosophy," Brad corrected him, "and that is neither here nor there." I had some free time between deployments."

"And during," said Lynette, "and before. On account of your lack of friends."

"What does that make all of you?"

"Hostages."

The group laughed as Owen returned with their drinks. "What's so funny?" he asked.

"Nothing much," said Jay. "Brad just thinks we're his friends."

"Well shit, that is funny," said Owen, taking a swig of his beer. "Next he'll be expecting civil treatment."

"I know better," said Brad, smiling wryly. "And thanks for the drink."

Owen nodded and sat. "You got it, boss. Hey, who was that girl earlier?"

Lynette let out an exasperated sigh. "Don't you pay attention to anything?"

"Not really. Who was she?"

"Her name was Isabella. She's an Astrophysicist."

"No shit?" Owen gestured to get Jay's attention. "You know her?"

Jay shook his head. "Not really. She's quiet. I might like to though..."

Brad spoke up. "Hey, I saw her first."

Jay looked at him, confused. "You already got shot down. Of the remaining contenders, I saw her first."

Brad puffed up. "Oh, well it's on big man. May the best man win!"

As the two men stood up, still joking and egging each other on, Lynette interrupted. "Guys, I wouldn't."

"Why not?" asked Jay.

Lynette hesitated. "I just don't think she's in the mood."

"Well, shiiiit," said Jay, "she better get in the mood. It's par-tay time!"

Brad regarded his small statured friend. "You are such a dork. You have no chance."

"We'll see mothafucka!" said Jay. "We'll see."

Lynette interrupted again. "Seriously, boys, she's not interested."

The two men looked at each other, shrugged, then sat back down. They knew Lynette wouldn't steer them wrong.

Alvin, now sitting in his own chair, donned his specs and started staring absentmindedly into space.

Lynette rolled her eyes and looked to the others for support. "There he goes again."

"You know what, why fight it?" asked Brad.

"Elaborate," said Owen.

THIRTEEN

"Why fight it? The man wants to game." Brad snapped his fingers to get Alvin's attention. "Hey, brother, do you still have that sport sim on your server?"

Alvin cracked a faint smile and nodded. "Yeah..."

"Are you able to project it on the main screen?"

Alvin's grin widened as he understood what Brad was suggesting. "Absolutely." He began wildly gesticulating in the air as he used his specs to interface with the Base computer.

"Brad, what are we doing here?" asked Owen.

"What kind of odds will you give me," asked Brad, "that the Cowboys will cream Washington this year?"

"Even. Both teams have been doing pretty well. You want to watch an old football game?"

"Heck no," said Brad. "I want to find out who's going to win. And I want to bet on it."

With a final flick of the wrist, Alvin took over the main screen. The movie montage that had been playing silently suddenly stopped, and a handful of groans filled the hall.

Brad dismissed them all with a wave. "Get over it! Those flicks all suck anyway. And you've seen em' before!"

Jay got Brad's attention. "What are you doing, man?"

"You'll see," said Brad. "Alvin, how are we looking?"

"Almost up...," said Alvin.

The screen flickered to life again, this time with a split view. One half showed a realistically rendered football field, with two football teams on the turf, prepping to begin play. The other half displayed a grid with Jay, Brad, Lynette, Alvin and Owen's names on it. Next to each name was a blank space. At the top, above all of the names, a ticker displayed the betting lines and point spreads for each virtual team.

"Why don't you go ahead and explain what we're looking at," said Brad.

"Sure," said Alvin, "on one of our previous tours I got bored, so I put together an algorithm that predicts future football wins based on past performance statistics. Nothing fancy, but it has an impressive prediction record. Brad and I used it to create realistic simulations of football games here on the base, so we didn't have to worry about delays or spoilers or seasons or whatever. We also bet on the outcomes."

"So," asked Brad, "what do you say gents?"

Jay already had his specs on. He made a gesture in the air and a figure populated next to his name on the board. "I'll take the over on Washington."

Brad smiled. "Very nice!"

Owen leaned forward, his own specs now on his face. "What folder do you make the deposits into?"

"I'll send it to you," said Alvin.

Owen turned to Brad. "Is the management aware you're co-opting processing space on the base computer to run a video game?"

"A simulation," corrected Brad, "and a sportsbook. But no, they aren't aware."

Owen shook his head.

"It'll be fine!" said Brad. "The mainframe has plenty of space. Alvin should know, he maintains it."

Owen shook his head again, then sighed. "Alvin, can you make a deposit for me? I can't open the folder."

"Absolutely," said Alvin, "you and anyone else that needs it."

Lynette spoke up. "I'm gonna' want some of that action."

Alvin nodded. "You got it babe."

Brad smiled. "Alvin, what is this, Martian super bowl number five?"

"Number six," replied Alvin. "We had number five last tour."

Brad tipped his glass in Alvin's direction. "Right you are, right you are. I'm going to go get a re-fill, then it's game on. Let's see if Jay can still get lucky tonight after all!"

...

Toby sat alone in the control room; the empty blackness of Mars stretched out before him. The stars were visible through the glass if he squinted, but the glare from the various screens and buttons on the control panel obscured most of them. Out of boredom, Toby flicked the night vision on and off, half expecting to see a monster lumbering towards the base from the inky void. The monster never came. He scrolled through the various camera feeds available to him, completing a thorough inspection of the base's perimeter. Most of the rest of the base was just as uninteresting as the rocky plane before his window. One of the cameras mounted on the east end of the living modules had some promise, though. It faced the open staging area that Alpha Base had been built around, which everyone called "the courtyard." From this vantage point in the courtyard, the windows of the recreation and chow module were visible. The resolution was poor, but Toby could tell they were having a hell of a time.

He sighed, spun his chair around, and opened a comm line to the powerplant and life support module. "Chris, you there?"

Chris responded promptly. "Where else would I be?"

Toby ignored Chris's sarcasm. "I got tired of listening to my own breathing. How are you?"

Chris sounded nonplussed. "Same as I was an hour ago. Listen, I'll be up there in two hours to switch with you. Calling me every few minutes isn't gonna' make it happen faster."

"Maybe I just want to talk to you. Dick."

Chris laughed. "Well, here I am. What do you want to talk about?"

"I'm looking at the party through the video feed up here. It looks fun."

"I'm sure it is."

"You mad you can't go?"

"Nope," said Chris, "I picked second shift so I don't have to go to things like that. I'll just stay down here in the boiler room and read my favorite book. Unless my shift-partner keeps calling to interrupt me every few minutes. Then I guess I'll just sit here and talk to him"

Toby shook his head. "You're just mad because I woke you up."

"Hey, I take this night shift thing seriously. I would never sleep on the job."

"Sure. I've never opened this comm line to hear you snoring before. Never."

"Hey, man," said Chris, "not all of us can be like you. Wide awake at all hours."

"Jesus," said Toby, "you say that like it's a good thing. I wish I could fall asleep. Like, at all. But I can't so...may as well put myself to use."

"That's really comforting, seeing as how you're at the controls to the whole base. Just try not to vent all the atmosphere when you start hallucinating, ok?"

Chris moved to close the line. Toby interrupted him.

"Hey, if you're so tired, why don't you take a break? Switch with someone else for a few nights."

Chris sighed loudly. "You say that like it's easy to do. Everyone has their own jobs around here during the day shift, you know?"

"Oh, come on. You could get one of the others to cover you for a couple of hours at least."

"Tried it. All of em' turned me down flat. After that I stopped asking."

Toby wasn't sure what to say. "Well, that sucks."

"Yup," said Chris, "such is life. You got anything else for me?"

"I guess not. See you in a couple hours."

"Enjoy the party."

Chris signed off, and Toby was alone again. He watched the silhouettes of the partygoers pass back and forth for another few minutes, then sighed and cut the feed.

...

THIRTEEN — | 209 |

Jeff stood frozen in the center of the dance floor. The room was bright and loud. His head hurt. He couldn't find James or anyone else he knew. His plan had been to walk into the party, find James, and follow his lead. But now...he couldn't find James.

Unsure of his next move, Jeff slowly backed away from the dance floor, drawing ire as he did so. Normally he would have realized how unusual it looked for a grown man to walk backwards through the middle of a crowded dance floor, but, at the moment, the ringing in his ears was too much for him to think through.

Safely on the shore of the dancefloor's edge, Jeff closed his eyes, shook his head, and tried to consider his options. He covered his ears to drown out the senseless, ceaseless thumping of the music.

He had just resolved to return to his room when he felt a light tap on his shoulder. Startled, he sprung upright and turned to face the tapper.

Melvin took a step back and lifted a hand up in surrender. His other hand held a drink. He leaned in and shouted. "Sorry to scare you! Was just wondering if you wanted to come join us in the lounge?"

Jeff saw Melvin's lips moving, and he heard noises coming from his mouth, but he had no idea what he was saying. "What? I'm sorry, I didn't catch that."

Melvin leaned in again and repeated his question.

When Jeff didn't respond, Melvin held up his hand again. "Hey, no pressure if you don't want to join us."

THIRTEEN

Jeff's suddenly realized what Melvin was asking. "No, I'd love to join you," he shouted, "thank you for the invitation!"

Melvin smiled, nodded his head, and gestured with his free hand for Jeff to follow him. Jeff did so, and the two men quickly found themselves in the far corner of the module, closest to the kitchen. The noise here was less overwhelming, and the lights were less dazzling. Jeff felt his head clear up some.

"Please, take a seat," said Melvin.

Jeff saw that a makeshift lounge had been made in this relatively quiet corner of the module, with chairs taken from the main lounge area. Two others were already sat, and they looked up in eager anticipation of a new arrival.

"I'm not sure if you've met," said Melvin, "this is Mark, my colleague, and Saul, a member of the life-sciences team."

Jeff shook each of their hands in turn. "I've seen each of you around."

Melvin sat down. "Saul was just elucidating his wedding plans. Did you say the date was set?"

Saul spoke enthusiastically. "Yes, it's scheduled for right after I get back. Hopefully she won't have changed her mind."

Jeff sat down. "And hopefully there won't be any delays getting you back home."

Concern flashed briefly over Saul's face. "Yes. Hopefully."

"I wouldn't worry," said Melvin, "this program has a very high reliability rate. All of them do, nowadays. No more surprise re-routes or tour extensions. It's all like clockwork."

Saul smiled in agreement and laughed politely; his enthusiasm gone.

Melvin quickly changed the subject. "So, Jeff, can we get you anything to drink? I see you've got two empty hands there."

"I'm fine," said Jeff, "I don't drink alcohol."

Melvin laughed. "Well neither do I...most of the time." He held up his cup. "This is pomegranate juice. They have a wide selection at the bar. They pulled out all the stops. I'm a little concerned they might have tapped a little too far into our juice reserves actually...I don't want to be stuck drinking nothing but lemonade and water for the next seventeen months...in any case, the bar is fully stocked with a variety of beverages. I suggest you go check it out."

Jeff nodded and stood. "Does anyone else want anything?"

Mark held up a bottle of water that had been on the floor next to his chair. "I'm fine."

Saul lifted his cup. "I do drink," he said, laughing, "So I'm fine."

The other men chuckled gently. Jeff smiled, nodded, and turned towards the bar.

...

Brad leaned forward as the simulated quarterback of his favored team threw the football downfield in a high and winding arc. When it was caught, he stood to his feet. The others all exploded in a cacophony of cheers and jeers that were indistinguishable from each other. As the runner got closer to the end zone, Brad raised his voice and joined them, in spite of the stares from the others at the party. The runner scored, the points went up, and just like that, Brad was guaranteed a payday. "I told you!" He screamed. "I told you they would beat ten in the first half! Suck it!"

Owen waved him away. "Sit your ass down. You got lucky."

"Luck, my ass! That's knowledge of the game right there, son!"

The others laughed while Owen folded his arms and shook his head. "Lotta' football ahead. We'll see how it ends."

Brad clapped him on the back. "That we will. I'm getting a refill. Anyone else?"

The group all gestured no, and Brad headed toward the bar.

He noticed Ira as soon as she entered the room. Her face was red, and her eyes were puffy, as if she had been crying. She walked directly to the bar, ordered a shot of something clear, downed it, then asked for another. She paused before downing the second shot, leaving it on the bar and staring intently at it, as if the answers to all of life's questions could be gleaned from its liquid sheen.

"Hey," he said, "Its Ira, right?"

She started, snapping quickly out of her reverie. "Yes. Yeah, that's me."

"You're a reporter?"

"Sociologist and author," she corrected him.

Brad nodded. "I see. So, one long article about us instead of a bunch of smaller ones?"

Ira smiled politely. "I guess that's one way of looking at it."

"So, what do you think of this place so far? Want to sign up and come back here every few years?"

Ira thought before she answered. Her face took on a shadow of pain. "This place is...complicated."

Brad wasn't sure how to respond. "Sure...sure. Lots of moving parts..."

Ira said nothing, tipping back her second shot and waving the bartender down for another.

Brad decided to be bold. "I hope you don't mind me saying so, but you seem like something has you down. Everything ok?"

Brad thought he saw tears well up in her eyes before Ira answered deliberately, her face smooth and controlled.

"Yes, I'm fine, thank you for asking. Tell me, what is your job, again?"

"I am an Aerospace Propulsion Specialist," Brad said, proudly. "It sounds complicated, but I'm basically a fancy gas attendant."

Ira laughed. "Gas attendant, got it."

"Well, I mean, that's a bit of an oversimplification...there's definitely more to it than just filling up tanks...we get lots of training in chemical composition, metallurgy...I mean some of these fuels are highly toxic and highly flammable..."

Ira interrupted. "I have no doubt. I'm sure it's a lot."

Brad nodded. "Yeah. Yeah, it sure can be."

After a beat of silence, Brad decided to be bold again. "Listen, I was wondering, would you like to dance at all? Or maybe I could buy you a drink?"

Ira smiled. "You seem nice. How about we head back to my room?"

Brad was speechless. "Well...ok, sure! I mean...listen, I would love to, don't get me wrong, but are you sure that's something you want to do?"

Ira fixed his eyes with a steely glare. "Absolutely."

...

Jeff returned with his drink - a cool seltzer water with lime.

"What do you think of winter initiation on mars?" asked Saul. "Is it everything you expected?"

"Well," said Jeff, "it's cold and dark outside. And snow is falling. That's about what I expected."

"Fair enough," said Saul, watching the party goers from afar. "Fair enough."

14

FOURTEEN

"Goddamnit! This is the second time this week!"

James stood quietly in the hanger as Dr. Jacobs unloaded his anger.

"How the fuck are we supposed to get any work done if this keeps happening?"

James held up his hands, appealing for peace. "Ok, Mark. Ok. I hear you. What exactly is missing?"

"Cabling. Meters and meters of cabling that we had laid out next to the unfinished accelerator sections, ready to go. Then, this morning, its gone. Just like the other spool someone 'misplaced' last week."

Mark stepped forward with a pointed finger, inches from James' face. "There is a thief in our midst, Wilmot, and it's your job to find them."

James took a step backward. "Please give me some space, Mark. I hear you. I will get to the bottom of this. I'm sure we're just dealing with a miscommunication of some kind. In the meantime, please help yourself to one of the reserve cable spools in the back."

FOURTEEN

"I thought those were reserved for station maintenance?"

"They are. That's why I'm going to ask you to only take one. And once we've recovered your missing spools, I expect that you'll donate one to the maintenance shed."

Mark nodded, still worked up but clearly happy with this turn of events. "How do I get it? They won't just let me back there..."

"I'll let Andre know you're coming."

"Fine. You'll do that right now?"

"Right after we're done talking."

"Ok. Ok, good."

Mark turned to go, then thought better of it. He turned around and spoke again, his tone markedly softer. "Thank you."

James nodded. "No problem. Let me know if you guys run into any more issues."

Mark hurried off.

James used his AR specs to inform Andre and the rest of the maintenance crew that Mark was authorized one spool of cable from the supply room. Green checkmarks appeared in his HUD as each recipient acknowledged the message.

James sighed and put his specs back in his pocket. No sooner had he done so than he heard a faint chime in his earpiece, indicating a new message. He put the specs back on and saw that Blaine was requesting his presence. He turned around and headed for the hangar stairs.

When he reached the control room, Blaine immediately started talking.

"So...I can't get ahold of command."

FOURTEEN

James made sure the door was shut behind him. "Say that again?"

"I can't get ahold of command. I've been trying all morning."

"Weather?"

"None. All clear down here and in space. Minimal dust. No solar flares. Nothing."

"Walk me through what happened."

Blaine cleared his throat. "So, the logs indicate we had a meteor strike last night. Nothing big - no seismic activity noted - it just showed up on the radar and blipped out of existence. Happens all the time, probably a pebble that burned up in the atmosphere. But it's the third one in our sector this month, and we had a couple close ones in the month before that, too. That's unusual and warrants a call back to home base - just to make sure we aren't passing through a shower we weren't expecting or something. I made the call, waited out the response delay, and got nothing. Tried again an hour later to see if the relay Sat. was in a better position. Still nothing. Then I called you."

James thought for a moment. "Is this the first time you've had any issues?"

"That I've noticed, yeah. I mean, we send out our regular reports, and the system always indicates they were transmitted ok. I honestly haven't tried to raise a real person in months. No reason to. Plus, it's against..."

James interrupted, muttering to himself. "Bandwidth and power policy. Yeah, I know..."

FOURTEEN

Silence filled the room as he mulled over the options. "When will the Sat. be in a good position to radio Ghez Station?"

Blaine checked the time. "I could probably raise them now, but the optimal window will be in a few hours."

"Ok...wait until then and give Ghez a call. See if they've been dealing with the same issues. If not, we can assume we're not important enough for a quick reply or there's a problem with our transmit equipment. If they have...I dunno'. Maybe there's bad weather back home or something. In any case, it will give us a better idea of what's going on."

"Are you sure you don't want me to try and raise them now?"

James shook his head. "No point in complicating things even more by trying to talk through static or getting cut off mid-sentence. See what they say in a couple of hours."

Blaine laughed nervously. "What if I can't raise them, either?"

"Then we make the SatCom techs earn their pay."

Blaine nodded. "Ok, will do."

James headed for the door, then turned. "Blaine...until we find out what's going on...let's keep this quiet, yeah?"

Blaine nodded again. "Yup. I got ya'."

James turned to leave again, then remembered. "Hey, by the way, do the logs indicate any unusual ground activity last night? Anything on the cameras or motion sensors?"

Blaine shook his head. "Not that I saw. Where area are we talkin'?"

"Out by the northeast accelerator sections."

"Oh, sorry boss. Sensors don't go out that far. Only meant for close in surveillance, so we can track single EVAs within the immediate perimeter of the base. Any further and you're supposed to have a buddy." Blaine laughed. "If you get lost alone while out that far...well, you better hope your suit's radio is working. Nobody is missing, right?"

James waived him off. "No, no. Nothing like that. We just misplaced some equipment and I thought...well I don't know what. Forget it."

"Right-o. I'll let you know what Ghez says."

"Good. Thanks."

James left the control room and headed back to his office. He sat down in his chair, sighed, and stared at the wall for a while.

"What kind of asshole," he thought to himself, "steals a cable?"

FIFTEEN

They hadn't heard from home in three weeks. Neither had Ghez Station, or six other facilities, scattered at various locations on the face of the planet. James wasn't sure what the comms issue was, but at least it wasn't on their end. He'd had the techs take a look at their equipment, just in case, and they couldn't find anything wrong.

The others weren't panicking - yet - but James could feel tension in the air.

The *Vectio's* automated systems were still pinging, so at least they had a ride coming. All they would have to do is survive for another month in complete isolation. Piece of cake.

The alarm took all of them by surprise. Unable to raise home, and out of new ideas for doing so, James had finally relented and returned to his room. Once there, he lay on his bed in silence, reading a pulpy science-fiction novel recovered from an antique bookstore - pure escapism, made all the more enjoyable by his current locale. It was exactly the kind of thing he needed to distract himself from the specter of imminent mutiny, death, or both. He read for hours, and when he next looked at the time, the hour had grown late. Most of his colleagues had gone to sleep. He resolved to do the same - in five more minutes.

The sudden claxon sound made his heart jump into his throat. Blue lights he hadn't even been aware of started blinking on and off in the corners of his room. He threw his vintage paperback down, jumped to his feet and rushed to the door. He was greeted by a half-dozen confused faces, blinking away sleep while standing still in their doorways.

"What the hell is going on?" someone shouted.

Others echoed the question.

"Stay calm, everyone," shouted James, "I'll go..."

James was interrupted by an automated voice over the Base PA system. *"Attention. Attention. The perimeter shield is down. Please take immediate protective action."* The voice continued speaking, repeating itself at three second intervals.

"Shit" said James, heading back into his room and throwing on his specs. He started to open a comm link to the control room when, thankfully, the automated message was replaced by Chris's voice.

"Everyone..." said Chris, "everyone head back to your rooms and shelter in place. Response team to airlock four. James, I need you up here!"

Chris's voice cut off and the automated message resumed.

James started running. As he did, he shouted behind him to the people gathered in the hall. "You heard him! If you aren't on the response team, head back to your room, grab your lead blanket and await further instructions!"

He didn't have time to gauge the group's response to the order, as he had already turned the nearest corner. He leaned into his sprint, making his way to the control room as quickly as he could.

Once there, he found Chris in a barely controlled panic.

"I followed the checklist! Response team is suiting up now!"

James knew he should try and reassure Chris, but his brain had switched to 'all business mode', as it often did in times of crisis. He brushed past the flustered man and began interacting with the control panel. "You were here when the alarm triggered?"

"Yes!" shouted Chris. "Yes! And I went right into the checklist."

James nodded to himself. "Ok. Ok, good."

Chris tapped James on the shoulder. "Can I take shelter? My girlfriend and I have talked about kids!"

James nodded wordlessly and Chris took off running for his room.

He couldn't blame the man for being scared. Whatever had caused the perimeter shield to fail, as long as it was down, they were all being exposed to hideous amounts of radiation. The shield, invisible and intangible, kept them all safe from the unfiltered onslaught of the cosmos under Mars' barely existent sky. With it down, their exposure had gone from standard background radiation levels to levels fifty times that.

He opened a comm line to Steve, head of the emergency response team. "You guys ready to go?"

Steve responded quickly. "Getting suited up. Two minutes."

"Copy. Let me know once you're outside." James brought up video feed from the perimeter cameras, trying to get a visual on the field nodes. There were eight nodes, each generating a portion of the overall field. All it took was one broken node and the whole field went down. He found the problem in short order - but it wasn't a broken node. He contacted Steve again.

Steve was clearly irritated. "Almost there. Need a few more seconds."

"It's not that. I wanted to let you know I think I've found the problem. Generator two in the northeast quadrant is missing."

"What do you mean, missing? Like it exploded?"

"No, I mean missing. Like it's not there."

There was silence on the line for a second. "We'll take a look when we get outside. Thirty seconds."

James could tell Steve didn't believe him. After all, where does a field node go all on its own? And yet, the proof was in the feed right in front of him. The generator node was gone.

"Ok," said Steve, "we're outside. Starting a perimeter sweep. Where did you say we needed to go?"

"Northeast quadrant."

"Copy. We'll head that way."

James switched the video feed to the cameras outside of airlock four. He could see the team: Alvin, Andre & Steven, ready to deal with any software, electrical or general engineering issues that arose, respectively. In their suits, outside, they were now more protected from radiation than he was, although all of them were getting far more exposure than they should be.

He watched as the men slowly made their way north-east, checking each generator node as they went.

James smiled ruefully. They didn't believe him at all. While it was probably advisable to check all of the nodes, each second spent unprotected from radiation was costing them moments of life. James considered heading back to his room and retrieving his lead blanket, but decided against it - he wasn't supposed to leave the control room unattended, and they would be at the missing generator soon enough.

Static came from the control room's speakers, then a voice. "Well, shit," said Steven, "you weren't kidding."

"You see the missing node?"

"Yeah. I mean, I see it. Having trouble believing it though."

Andre chimed in. "Who the hell would put us all at risk like this? They think it's a joke?"

"Let's not jump to conclusions just now," said James. "Focus on finding the unit."

"I don't think that approach is going to work, boss," said Alvin. "We can see for a ways in every direction. No rocks big enough to hide a node behind. That thing is gone."

Steve took a knee and assessed the empty lot where the generator node once stood. "The connectors are intact, at least. Whoever did this didn't rip anything loose." He stood up. "We can fish the spare out of storage. Swap it out and get the field back up."

"We only have one spare?" asked James, already thinking ahead.

"We didn't expect an entire unit to go missing. We have plenty of replacement parts, but only one assembled spare. Why, do you expect this to happen again?"

James shook his head. "Nevermind. Just get the replacement please."

"We need to find the missing node." said Andre. "We've got a serious fucking problem if someone is stealing critical components for a laugh..."

"I'll address that," said James. "You have my word. I'll call an all-hands to discuss. In the meantime, please just swap in the new unit."

"Already on it," said Steve. "Recommend you go and take shelter while we complete the install."

"But the procedures state..."

"I know what the procedures state. They were also written by someone who wasn't getting actively French-fried by radiation. Go back to your room and shelter. We'll call you when we're done."

James nodded to himself. "Ok. Ok, thanks Steve. Let me know if you need anything and its yours."

Steve grunted an affirmative response, already on his way to the hangar for a replacement. The other two men followed, all three engrossed in their new task.

James linked his specs to the console and quickly downloaded the last forty-eight hours of security footage from the perimeter cameras. He'd get to the bottom of this before he faced the crew. If it was what he thought, it was going to be a hard conversation.

...

Everyone was assembled. Even Dewey, who should have been tending the powerplant. If there was ever a time to set protocol aside for a short time, this was it.

The timing of the breach was fortuitous. Although it was hard to tell in the near-constant darkness of late winter, the alarm had rung close to the shift-change between "day" and "night" crews. That meant everyone was awake for the meeting, even if night shift was starting to look a little punchy. James would have to keep it short.

"Listen, everyone. I know you have questions about what happened today, and what has been happening over the past few weeks. Blaine and I are going to answer those questions. Blaine, can you please come up here?"

Blaine's eyes widened and he sat up straight. Reluctantly, he stood and took his place beside James.

"What has been going on," said James, "is this: we haven't had contact with earth in three weeks."

He paused while murmurs of surprise and indignation wove their way through the crowd. Many of them had been suspicious, and now their suspicions were confirmed.

"We've tried all avenues to regain contact that we can think of, including signal frequency changes, polarization changes, increasing the gain of the antenna, pointing in different directions, signaling on different times of day, and so on. Nothing has worked, for us or any of our sister facilities. The good news is that we do still have full communication with all of our sister facilities, as well as the orbital comm relays and other satellites overhead. So, the problem isn't with us or our equipment."

James paused again to let the group take in the news. Being that the room was full of scientists and technicians, James half-expected some questions, objections or suggestions of what they could be doing better. To his surprise, he heard none.

He continued. "The other problem we are facing - tangential, but related - is...a little harder to explain. I'll let Blaine tell you what he knows."

Blaine cleared his throat. "Around the time we started having issues with our comms, we started to get some odd readings on our radar."

"Like what?" said Alvin, the first among the group to speak.

"Meteor strikes, I thought. Only one close enough to pose a danger. But we never felt an impact, so I assumed it burned up in the atmosphere."

"Did you get a visual?" asked Lynette.

"No," said Blaine, "no visual. But the signature wasn't unusual, or large enough to warrant undue concern. When I passed on the news about comms to James, I also let him know about the detects. We both figured it was nothing. But then..."

James interrupted. "Things started going missing. You're all aware of that. I think all of us assumed items were simply being misplaced within the expanse of our facility, or possibly borrowed by other team members. After the events of last night and this morning, it became clear to me that things are escalating, and a more thorough investigation was warranted. I pulled the footage from the security cameras on the perimeter and...well, see for yourself."

James gestured to the large viewscreen behind him and stepped out of the way as it flickered to life. Blaine followed.

The entire room seemed to lean forward with anticipation. In grainy black and white - the company never sprung for high quality cameras - the group watched as a figure approached the now-missing generator. It seemed humanoid and average height, but its proportions were off - whatever it was wearing wasn't a standard issue exosuit. They watched in stunned silence as the figure was joined by four or five others, who helped it surround and remove the generator, dragging it off-screen.

The footage stopped and James resumed his place before the group. "The best explanation that I can think of for what you have just seen is that we are not alone in this area. The prolonged radio silence from home, combined with multiple unexplained radar detects, suggests to me that something on Earth has prompted an unannounced mission of some kind - unannounced to us at least. These newcomers, whoever they are, appear to be running short on supplies, and they've been surreptitiously borrowing ours."

The room was silent while the crew mulled over what they had just heard. Then, all at once, hands started popping up. James called on Alvin again.

"What sort of event causes a complete comms blackout, followed by unplanned arrivals? Arrivals who proceed to take our stuff? Are we under attack here?"

The room grew riotous as the group joined Alvin in his call for answers.

James raised his hands for quiet. "Please, everyone, one at a time or I can't make out what you're saying. Yes, Alvin, I won't lie to you - that is a possibility. I don't want to jump to that conclusion, but we can't rule anything out."

Alvin spoke again. "Well, what do you think the chances are?"

"I'd hate to speculate."

Alvin wasn't having his evasiveness. "Please, speculate."

James smiled ruefully. "Like you said, a complete comms blackout is cause for alarm. I lean toward war or a major disaster of some kind."

The room went quiet. Another hand went up.

"Yes, Jeff?"

"Have you tried raising the Europeans?"

"I'm glad you asked. We have successfully raised the Europeans, as well as the Chinese and the Russians. They're having all of the same problems we are, and they claim not to know anything more than we do. I have no reason not to believe them."

"Doesn't that rule out war?" asked Kate.

"I wish it did, but not necessarily. A conflict may have broken out that nobody had time to inform us of before communications were lost. And that may extend to all of the bases on this planet."

Isabella raised her hand. "How are we getting home?"

"The *Vectio* is still fully operational, responding to pings and on its way to us. In one month, it will be here. Getting home shouldn't be a problem."

A wave of relief rippled through the crowd.

Charlie raised his hand. "So, let me get this straight...there's a bunch of unidentified people running around outside, stealing our stuff? Including our life-support equipment? What exactly do you plan to do about this?"

The crowd rumbled in agreement.

"Well," said James, "that's part of what I wanted to discuss at this meeting. A response of some kind is obviously appropriate. The question is what..."

Charlie interrupted. "There's no question. We need to go get our equipment back. And make sure these people aren't a threat!"

Half the crowd agreed. The other half remained silent.

"What if," said Jeff, "there's some other explanation? What if they didn't know how important that piece of equipment was? On the other hand, what if they're armed and here to kill us? We might show up and knock on their door only to get shot!"

"Oh, please," said Miguel, "you don't accidentally steal a field generator node. They took it to put us at risk!"

"We can't jump to conclusions," counseled Cecilia.

Miguel rolled his eyes. "I know an attack when I see one."

There was general disagreement amongst the crowd.

Melvin spoke. "Do we even know where to find these people?"

"We think so," said Blaine. I've roughly projected the landing area of our last detect, based on its trajectory. Assuming that detect is one of our...visitors...we should be able to drive right up to their location."

"Well, what the hell are we waiting for?" asked Charlie. "Let's go!"

The crowd was silent, uncertain.

Charlie insisted. "We've got to take a look at what these fuckers are up to!"

"I agree," said Melvin. "We should at least take a look. What about sending a drone?"

James shook his head. "We thought of that. Our drones aren't built for long flights: their battery packs are too small. Adding packs adds too much weight."

"What about flying straight up for a distant view?" asked Isabella.

"Tried it," said Blaine. "It doesn't tell us much that we don't already know. We can see an object at the target location, but the resolution at that distance is poor. We're still in the transition from late winter to early spring, so the lighting is crap, which doesn't help. Plus, peeking over the horizon uses up a lot of battery; not much loiter time."

Melvin thought for a moment, then nodded. "So, we have to send someone. But the group that goes should be small, with the goal of making contact and determining intent. We can't make any useful decisions unless we have more information."

There was a general murmuring of agreement as the gathering considered the wisdom of Melvin's words. Then, an inevitable silence followed, as the assembled realized the next step required volunteers.

"I'll go," said James, "and I'll take one other person with me."

He scanned the room, then picked. "Charlie, you can come with. Everyone else, please keep your eyes peeled but otherwise go about your regular routines. We still have milestones to hit this week. Steven has site authority until I get back."

Charlie stood, already shaking with fear, suppressed aggression, or both. James briefly reconsidered his choice, then shook off his doubt. Leadership meant sticking to a decision, sometimes, even if you weren't sure it was the right one. The last thing anyone needed during a crisis was more uncertainty.

With thin lips and wide eyes, the group disassembled, everyone processing the news in their own way. The solace of routine would be welcome, and James hoped it would be enough to keep order until they had a better idea of what was going on. Taking a deep breath, he gestured for Charlie to follow him toward the hangar.

A few steps later, he was stopped by Dr. Boss and Connie.

He told Charlie to keep walking, that he would meet him there, then cleared his throat. "Carolyn. Connie. What can I help you with?"

Connie was practically shaking. "Dr. Boss has some information she thinks you should have."

Carolyn shot Connie a hard-to-read look. "It's not...its something I have been advised to share..."

Connie interrupted. "Charlie has a drug problem."

FIFTEEN

The doctor looked furious. "Connie, lower your voice! James – that is not something we have any evidence for."

Connie interjected again. "And he assaulted me."

"Connie! Enough!" Dr. Boss collected herself, then continued in a hushed tone. "I'm sorry. I don't know where any of this is coming from. I haven't seen any evidence of these allegations and this is the first I'm hearing of them...I apologize, James, for dropping this information at your feet...Connie, when did this happen? And why didn't you share it before now?"

Connie blushed. "I wasn't going to."

James ushered both women toward a quiet corner and waited for the crowd to thin. "Connie, I'm so sorry this happened to you. Tell us everything."

Connie quickly recapped the events in the med bay. "Andre can back all of this up. He was there."

James held up his hand. "That's not necessary. We believe you. But...Connie, why are you only sharing this now?"

She paused. "Do either of you know Charlie's last name?"

Dr. Boss frowned. "Gibson, right?"

Connie nodded. "That's right. Of the Gibson family."

The doctor's eyes widened. "THOSE Gibsons?"

Connie nodded again. "Those Gibsons. They're wealthy. Well connected. Not a group I want trouble with. Nothing really happened, thanks to Andre, and nothing else has happened since, so I let it go. I encourage you each to do the same. But...you're about to go out alone with him, James. Maybe take someone else is all I'm saying."

FIFTEEN

James nodded, thinking. After a time, he spoke. "I really appreciate you sharing this. But I've made a call and there are too many moving parts to change course now. But seriously, thank you."

Connie grabbed his sleeve. "Be careful. Watch your back."

SIXTEEN

The two men drove in silence, their seats rocking gently with the vagaries of the terrain. James had opted for an open topped buggy, in order to retain the lowest profile and travel the most quickly. The downside of that, of course, was that both men were confined to their exosuits for the entire journey, which was uncomfortable. Breathable air was also a slight concern, but he figured they would have enough to get to their destination and back, so long as no major obstacles presented themselves.

The real issue was that, due to their polar location, the relay satellites overhead weren't always within range, and the base's antenna mast only rose about one meter from the roof of the hangar. Factoring in terrain, they would have to make do with spotty comms and dead zones for the duration of the trip. That made James nervous.

He tried to strike up a conversation with Charlie to distract himself. "So, we haven't gotten much of a chance to get to know each other. What brought you out here to Mars?"

SIXTEEN

Charlie answered in a deadpan. "Trying to get away from people asking me questions."

James said nothing in reply. Clearly there was a reason they hadn't talked before. He remembered Connie's warning and fought a sense of dread.

They both saw the crash site from a long way off. Whatever vehicle it was that had brought the visitors to Mars, it had suffered an ignominious end. Its landing had been hard, and the small crater that marked the impact site now housed a bent heap of metal which vaguely resembled a craft. As they got closer, small pieces of debris blocked their path, and they had to swerve back and forth to avoid them.

"This looks bad," said James. "It's a wonder there are any survivors at all."

"Maybe our thieves came from somewhere else," said Charlie. "Didn't Blaine say he picked up multiple landings?"

"Yeah," said James, "maybe. Keep an eye out."

Seeing no signs of life, James brought the buggy in for a closer look. He tried raising Blaine on the radio, to let them know they had made contact, but heard nothing in reply except static.

As they came within a hundred yards of the crash site, James slowed the buggy to a crawl. The terrain in the immediate vicinity of the shallow crater was uneven, with a few rocky raises and a couple of ditches, and James didn't want to risk getting stuck.

With eighty yards to go, Charlie grabbed his shoulder. "There! There's someone there!"

James turned his head to look. A figure darted behind a rocky outcropping, moving too quickly for James to see more than a blur. Frightened, James involuntarily slammed the full weight of his foot on the accelerator pedal, and the buggy raced forward.

"Is it armed?"

"How should I know!" Charlie shouted. "Just get us out of here!"

James turned the wheel hard, trying to spin the buggy so they could get some distance between them and the unknown figure.

"Watch out!" Screamed Charlie.

It was too late. The buggy tipped over into a ditch, throwing both men into the sand.

Charlie spoke first. "God damn it! You fucking idiot!"

"Are you ok?"

"Yes, I'm fine! Help me flip this thing back over!"

The buggy was equipped with a light, hollow frame, and the reduced gravity made it easy to lift. The two men each stood on one side of the vehicle, reached up and grasped the wheels firmly, then pulled down. The buggy righted itself with a thud - more felt than heard.

Charlie re-boarded first, planting himself behind the wheel. "Get in!"

James made his way over to the passenger side, then froze. The figure was watching them. James could just make out what he assumed was the top of a helmet, peaking at him from behind a boulder. Another helmet appeared, behind a sand dune to their west. He realized they may already have been surrounded.

"Hang on, Charlie. They're already here. No point in running."

James scrambled up the side of the ditch they had fallen into, raising both hands to show that he meant no harm. The figure did not respond. He began walking forward, toward the closest one.

"God damn it," said Charlie over comms, "get in the buggy and let's get out of here!"

"We came to find out who they are and why they're here. They've seen us now. May as well ask."

"Fuck this," said Charlie, "I'm leaving. Get in the buggy now or I'm leaving you behind!"

James stopped walking. He stood frozen in indecision for a beat before turning around and walking back toward the buggy. "Fine, Charlie. Stay put. I'm on my way."

Charlie said nothing, but didn't leave.

James could see the vehicle, facing up and out of the ditch, ready to go. Charlie waved him on eagerly from the driver's seat. James walked toward the buggy at a steady pace.

Suddenly, Charlie's demeanor changed. His body stiffened, his shoulders reared back, and he pointed frantically over James's shoulder.

The design of the arrow — if you could call it that — was simple, really. Almost primal. A sharpened tip connected to a pressurized cylinder no thicker than a pencil. Filled with standard Earth-atmospheric mix and pressure, the projectile was fired on an improvised rail system. The assailant simply aimed, then pulled a plug on the end of the cylinder. The atmospheric pressure on Mars was so low - nearly a vacuum – that the Earth air rushed out of the cylinder, propelling the projectile an impressive distance.

The first shot missed James, but he heard a faint metallic ring as it struck a nearby rock. Given the poor sound conduction of the Martian atmosphere, that could only mean one thing: that the arrow had hit the rock very hard.

James spun around quickly to face his attacker.

He had just enough time to register a faint, silver-grey blur before the arrow pierced his thigh.

His suit's alarms began blaring immediately, drowning out his cry of surprise and pain. His ears popped as his air tanks began dumping atmosphere into the suit as quickly as possible, trying to avoid catastrophic depressurization by replacing atmosphere as rapidly as it was lost. The increase in internal pressure caused the suit to become dramatically overinflated. Suddenly barely able to move, James tried to turn around and run for the buggy, but found himself on the floor, arms and legs flailing.

Struggling against panic, James tried to prop himself up on his elbows to assess his assailant's position. This proved impossible. He watched, helplessly, as the atmosphere gauges on his HUD began plummeting to zero. Soon the air would be sucked from his lungs; assuming he hadn't already been shot in the head by then.

A moment passed. Then another. The alarms continued to blare. No more projectiles pierced the thin second skin of

SIXTEEN

his suit. Nothing else but the tortured whistle of venting air met his ears.

Disbelieving, James rolled his body to face the general direction of his attacker. From what he could see through his rapidly fogging faceplate, no one was there. He relaxed a little and rolled onto his back. He checked the HUD again. The suit was almost out of atmosphere. He noted grimly that the readouts indicated more oxygen left in the tanks than nitrogen. At least he would be conscious until there was no more air to breathe.

Things moved too fast and too slow all at once as James reached for the patch kit on his other leg. With an agonizing awareness of each passing second, he fumbled at the Velcro of his suit's cargo pocket with stubby, gloved fingers.

The voice alarm activated: *Twenty percent reserve atmosphere remaining.*

One attempt to open the kit-packet, brittle in the Martian cold. Failure.

A second attempt. Success.

Fifteen percent reserve atmosphere remaining.

James ripped the adhesive cover from the patch and felt for the hole. Shit – the projectile was still there, lodged firmly into his upper thigh.

Ten percent reserve atmosphere remaining.

With the patch in his left hand, James grasped the body of the tube sticking out from his suit and pulled firmly. Stars clouded his vision, and the pain came in waves.

Eight percent reserve atmosphere remaining.

Desperate, he pulled again, pushing himself to the edge of unconsciousness. Finally, a ripping sensation, as muscle and tissue separated from bone, and the projectile was free.

Atmosphere immediately began pouring out of the hole.

Six percent reserve atmosphere remaining. Five percent reserve atmosphere remaining. Four percent...

James slammed the patch on the hole and held it there as firmly as he could. Almost instantly, the whistling stopped, and he felt a pulsing in his inner ear as the pressure stabilized.

Suit breach sealed. Pressure stable and holding. Three percent reserve atmosphere remaining.

The suit slowly deflated to its normal size. James watched as the HUD indicator for reserve atmosphere went up to three and a half percent after the suit had finished sucking the extra air back into the tank. He was alive and would stay that way, at least for now.

After three breaths to collect himself, James was back on his feet, looking for Charlie - until he took a step and his right leg collapsed underneath him. Strange noises filled his suit as the outer material stretched and the patch seams strained against near-vacuum. His suit was leaking again, but slowly this time.

He carefully stood up, hobbling now instead of walking. He couldn't see his attacker anywhere, and soon he stopped looking. If his assailant wanted him dead at this point, there was little he could do to stop them.

James reached the crest of the small hill he had been shot from.

Two percent reserve atmosphere remaining.

SIXTEEN

Charlie was nowhere to be seen, presumably having made a run for it in the buggy. He wasn't responding to calls. There was nowhere left for James to go but the abandoned wreckage of the visitor's craft, not fifty yards away.

He started limping toward the craft, assessing his environment for threats all the while. The wreckage was a sight to behold. It had clearly been put together from scraps.

One percent reserve atmosphere remaining.

James stopped at what he assumed was an airlock, afraid to touch it. The entire cobbled together shelter looked as if it was one small disturbance away from collapse. He explored the surface of the door, looking for a handle of some kind. Eventually he found one and pulled.

No response.

He could feel the blood pouring from his leg, filling his boot. He was starting to feel lightheaded and just...bad. He recognized the feeling from his altitude chamber training – he was going into hypoxia. Or hypovolemic shock. Or both.

He placed his helmeted head on the hatch, trying to think of a way into the shelter that wouldn't cause a permanent breach. It was hard to think. He felt out of breath, even though there was plenty of oxygen in his...

Warning: atmospheric tanks depleted. Seek pressurized shelter immediately.

Shit.

His ears had already started to pop. Each particle of air that escaped his suit brought him closer to death. Think. He had to think. How would a person enter this damn thing?

SIXTEEN – | 243 |

His hands searched the surface of the door for a lock of some kind, to no avail. His eyes scanned about. Nothing.

He was more lightheaded now. So lightheaded. His thoughts were cloudy. He drew deep, desperate breaths. He couldn't fill his lungs.

The alarms of his suit were fading away to nothing. The only thing keeping him conscious was pain. His head hurt – badly. Internal gasses in his ear canal and sinuses pressed against his skull as the atmosphere leaked out of his suit.

Where was the way in?!

At last, his eyes settled on a latch, flush with the seal of the door. He pulled it, then the handle, and the door swung open.

Using what felt like the last of his strength, James stepped inside and closed the door behind him. Expecting an automatic pressurization sequence, he waited. And panted. And waited. What was going on? What? Wh...

James fell to his knees as his last exhalation was drawn involuntarily from his lips. His air was gone. Every blood vessel under his skin started to rupture. His eyes felt like they were on fire. The saliva on the end of his tongue began to boil, forming a thin foam.

Soon his nose would begin to bleed, and his body would swell. In a matter of seconds, the last bits of oxygen in his blood would be used up, and his brain would be unable to sustain metabolic activity. He would lose consciousness and die.

In a final surge of energy, he leaped forward and leaned against the interior airlock door, leading into the rest of the wrecked craft. He popped the seal on his helmet, lifted it off

| 244 | - SIXTEEN

his head and opened the interior airlock door anyway, pressure be damned.

After that the whole world was chaos, a swirling whirlwind. Then, only darkness.

17

SEVENTEEN

When he woke up, James found himself on the other side of the airlock, pushed against the habitat's closed outer door. His ears and sinuses hurt from the rapid pressure change. He couldn't see very well. His body was bruised from the concussive force of being thrown backward. The inner airlock door might have broken his nose when it swung open. But he was alive. His last-minute gambit had worked.

Rather than wait to equalize the pressure between the airlock and the habitat, he had opened the inner door and allowed it to equalize all at once. The airlock chamber had filled with atmosphere, giving his body the pressure and oxygen he needed to survive. The craft itself had stayed together as well, which was a wonderful bonus.

James wasn't sure how long he had been out, but it couldn't have been long, because he hadn't yet bled to death. He sat up and moved each limb, assessing himself. No other broken bones that he could see or feel.

He rolled over and stood to his feet. His wound was throbbing, and he still couldn't put his full weight on his right leg, but at least he could stand.

He hobbled toward the inner airlock door, stepped through it and closed it behind him. It wasn't much, but the extra few feet of protection against the near-vacuum outside made him feel more secure.

He looked around – the place was a mess. Objects had scattered all over the room when he opened the internal airlock hatch. He couldn't be sure, but it seemed like the place might have been a mess before he opened the door, as well. There were discarded wrappers and other pieces of debris that could only be described as trash strewn about. It appeared that the inhabitants of this craft had been living on top of each other for some time, with no place to put their waste.

James knew he couldn't spend any more time assessing his surroundings. He had to tend to his wound and stop the bleeding.

He quickly began the process of removing his suit, feeling himself die all the while. His body ached – a deep, painful, sickening ache. He was nauseous. His limbs felt as if they were slowly slipping into a bath of ice water. Every move cost him a fortune in energy.

As he undid the metal clasps and Velcro straps holding his suit together, he honestly started to wonder if he cared anymore. Maybe he should just die – whatever would make this feeling stop.

He couldn't, of course. He had children. He had a wife. His beautiful, beautiful wife. He had to remember how all of this would feel the next time he made love, or shared a laugh, or sat in a comfy chair, or ate a good meal, or picked up his children and spun them around. It would feel like a bad dream, then, and he would be infinitely aware of how worth it not giving up had been. But he'd have to take all of that on faith, because right now, dying seemed much easier.

At last, his suit was loose enough that he could step out of it. Doing so ripped open his half-clotted wound, which had started adhering to the lining of the suit. The blood poured out now, cascading down his leg. The arrow might have nicked an artery.

James quickly surveyed the mess around him for something he could use as a tourniquet. His eyes settled on a piece of cord that, he assumed, had previously been used to tie down some loose equipment. He positioned the cord a few inches above the wound and tightened it as hard as he could. The flow of blood slowed to a trickle.

He had bought himself some time. He knew he couldn't leave the makeshift tourniquet on forever – not only was he still bleeding slowly, but the lack of blood flow to his leg would result in gangrene if left long enough. He didn't want to lose his leg to amputation if he could help it.

James hobbled around the wreck, searching for something he could use to permanently close his wound. The area he was in constituted the bulk of the craft. A single door in the south-facing side of the structure led to a hallway which opened into two small rooms: one for sleeping, and the other for...he couldn't tell. It might have been the dining area once. Or an area for storage. Now it was a semicircular room with a depth of no more than ten feet. The reason for this was the floor-to-ceiling makeshift wall of empty cargo boxes and hardened, translucent sealant-foam which took up the rest of the space. On the other side of the wall was a gaping hole, invisible from the outside due to its angle relative to the rest of the structure.

Clearly, the room had breached at some point, and the wall was the crew's answer. He wondered how many lives had been taken when the breach occurred. How many had survived? Where were they now?

James watched his breath rise to the ceiling of the structure. It was cold in here. Much colder than the other rooms. He surveyed the boxes and the foam sprayed in-between them. He stopped at the left-hand corner of the wall and peered closely. He could see the vague outline of the Martian surface through the thin layer of foam. Red and light-yellow rocks appeared white through the thin gossamer of sealant separating James from the void.

"My God..." he said quietly to himself. It was a miracle the wall had held for more than a few moments, let alone the pressure changes he had just put it through. He very slowly backed out of the room and reached for the hatch, sealing it behind him. He wouldn't be going in there again.

James headed back down the corridor toward the main room. He became aware again of how lightheaded he was. He looked down at his leg. The tourniquet was soaked through with blood. All the movement must have loosened it.

He reached down to tighten it again, and the pain of the cord biting into the skin around the wound made his knees buckle. Evidently, the arrow had pierced an area that was also close to a major nerve.

James fell on his ass and tried to regain his composure. He placed his head between his knees and waited for the nausea and dizziness to pass. "Come on, man." He thought. "Dig deep. No way you got this far to bleed out."

He struggled to his feet again and resumed moving toward the main room. He didn't have much time left.

There didn't appear to be any medical supplies anywhere, so he'd have to improvise. He looked around the room for something he could use as a cauterizing agent – a chemical, perhaps. He didn't recognize anything useful.

Maybe he could use the cold of the Martian atmosphere to close the wound? Cut a hole in his suit exposing his leg, seal the rest off, and go back outside for a moment? No, no, it wouldn't be quite cold enough. The bleeding might slow as his capillaries constricted, but that's it. On second thought, the lack of pressure outside would make the bleeding worse. Much worse. That was out then.

Perhaps he could use the old-fashioned method, and burn the wound closed? He looked around for something that might be used to generate heat. His eyes settled on some exposed wiring on the north facing wall.

He moved haltingly toward the wall, stopping only to grab a pair of pliers resting on the floor near an overturned workbench. He carefully stripped the ends off of each wire, exposing the conductive material beneath the insulation. He held his breath, pushed the ends together, and prayed he wasn't about to blow any important circuits, or start a fire.

The lights flickered and a spark leapt from the area where the two wires met. Nothing else happened. Good. He had a charge, and it didn't seem to break anything.

James spied a metal pipe on the floor. It looked like it might have been intended for a piece of furniture, once. He retrieved the pipe and walked back to the wires. Being careful not to have the exposed ends touch, James placed the pipe on the ground and gently wrapped the wires around the end of the pipe several times. Using the pliers, he stripped a little more insulation from the end of each wire, then crossed the ends and pushed them onto the surface of the pipe.

There was a brief flash and the smell of ozone. The lights flickered again. Then, nothing. Had he tripped a breaker? How did he know if the pipe was receiving a charge? Without touching it, he couldn't be sure. At least not until it had gotten hot enough. Nothing to do but wait.

An eternity passed. James, tired from exertion, injury and blood loss, began to drift off. He was so cold. So exhausted. He would just close his eyes for a moment...let the pain fade away. He would just...float...

...

He woke with a start an indeterminate amount of time later, sucking in air madly. He must have stopped breathing in his sleep. Stupid. He had to move. Stillness was how bleeding men died.

As he stood up, he glanced at the pipe. The end attached to the wires was glowing red-hot. He glanced down at his leg. He couldn't have been out that long, as the tourniquet was only slightly more wet. Apparently, the pipe was receiving a charge, and lots of it. Time to bite the bullet.

James hobbled to his suit and picked up the left-hand glove. He figured its insulating properties should enable him to grab the pipe for at least a moment.

James donned the glove and used the pliers in his right hand to snip the wires in half, disconnecting the portions still on the pipe from the portions coming from the wall, stopping the current flowing between them. The parts of the wires still connected to the wall now hung limply, menacingly, like two cobras taking a nap. Forget they were there and they would remind you quickly, but they were harmless for now.

James had to be quick, before the pipe cooled. He picked it up, feeling the heat in the non-glowing end penetrating his glove. He loosened and removed the tourniquet. As soon as he did so, blood rushed out again, dark and sluggish at first, then a bright, vibrant red.

James swung the glowing end down at the wound and pressed it against his thigh as hard as he could. The pain was excruciating. He almost dropped the pipe, but to do so would be certain death. He had to push the pipe deeply into the wound – deep enough to sear it completely shut.

He kept pushing, deeper and deeper. He realized after a moment that he could no longer feel anything – not the heat, the wound, not even his hand holding the pipe. He was out of his body, watching himself scream with detached curiosity.

As his screaming grew softer, James watched through narrowing vision as his arm weakly threw the pipe to his left, where it rolled to a stop barely a foot away.

James thought of how much he had missed BBQ, and the smokey sweet smell of a fire on the beach in the summer. He thought of the breeze, and the sound of crickets at night. He thought of stars. But the darkness before his eyes now had no stars. It was black. Only black.

EIGHTEEN

James came to hours later. His leg felt equal parts sore and numb. He realized he might have nerve damage, but that was better than being dead.

He lay on the floor for a moment, head slumped against the wall, unsure of his next move. He quickly realized he had been in the same position for many hours. Something in his neck and upper spine felt pulled.

Using his good leg, he scooted down so that he was completely prone. Tilting his head to the side, he noticed a porthole that he hadn't seen before. It was small, barely big enough for a person to press their face to. He thought it strange that it should be located so low.

The light outside the porthole had gone from a pinkish red to a dull yellow. He could see hints of blue in the sky outside. Sunset.

James took in a deep breath and let it out slowly. It wasn't safe to travel alone at night. Too cold. Too many opportunities to lose his footing, or his way. The wrecked craft would have to be his accommodation for the evening.

EIGHTEEN

First thing was first: he needed to check the life support status of this heap, make sure it could keep him alive for the next sixteen hours or so. He would need heat very soon. He would also need air. A lot of atmosphere had been vented when he opened the airlock, and he had no idea if there was a replenishment system in place. Depending on the composition of the room's air before he entered, what was lost in the vent, and how the craft's life support system was working now, he might be on the verge of suffocating on his own exhalations or, conversely, bursting into flames from the smallest spark.

After that, he had to make a phone call. Well, not a phone call exactly, but a radio call to home base. If possible, he had to let them know he was alive.

Lastly, he had to think about piecing together a suit for the trip home. His suit was toast. The patch he had made outside saved his life, but it wouldn't hold up to a long journey.

He rolled to his feet slowly, testing his injured leg. He didn't collapse right away, which was a good sign in terms of nerve and soft tissue damage. The angry, black, charred welt on his thigh didn't bleed, which was an even better sign. He wouldn't need to cauterize himself again.

He suddenly remembered the pain of the hot pipe he'd used to seal the wound and turned in frantic circles looking for it. He found it laying where he had thrown it, no longer burning red hot and, miraculously, not surrounded by flames – more good news. He also looked to the live wires he had

EIGHTEEN — | 255 |

used to electrify the rod. They protruded silently from the wall – no sparks, no free movement.

He moved toward a console in the interior portion of the room. He looked carefully at its knobs, switches and glass panels. None of them were labeled. Rather than touch things at random, he decided to check the whole room before choosing what to manipulate.

Moving counterclockwise, he surveyed everything that looked important. At last, he came to a panel with some writing on it. Well, not writing exactly, but a graphic of some kind. A pictogram had been etched into the metal of the panel's body, above a gauge or readout of some kind. He rubbed dust and old shavings from the carving and peered at it in the rapidly dimming light. Did it depict a thermometer?

Next to it, three more readouts. These readouts each had a letter scratched underneath them: "C", "N" and "O." Carbon Dioxide, Nitrogen and Oxygen? He assumed so. He had found the life-support panel, then.

The readouts indicated adequate oxygen and minimal C02. The craft must have been equipped with some kind of basic C02 scrubber. The Nitrogen content seemed low, so the overall pressure in the room was likely reduced – probably from his entry into the habitat – but it was more than enough to stay alive comfortably.

He hoped that the readouts captured all of the gas in the room. If not, he might suffocate from oxygen displacement, or the habitat could over-pressurize and burst without warning, killing him instantly.

EIGHTEEN

There was also the possibility that the readouts were broken or had never functioned in the first place. Additionally, he still hadn't found any means of adding or taking away a gas in the room, assuming the builders had even included a means to do so. The panel had no buttons to press – just the readouts and their improvised labels.

On the plus side, he was still breathing and that was definitely a point in the readouts favor. Better just to assume they were correct and get through the night. He only had to live here a short time.

He continued to search the room, gliding his hand just centimeters over unlabeled panels, buttons and switches. He saw nothing useful. A pile of discarded food wrappers and plastic cups in the corner revealed nothing underneath but more cups and wrappers, followed by floor.

Shit.

What was he going to do? He couldn't go around just testing buttons, hoping for the best. Without an identifiable radio he couldn't call home, and without a heater he was going to freeze. The temperature of the room had already dropped noticeably, and the sun had dipped completely below the horizon.

He searched the room in the southern end of the shelter again, being careful to avoid disturbing the adjacent room with the barely contained hull breach. He found nothing useful for storing heat, generating heat or sending a signal. The builders, whoever they were, had clearly scoured the place for everything worth taking before they left to...wherever they left to. Even the bed sheets were gone.

EIGHTEEN — | 257 |

James surveyed the pool of trash before him. He let out a deep sigh and watched his breath rise to the ceiling. His leg hurt. He was hungry. He was tired. He was cold. All he wanted was the simple pleasure of climbing into a safe bed and resting for a while.

He had never been without a bed he could go to when he needed it. A safe bed, where he could forget about his troubles for at least one night. There were places to sleep here, certainly, but none of them were safe. He knew that sleeping here might end with never waking up. Of course, at the rate he was going, staying awake would result in the same outcome.

He wondered how the shelter had remained as warm as it was. He had no idea. Perhaps the heater had worked until recently and was now broken. Perhaps the computers and other machinery still working had just enough of a heating effect in the daytime that the craft was semi-habitable. Perhaps all of the heat in the wreck was left over from the previous inhabitants, and the walls simply had damn good insulation.

He looked around at the barely concealed piping, jury rigged consoles, piles of trash and unfinished paneling and laughed to himself. It probably wasn't the insulation. He was going to freeze to death in this hunk of junk. He may as well be stranded outside, the first homeless man on Mars.

Homeless. A homeless man. He looked over the debris once more. What did homeless men in old movies use to warm themselves? Newspapers, leaves, things they could find on the street or other outside places. Like trash, for example. Sometimes they used trash.

James smiled. Of course, he had plenty of ways to store heat here – he was swimming in them! Each one of these pieces of trash could be used for insulation, and he had most of his suit left. The suit itself had run out of power by now, and the heating system wouldn't work, but it had an insulating layer built in. He could stuff it full of debris, then put another layer or two of debris on top of himself. It would be disgusting, sure, but it was better than freezing to death.

He began grabbing fistfuls of debris – mostly paper based – and piling them up near what was left of his exosuit. As he did so, his eye once again caught the metal pipe he had used on his wound, now cold and still on the habitat floor. He was very lucky it had landed in one of the few areas of bare floor in this place - otherwise he might have started a fire.

His eyes drifted to the small lengths of live wire still protruding from the wall. A fire. He could start a fire. But did he dare? If it got out of control he would burn the place down, and fast. How would he get rid of the smoke? What if the smoke was toxic? More toxic, that is, than garden variety smoke. Then again, could he risk not starting a fire if it was an option? The debris in the room would certainly help warm him if he had nothing else, but it might not be enough to keep him from freezing to death. A fire would be.

He stopped what he was doing for a moment to consider the possibilities. He didn't have long. The temperature was plummeting – he could feel the cold creeping in from the walls.

He hung his head between his legs. "Ugh, God," he thought, "why is this so hard?" His brain felt like it was swimming in molasses. He wondered suddenly if he might have a concussion. He had fallen or been violently blasted into walls several times in the last few hours. Assuming he lived through the night, a trip to the med bay was definitely in order.

He glanced around the room once again, hoping, praying for an idea to present itself. Could he use the live wires to recharge his exosuit and use its heater? Too risky. Assuming he could even make that work, if he shorted something and broke the suit permanently, he'd never be able to leave.

What if he piled some of the debris into the airlock, set it alight, and sat near it on the interior side? That way, once the smoke got to be too much, he could close the inner door and vent the airlock, removing the smoke.

But what about the fire? It would go out each time and need to be restarted. Restarting a fire over and over would take much more fuel than keeping a single one going continuously. Plus, he would have no way of safely removing the smoke that had drifted through the inner door into the main habitat. He also didn't know how to vent the airlock without manually opening the external door. And he couldn't repressurize it without opening the inner door and allowing the air to flow back in, as he had when he first entered. To do that would mean putting the remaining structure of the craft under significant physical stress, multiple times.

He would also be risking his safety during the violent procedure, from avoiding burns as he ran across the gap between doors with the debris aflame nearby, to being flung backwards or outside each time he opened one of the airlock doors.

Finally, there was only so much atmosphere in the base as far as he knew. To continually vent it would place him at risk of suffocation, depressurization, or both. Oh, and his suit was broken so he had no way of surviving in vacuum. A bad idea, then.

He watched as the first threads of frost formed on the wall to his left. He glanced over and saw that the porthole had threads of frost forming at its edges as well. No more time to think.

He slid his suit on as quickly as he could, then began stuffing the half-open hole in the leg with debris, trying to create a barrier so warmth couldn't escape. He also stuffed the open collar of the suit with debris and shoved as much of it down into the torso area as he could manage. Finally, he filled the back and sides of his helmet with as much paper or plastic based trash as he could find, then placed it on his head and locked it into place. He left the visor open. No point in suffocating.

The gloves went on last, wrapping his hands in a warm embrace. He hadn't realized how cold his hands had been. They prickled as they thawed, little pins and needles of pain reminding him that he wasn't dead, but that without gloves, his hands soon would be.

Finally, he cleared a spot on the floor, lay down, and began scooping handfuls of nearby trash to cover himself. Soon he was at the bottom of several layers of trash, with only a tiny space for his head to poke out so he could breathe.

Keeping his feet covered proved difficult, as the trash fell to the left and the right of his boots every time he shifted even

EIGHTEEN — | 261 |

the tiniest amount. No matter – the majority of his body was covered, and he felt much warmer than he had.

The room was dark now, save for a soft glow from a few of the unlabeled panels. He lay in the darkness and contemplated the ceiling. He was reminded of playing in leaf piles as a child. It wasn't an experience he had had too often, but sometimes, when the weather was just right and the crowds had thinned, he had been able to find a corner of the city park with enough living trees and open ground to make a pile of leaves to play in. He would pile them up, as high and deep as he could, before running and jumping back into them, savoring the sound of each crunch and rustle. Then he would fall backward, as if onto a pillow, and gaze at the sky through the barren branches.

A few more moments went by. He rested – not sleeping, exactly, but not thinking either. Just trying to pass the time. His cheeks grew cold. Then the rest of his face. It wouldn't do. He might get frostbite on the tip of his nose or something.

He tried placing handfuls of trash on top of his face, with a small area around the mouth left uncovered for him to breathe. It soon became too uncomfortable, and he shifted. This made the trash slide off of the uneven contours of his face. Even the smallest adjustment or accidental disturbance left a part of his body uncovered, and that part became much too cold.

He rebuilt the pile on his body, resolving to tough out the numbness on his face and pledging to himself that he would see a surgeon for his frostbitten nose. Not long after, the cold began creeping up from the floor.

EIGHTEEN

He sat bolt upright and stood, trash falling from his suit like dust blown from a shelf.

The room was absolutely freezing. Past freezing, technically. It hurt to breathe. He placed his gloves over his mouth and nose, trying to create a pocket of warmth. His eyes felt as if they would freeze in their sockets. If it got cold enough, perhaps they would.

What was he going to do? He searched the room for answers yet again, swallowing a rising panic that hadn't been present before. It quickly dawned on him that he didn't have a choice: he was going to have to start a fire, even if it killed him.

He turned toward the back of the craft, considering his options. Perhaps if he started the fire in the back bedroom, it would increase the time he had before the air in the main room became too toxic to breathe. After that he could move into the airlock. After that...he didn't know. He could vent the atmosphere, he supposed. Hopefully he would have figured out a way to repair his suit by then.

As he headed toward the bedroom, he passed the room with the breach and stopped. On a hunch, he opened the door again. He instantly regretted doing so, as a wave of even colder air hit him directly in the face. He stepped back, gasping.

From a distance, he looked through the open door. He could see the wall of boxes and sealant separating the breached room from the void. Starlight lit the surface of Mars, beyond.

"How good is that seal?" he wondered aloud.

EIGHTEEN

His voice startled him in the otherwise silent enclosure. He hadn't realized how quiet things had gotten. He cleared his throat and spoke again, louder, in defiance of the despair he could feel creeping up. "How good is that seal? Not very good, I'd bet. Hopefully, not very good at all."

He would have to take a small risk to test this, but it was a risk he couldn't afford not to take. He quickly ran to the pile of debris he had made in the main room. He grabbed two pieces of trash and approached one of the live wires, still hanging benignly from its place on the wall.

He crouched down, then hesitated. Was this a mistake? He had to be incredibly careful. One stray spark and the whole pile might go up.

To be safe, he cleared a path between the open door of the breached room and the live wire, kicking any trash in the way to the left and the right. He made sure to push any trash in the immediate area of the wire even further back, so it wouldn't catch a stray spark. He crouched down again, took a deep breath of the painfully cold air, then held one of the pieces of trash up to the exposed end of the wire.

It caught immediately, flashing a strangely colored blue and green flame. It went out almost as quickly, leaving most of the debris piece intact and an acrid, sour smell in its wake. A single, slim sliver of smoke drifted up toward the ceiling, out of sight.

Now he was panicked. Perhaps the trash wasn't as flammable as he had thought. He discarded both plastic pieces and ran back to the pile, rummaging for something paper based. He found two items and ran back to the wire.

EIGHTEEN

The first piece caught quickly, then burned away into nothing before he could take a step. He cursed and held the second piece to the wire. It caught and began to burn steadily.

He rushed as quickly as he dared toward the breached room, watching for stray embers and praying the debris wouldn't burn all the way up before he got there. As he got closer to the open door, the cold became unbearable again. He held his breath and narrowed his eyes to slits, pushing forward into the breached room.

The last few bits of the paper burned into ash and smoke just as he entered the room. He watched as the smoke drifted slowly upward, curled upon itself, and moved toward the box/sealant wall. It hovered for a moment where the edge of the boxes and the sealant met. Then it was sucked away, into the Martian atmosphere and out of sight.

James was so relieved, he could cry.

NINETEEN

James sat in the doorway of the breached room, leaning on the door-jam. To his right, a small fire burned from a handful of plastic and paper-based debris. To his left sat a large pile of trash – all he could find and drag over to the area of the fire.

James periodically reached into the pile on his left and fed the fire on his right, keeping the flames alive. The area he sat in, and much of the craft, was filled with a thin layer of smoke; just enough to make the eyes burn and the throat tickle. It smelled awful. James was almost certain the smoke was toxic and killing him, but as long as it did so more slowly than the Martian cold, he could tolerate it.

The lion's share of the smoke was being sucked out into the Martian atmosphere via the imperfect seal of the box/sealant wall to his right. James had been careful to position the fire in a way he thought unlikely to melt or burn any part of the wall. Still, he fought existential terror whenever he stared at the nighttime Martian surface, blurry but visible through the translucent sealant. Millimeters from death, he was so scared that, in a way, he had stopped being scared. Instead, he felt like he was over his own shoulder, a ghost watching the first trashcan fire on Mars. At least the flames were doing their job. He was much warmer now, and confident that he wouldn't freeze to death so long as the fire was burning.

He stared wistfully at the dim light of the fire, a strange peace falling over him. He closed his eyes, grateful to be out of immediate danger for a moment. After a while he took a deep breath, opened his eyes, and fed more trash into the fire. It crackled, sputtered and sparked, a few embers drifting harmlessly into the air before winking out of existence.

He had to plan his next move. He was unable to leave the immediate area of the door-jam. Any further than that and he got too cold. He had only dared venture into the main room to check the atmosphere gauges once since he started the fire. Since then, he had learned his lesson. The air beyond the area of the fire was so cold it felt hot - the kind of hot that took the flesh from your bones. Any warmth he had stored from sitting near the flames leeched away almost instantly when he left them, leaving in its place an ache he could feel to his core. Any further movement, in search of survival supplies or rescue, would have to wait until daylight.

The first thing he would need to do once the sun rose was figure out how to replace the hole in his suit. After that, he had to find a way to charge and pressurize it. Doing the latter could prove impossible if he wasn't able to find the craft's atmospheric tanks. It obviously had an air supply of some kind, but nothing he had seen so far gave him any indication of where it might be. If he had taken more time to assess the outside of the wreck before he entered, then maybe...but that was easier said in hindsight. While fighting for his life he hadn't exactly had time to assess structural details.

As for resealing the suit, he had one more emergency patch available, but he had seen how well those stood up to punishment. Which was to say, not very well at all. He was highly doubtful the patch would hold for as long as was needed to walk back to base, which he was increasingly certain he would have to do.

He hadn't seen any vehicles coming for him since the attack. No rescue party from his team. Which probably meant they thought he was dead. It probably also meant that Charlie *was* dead, gunned down on his way back for help.

James shook his head sadly, then adjusted his position against the door-jam. No point in ruminating on Charlie's fate. There was nothing he could do to change it now. Better to save his strength for the tasks to come. He couldn't sleep, of course, or else the fire would go out. But he could rest his body and allow his mind to drift.

The morning came slowly, star-lit darkness giving way to dusky dawn. The horizon glowed blue for a moment, providing a precious reminder of home, before taking its normal yellow/red hue. The sun itself, pale and distant, hung in the air like a specter, casting an otherworldly glow on the barren land outside.

After an hour or so, James let the fire die, then waited to see if he would die as well. He got colder, but kept on living.

He stood and began to work. To seal his suit, he layered debris on the inner and outer sides of the torn leg material, holding the pieces together with tiny dabs of extra sealant glue from his one remaining kit. He then filled any spaces left in the hole with a small amount of sealant foam he had been able to scrounge up in the halls of the craft. To top it all off, he used the remaining drops of sealant glue to reinforce the patch from his kit when he affixed it on top of the hole. After a few minutes of letting it dry, he re-donned his suit and gently flexed his leg to test the repair. It appeared to hold well – much better than the rushed job he had done the first time.

James took one more lap around the craft, searching in vain for the location of the air tanks. He found nothing. Wherever they were, they weren't on the inside. At least not the readily accessible portion.

He checked the atmospheric readouts. They indicated a moderate level of nitrogen, standard earth-atmosphere oxygen levels of twenty percent or so, and an elevated level of Carbon Dioxide. It wasn't enough to be a problem – yet – but whatever scrubbing technology had kept the air clean up to this point was no longer keeping up. It was a good thing he didn't plan on staying much longer.

James stood still, contemplating the air vent located above the readout console. If the air tanks were accessible from inside the facility, chances are it was through that vent.

James found a flathead screwdriver on the ground near the overturned workbench. He doffed his suit once again, ignoring the sudden chill that met his skin, and piled two empty metal boxes on top of each other, with a third at the base. Using the third box as a stepping stool, he climbed to the top box and began unscrewing the screen of the vent. Once it was loose, he removed it and placed it on the ground next to the bottom box, then placed his head inside the vent shaft.

The air inside the vent was, predictably, cold. The vent shaft extended forward for a foot or two, then upward and out of site. James hoped it led to the facility's atmospheric tanks, but he wasn't certain. Yet he couldn't think of any other plausible end point.

James extended his arms into the vent shaft, placed his palms flat on the metal surface of its interior, then applied pressure to see if it could hold his weight. Not only did the vent make a very unsettling groaning sound, but his palms immediately reminded him why it was bad to touch freezing cold metal with bare skin. He pulled his hands back with a yelp and settled his body weight back onto the top of his makeshift ladder.

If climbing up the vent to find the connections to the air tanks wouldn't work, he would have to go outside. He looked at his suit, doffed and lying on the floor beneath him. How could he go outside with empty atmospheric tanks?

The suit's seal should hold now, which meant he could wear it outside. The air that had filled it from the inside of the craft would remain inside it once he exited, providing his body with plenty of external pressure. The nitrogen in the suit was inert and wouldn't cause narcosis at normal pressure in normal amounts. He could rebreathe it a thousand times and it would remain the same – not life giving, but not life taking either. The carbon dioxide in the suit would be removed by the scrubbers, so that wasn't an issue. Oxygen, though. That was a problem.

NINETEEN

The suit would have whatever oxygen it had in it when he left, and that was it. Without a fresh supply to replenish what he breathed, he would eventually pass out. How long would that take? Hard to say. Some oxygen would be broken free by the scrubbers and could be re-used. But, eventually, it would all be gone, expelled along with the excess carbon or consumed by his body.

Come to think of it, even the carbon dioxide would be a problem while the exosuit was still without power. He had to charge it.

James stepped down and picked his suit up off the floor. He moved over to the live wire he had used to set the fire and sat down in front of it. Using the tools he had originally used to strip the wire of its insulation, James unscrewed the chest plate of his suit and searched for the battery. He found it and gently probed at it, trying to pry it loose. He couldn't find a way to remove it from the body of the suit. The battery was too well integrated with the rest of the electronics.

To the right of the battery itself he saw what he assumed was a charging port. He sighed. Despite wracking his brain for ideas all night, removing the battery and charging it separately - to avoid any electrical shorts in the suit while charging - was the best he had come up with. Since that hadn't worked, well...what he was about to do might fry the suit's circuits completely and strand him here, but he didn't have a choice.

James gently stuck the live wire into the charging port. The suit beeped and a few lights flashed as power coursed through it, then all noises and flashes stopped, save for a single green light that was flashing right above the battery. Did that mean it was charging? He hoped so.

James gently inserted the whole exposed length of the live wire into the charging port, so that all that protruded was insulated wire. That should prevent the other surfaces of the suit from contacting the current and starting a fire.

He sat back and waited for the suit to charge. It didn't take long. The live wire was probably pumping out much more electricity than the suit was designed to take. Within twenty minutes the green light above the battery had stopped flashing and was a solid green.

Shaking from the cold, James disconnected the live wire, carefully placing it back into its free hanging position, then reattached the front of the suit's chest plate. He then activated the suit while still sitting on the floor beside it. Once it was fully booted, he consulted the status indicator on the suit's left wrist. The status indicator only provided the most basic life-support and system status information, in case the more detailed HUD within the helmet failed. One of those pieces of information was the suit's power levels. The readout indicated that the suit was at one hundred percent power.

"Very well, then." he thought. His latest gambit had worked. Now there were only two more risks to take: go outside to get air in his suit, then survive the trip home.

The sun was higher in the sky, now, and the air around him had warmed considerably, although it was still very crisp. The Carbon Dioxide gauge on the panel behind him was still rising, meaning his time was limited. No point in delaying any further. Either this would work, or it wouldn't, but the time to find out was now.

James detached the empty air tanks from the back of the suit but kept their cabling and hoses connected - that way he could more easily refill them. Next, he stepped back into his suit, placed the helmet on top of his head, lowered the visor and sealed it. Once the HUD was up, he checked his systems one more time. Power was good. All systems online, save for the empty tanks in his hands.

His heater was already busy warming his body, and he cursed himself for not taking the risk of charging the suit sooner. The liquid recirculator was also up and running, and James suddenly realized how thirsty he was. He took a deep drink from the spout in his helmet.

Normally he was grossed out by the knowledge that most of the water provided by the suit was his own purified urine, but this time it didn't bother him at all. It had been almost a full day since the last time he drank water, and it tasted like ambrosia.

One more deep draught from the spout and James opened the airlock door, stepped into the airlock and closed it securely behind him.

James was scared. The act of compressing the airlock the first time had been violent, and decompressing it would be no different. He stood at the external airlock door with his hand on the handle, ready to pull down. James knew that as soon as he opened the door he would be sucked – well, pushed really – out of the door and onto the barren landscape outside. He would likely be thrown several feet, after which he may incur more damage to his exosuit, already compromised.

If his suit's seal broke again, he was done for. If he broke a limb, sprained an ankle, or received any other type of injury that might limit his mobility, he was done for. If he kept standing mutely at the door, struggling to control his panic and using up precious oxygen, he was done for.

James took one long, deep, breath to calm himself, then began consciously controlling his breathing, keeping each breath steady, even, and short, with as long an interval between breaths as he could handle.

He centered himself in the middle of the doorframe, then crouched down and hugged his knees with one arm. He assumed that tucking his body into a ball would minimize his chances of injury. He used an adjustable strap on the side of each calf – originally meant to hold digging and excavating equipment, such as a pickaxe – to secure the two air-tanks, one on each leg. He lowered his head, then reached up for the handle of the door with his free hand.

He opened the door.

The world was chaos again. He turned end over end, quickly losing his grip on his knees, his tightly tucked-in ball of a body flattening out into a flailing missile. The world moved in slow motion as he arched over the Martian sand, then lost momentum and headed for it face first.

As the ground rushed towards him, James twisted his body in the air, trying to turn over onto his back. A direct impact to his faceplate would be devastating, but his back should be ok

– with his air tanks on his legs, his suit had relatively few important and fragile components in that area.

He only made half of the turn before impact. His left shoulder hit the gravel and sand with a thud. He felt a small pop as he hit, and his left arm went numb, as if he had struck his funny bone. The back and side of his helmet hit the ground next, followed by the rest of his body. His legs flopped over in the air as he did a half tumble and slid to a stop.

He lay still for a moment, face up, regarding the Martian sky. He waited for signs of a suit breach or impending decompression and detected none. He moved his hands and legs, testing if they still worked. His left hand was a bit numb from the impact of his shoulder, but still did as it was told.

Not wanting to waste any time, James rolled on his side and got to his feet. His back groaned as he did so, reminding him that he was too old for high falls and front flips.

He quickly scrambled up a nearby rise and looked toward the top of the craft. There, in the dead center of the structure, was an assembly of some kind. James could see a few solar panels and lots of cabling. That was where James hoped to find the air tanks.

He began frantically circumnavigating the structure, looking for a way up. He realized too late that he had already lost track of his breathing, and it was no longer steady and even. Instead, it was ragged and quick. An alarm chimed in his helmet, startling him further.

Warning: Oxygen level low. Replenish atmospheric tanks immediately.

Crap.

NINETEEN

He had already burned through too much oxygen. He calmed himself and began regulating his breathing again. He had to make the most of whatever was left.

James finished his circle of the downed ship at a steady pace, his steps fast but measured. There was no ladder to the top. He would need to find another way up. He walked a few steps backward, assessing the structure as a whole and weighing his options.

He spotted a handhold on a low area of the hull, where it extended a small amount past the body of the wreck to form a kind of overhang. He reached up to grab it and found that it extended just beyond his reach. He jumped for it with both hands, missing several times and expending precious oxygen in the process. At last, he grasped the handhold, legs dangling freely. He was grateful for the low gravity as he pulled himself up high enough to swing his right leg up. He was hanging with his back parallel to the ground now, his left leg drooping downward. His alarm sounded again.

Warning: Oxygen level low. Replenish atmospheric tanks immediately.

"Yeah, yeah" he muttered to himself. "Working on it."

James gritted his teeth and dragged his body the rest of the way up onto the overhang. He had nothing else to grab a hold of as he did so, so he spread the fingers of his free hand as widely as he could, swung his arm up, pressed hard, and used the static friction of his glove against the overhang as leverage. It took some wiggling, and hurt muscles in his abs and back he didn't know he had, but he was finally able to swing himself over the ledge and onto his back.

NINETEEN

He was breathing hard again, and exhausted. He felt the familiar pins and needles feeling in his extremities and remembered that he was going hypoxic as well. No time to waste, he had to keep moving.

James slowly got to his feet and stood on the overhang, leaning against the main body of the ship. Now he had to figure out how to keep climbing. He couldn't see any more handholds from his current position, so he'd have to search elsewhere.

Being careful to press his torso against the hull, James began slowly circumnavigating the wreck via the narrow ledge of the overhang. He faced the hull as he did so and continued looking upward for another route to the top. He got about a quarter of the way around, with no luck, before he realized he had to improvise a way up from where he was now. His head was swimming, and he could barely feel the tips of his fingers. A red light indicating critically low oxygen status had begun blinking in the corner of his faceplate's heads-up display.

James spied a black cable to his right. He followed it with his eyes to the top of the craft and saw that it was partially responsible for keeping the machinery at the apex tethered in place. He grabbed it and pulled gently, testing its tensile strength. It seemed capable of supporting his weight. He pulled it again, looking to see what affect the pulling had on the machinery. The tether lifted from the hull somewhat and the machine vibrated hard, but held fast.

He began his ascent. The climb was hard. He used both hands on the tether, pulling arm over arm, with his torso against the hull and his legs pushing from below when they could find traction.

He was halfway up before the first bolt flew past in the periphery of his vision.

James looked up and tried to see exactly where it had come from but saw nothing. He kept climbing. He was really struggling for air, now. The muscles in his arms were screaming. He cried out in frustration and desperation, his own voice resonating in the tiny confines of his helmet. Oh, God, he wanted to stop. Everything hurt. He wasn't sure he could continue.

Then, just like that, he didn't have to. A second bolt flew past his helmet like a meteor. The line grew slack in his hand, and he began sliding backwards. The sky above him was eclipsed by the profile of the machinery as it toppled all the way onto its side. James closed his eyes and waited for the crushing weight of the apparatus to fall on him.

The line snapped taught again, and James nearly lost his grip as his backward slide was violently arrested. He opened his eyes and looked up. The equipment had toppled over, and was now perched precariously on the edge of the craft's 'roof,' but it wasn't falling any further.

He blinked twice in rapid succession and realized he couldn't see colors anymore. He looked around at his newly black and white surroundings. He was close to the ledge of the overhang again, and his body was tired. He tried to think of what to do next and drew a blank. All he knew was that he needed rest.

He slid back down until he was standing on the overhang. He faced outward and leaned, back to the hull, struggling to catch his breath. God dammit it was so frustrating! He just wanted to breathe! His helmet was stifling him. He reached up and considered taking it off.

As his finger was moving toward the slide, he remembered where he was and what he was doing. Shit. Fuck. This was it; he was losing his shit. It was about to be game over.

What was he supposed to do? He looked up in a fog, vaguely panicking that he wasn't more panicked. There was the machine, still looming over him. It still hadn't fallen...maybe it was stuck fast. It didn't matter. He wasn't going to make it up there. He lacked the strength. He'd be better off at this point if it just fell...

Somewhere deep in his now dull brain, a light bulb went off. James reached out, took a firm hold of the line, now hanging slackly to his side, and pulled with all of his might. The machinery moved but did not fall. He pulled again, then again.

His vision was beginning to narrow into a tunnel, and he could barely feel his arms.

With a final mighty heave on the line, he collapsed to his knees on the overhang. He was spent. He rolled to his left – off of his knees and into a sitting position. As he sat with his back to the hull, gasping for breath, he took in the otherworldly, colorless landscape before him. If he could have thought, he would have considered that there were worse sights to die to. As it was, he merely sat and stared.

The hull began vibrating behind him. An enormous blur passed to his left, then hit the ground with an impact hard enough to hear in the rarefied air.

James stared, uncomprehending, at the shape below him. Steam or smoke floated up from it and quickly dissipated. Sparks flew from it and parts took turns falling off and rolling into the sand.

Almost instinctively, James leaned forward and lowered himself over the lip of the overhang. He hung from his gloved hands for a moment, feet dangling, then dropped the last few inches to the ground. His legs gave way as soon as his feet made contact with the dust below.

He lay on the ground listlessly and considered the broken, amorphous blob spitting out sparks in front of him. He crawled closer to it and continued to stare. He was supposed to care about it. This thing was important. But...he had no idea why. He was so tired. He thought he might sleep here.

He closed his eyes and allowed his head to drift down onto the Martian sand. All was peaceful for a few precious seconds. He floated toward oblivion, toward nothingness. Just as he was slipping over the ledge of unconsciousness, a sudden flood of primal rage filled him.

"No!" he thought, "No God damn it! No!"

He was so close - on the cusp. But of what? Why couldn't he sleep?

It didn't matter.

The anger prompted his eyes to open and his head to raise. He pulled himself closer to the shape before him, until he was inches from it. He reached out and took hold of the object, furiously shaking and punching it, as if he could intimidate the lifeless hunk of metal into giving him answers. He grew tired and stopped moving, proceeding to stare at the object and breathe heavily.

One of the many shapes on the surface of the nameless thing before him felt familiar. It was a rounded container of some sort with a neck which connected to a tube, which connected to the machine. James was dimly aware that he shouldn't trust the container – that it could be full of things which might kill him. But he no longer cared.

He disconnected the container from its tube, removed one of the tanks from the strap on his leg, and connected the now free tube to the neck of the tank. Then, he promptly passed out.

TWENTY

James awoke to the sight of the Martian sky. De ja vu overtook him for a moment and he wasn't sure when or where he was. Had the last day and a half been a dream? Was he still on his back with an arrow in his leg, bleeding out onto the sand? He reached down to his thigh and felt the new, reinforced patch he'd made, still intact.

He rolled to his right and looked at the craft's life-support machinery, previously perched high on the roof and now crumpled in a heap on the ground. One of his tanks was connected to it via a hose, whose other end was lost inside the tangle of wires and metal. He looked around for the discarded canister his tank had replaced and found it a foot or so away. There on the front was the reassuring sight of the letter "O" followed by the number two.

James searched the contraption for more air canisters. He found them quickly, hung in concentric rings around what was left of the machine. He couldn't tell how many there were, or how deep they went, but there were lots of them. Each canister was connected to the life-support machine via its own hose. It looked like the machine drew oxygen from hundreds of individual canisters into a central reservoir, and from there into the craft itself. His tank had taken the place of one of the canisters.

James assumed the machine usually only drew oxygen in one direction: from canister to reservoir to craft. In this case, since the machine had no power after falling from the roof, and since his suit was trying to draw oxygen from the empty tank he had connected, air had been drawn from the reservoir into the tank, rather than the opposite. Lucky.

Since he couldn't take the giant reservoir along with him, James began harvesting canisters. First, he made sure the air tanks he had brought with him were disconnected from his suit and completely emptied. Since his suit was already pressurized he didn't need any more nitrogen. He would be just fine with what he had. He was going to fill both air tanks with nothing but oxygen, and he wanted to make sure he had as much room as possible in each tank. If his suit got another breach he would die from oxygen toxicity, but he had no more sealant or patches for his suit, so it wouldn't really matter – if he got another leak he was dead anyway.

James disconnected an oxygen canister from the life-support machine and started filling his tanks. One oxygen canister filled about half of one air tank. James marveled at how many canisters it must have taken to fill the base with breathable air. It wasn't a smart design. How desperate had the builders been to piece together whatever they could find like this? What had motivated that choice? James shuddered at the implications.

His first tank's valve display indicated that it was full. James quickly reconnected it and listened to the whirs and hums of his suit as it adjusted his atmosphere. Carbon dioxide was released into the Martian air and fresh oxygen took its place. The HUD indicated that his pressure and oxygen levels were now optimal, with no loss of nitrogen and plenty of breathable air. He let out a great sigh of relief.

James quietly filled his second tank with oxygen. Once it was full, he reconnected it to his suit and slid both tanks back into place on his back.

He stood and took stock of his situation. His air tanks were full. Combined with the C02 scrubbers, they would provide him with about eight hours of breathable air. He had a little less than a quarter gallon of water left, which, when combined with his suit's liquid waste recycler, should yield about forty-two ounces or so. That was…what? Five cups? Should be plenty. He was still thirsty despite the deep draughts of water he had taken earlier, and he had a decent amount of exertion ahead of him, so he would have to be mindful of his intake lest he become dehydrated. Still, it should be enough.

Physically he was ok. His wound was sore and would probably get infected soon. The wrecked craft hadn't been the most hygienic environment. No matter – he could get some antibiotics from the med bay on base if needed. His body was sore from all of the falls he had taken, as well as a crappy night of no sleep, but he could walk well enough. As far as his energy levels, he was tired and hungry, but he had no food and he couldn't stop and rest, so no point in dwelling on that.

TWENTY

With nothing left to do but get started, he tapped the voice-command key on his wrist console and spoke. His voice, dry and tired, startled him. "Show me the way to Alpha base."

Alpha base is approximately eighty kilometers to the NNE.

A graphic display popped up in his HUD, with a small map of the terrain and waypoint markers showing his current location and his destination. "Holy crap" he thought. Eighty kilometers was some walk. It was about...Fifty miles. That made sense. The buggy ride here had taken about two hours, and the average speed of the rover was twenty-five miles per hour.

The average human only walked at three miles per hour. James had no reason to think his walking speed would be any different than average, especially considering the sandy, rocky terrain, his injury, his exhaustion, and the clunky exosuit he was wearing. At that speed it would take him...somewhere in the ballpark of sixteen hours to get there.

Jesus. Sixteen hours.

Suddenly daunted by the task before him, James did some more math, then turned and kneeled toward the life-support machine. He would need at least four more canisters if he wanted to make it there alive. He stored the first two canisters the same way he had secured his tanks earlier: in the straps on the lower parts of each leg.

He held the other two canisters in the crooks of his arms. The canisters were fairly light, especially in the reduced gravity. Most of their weight came from the material of the canisters themselves, and not their contents. They would be uncomfortable to carry, but not preventatively so. Besides, the journey would only get easier as he used more and more oxygen; he could discard the canisters once they were empty.

James took one more deep breath and oriented himself NNE. Less than twenty steps into his perilous journey, a faint popping noise behind him caught his attention.

He turned to see the wrecked craft collapsing on itself, a hole in the south-eastern side spewing debris into the open air. The debris was the contents of the craft, of course: all of the trash wrappers, worn power cords and half-built machinery that had kept him alive for one fraught night.

Smaller artifacts he hadn't noticed when they were in piles on the floor caught his eye. Toothbrushes. Worn clothes. A blanket or tapestry of some kind that looked hand woven, like it had taken its maker real time and effort.

The walls of the craft finally collapsed and the structure appeared to topple over. The strain of multiple airlock breaches, rooftop ascents and toppling machinery had finally worn a big enough hole in the sealant-foam to make a difference.

With no time to spare and nothing left to say, James bid his temporary shelter goodbye, then turned toward home.

21

TWENTY-ONE

The journey was longer than James had expected. He trudged, one foot in front of the other, through the Martian sand. Many times, the sand gave way to a hard gravel, as if the individual grains had grown by magnitudes. Then there were flat areas – stretches of hardened dirt that looked like baked clay, despite the freezing temperatures. James trod through all of these, his feet growing wearier by the step.

He had nothing to accompany him but the occasional whir of his atmospheric regulators, his own breathing, and the suit's AI. It would alert him to his wandering course sometimes, with gentle chimes at first, then words if the chimes didn't get his attention. It would also speak up when his air tanks were low and it was time to make a swap. Otherwise, he was confronted with an all-encompassing, eerie silence.

He had known that silence was coming, but he had underestimated the power of it. Normally, a journey of this distance would have been filled with sound: the noise of a rover's wheels crunching and sliding over the landscape, the vibrations of their movement traveling from the tires, through the rover's hull and into the cabin. The beeps and bops of the rover's control console as it provided directional guidance and system updates to the explorers inside. The human noises of his traveling companions, whoever they might be – small sighs, movements and scratches, half-concealed burps and other expulsions, occasional laughter – all of it was gone, replaced with nothing. Nearly complete silence, as loud as a crowd of a hundred.

His blood pumped within his ears. The sparseness of this world struck him anew as he traversed its craters and dunes on foot. It was dead.

He sang songs to himself as he walked – half remembered tunes from his childhood. Most of them were wordless, nothing but a few lines of melody. For others he could recall a word or two; usually the chorus. He sang and hummed until his voice was hoarse, even though he had been singing quietly. Then he drank from his water line and kept on moving.

Occasionally the silence became too much. He felt engulfed by it. He looked around at the emptiness around him and realized how truly alone he was. The madness of his situation, the overwhelming danger of it, threatened to take his mind. He wanted to scream – to rip the helmet from his head and shout at the top of his lungs, to fill the world around him with life, with movement, with color, with sound.

A moan slipped from his lips as he fought the wild impulse.

He stopped and doubled over in emotional pain, pushing down rising panic. He swallowed hard and tasted bile. He knew that if he let that scream out, he wouldn't stop. He really would remove the helmet from his head and lose everything. He closed his eyes and breathed slowly, vowing to hold on until he could fall apart in a safe place. He was so close to safety. So close.

A strange sensation filled him – a calming presence, urging him to keep moving, to not give up. It was almost as if he wasn't alone. He looked around him, bewildered at the certainty of the feeling, yet saw no one. Still, the feeling remained: an urging to continue, almost loud enough to be audible. He felt his children in that urging. He felt his wife. He set his jaw and kept walking.

His suit's AI gently reminded him to refill his left air tank. He did so, dropping one of the empty oxygen canisters in the sand at his feet. His arms were free now, and his legs were lighter.

He kept moving.

His heels hurt. He thought he might be getting a blister. It occurred to him that this was probably the most walking he had done since arriving on this strange, alien world. His entire life had been lived within a few thousand feet for months. Ironic that he felt so trapped when he had never been more free.

Once, during a single moment out of thousands of interminable moments, he tripped and fell. The pebbles and rocks under his feet had given way as he traversed a small decline, and he fell on his ass, hard. The fall shocked his senses. What had been routine and drudgery blossomed once again into panic as he waited to see if he had damaged his suit. To his great relief, no alarms sounded. He shifted his weight back

TWENTY-ONE — | 289 |

and forth as he rolled to his side and stood up. Nothing in his back or legs complained. He was unhurt, still capable of movement. He got back to walking.

He started to play mental games to pass the time. He glanced at the sun as it made its lazy arc through the sky. He planned what he would do once he arrived safely at home. He rehearsed the story of what happened to him in his mind. He ran through all of his knock-knock jokes. He tried urinating and drinking at the same time, then rejoiced in perverse pride at his success, and his efficiency. He began to count his steps, then stopped when he passed five hundred.

He was almost certain his feet were bleeding now. Each step was painful. Aches began cropping up all over his body, most of them in places he hadn't realized were sore. He briefly considered the possibility that he had gotten the bends from depressurizing so quickly at the wreck, then dismissed the notion and reminded himself that his body had been through plenty of other traumas.

The sky above him began darkening as the sun lit the horizon in bright azure. James was grateful for the south-Martian springtime, that it had risen at all. He emptied his last oxygen canister. One of his two air tanks ran dry. His water line ran dry - his urine too full of impurities for further filtration. His wound hurt. His knees hurt. His HUD indicated low battery power.

There was still no sign of the base. He picked up the pace.

Finally, in the distance, James began to see the tops of the structures he now called home. He quickly checked his radio to see if he had comms. Reception was terrible, but he was getting a faint signal. No point in trying to radio for help now – they would just hear static and dismiss it as random interference – but he would be able to call soon.

James walked a little faster, believing for the first time since the arrow strike that he would be ok, that he would survive.

He glanced upward. Thousands of twinkling points of light met his gaze. In his hurry they all blurred together. Which ones were stars? Which were planets, or one of the twin moons hurrying across the firmament? James wasn't an astronomer, nor had he spent enough time outside to know the difference. The tiny lights were innumerable, so clustered together in spots that they seemed to constitute a solid mass. It was an odd time to realize it, but James was once again in the presence of majesty. If he had had time he would have fallen to his knees in awe. But he didn't have time, and the alarms in his suit chose this moment of sublimity to remind him of that.

One after another, they went off: *Low oxygen. Low power. Nearing Destination. Radio signal detected.*

He smiled to himself. At least half of the news was good. He checked his battery's charge. It was at twelve percent – normally terrible but plenty in his current situation. He checked his oxygen level.

Shit. Five percent.

"Here we go again," he muttered. Nothing was ever easy on this planet.

James opened a comms channel: "Alpha Base, this is EXO-1. Over." He was met with silence. He tried once more. "Alpha Base, this is EXO-1. Do you read me? Over." More silence. Either he was still too far away or someone wasn't manning the comms station like they should be. In any case, James had no choice but to keep walking.

Warning. Oxygen level at three percent. Please re-charge atmospheric tanks immediately.

"Alpha Base, this is EXO-1. Come in please, over."

More static.

He tried again. This time he could hear the rising panic in his own voice. "Alpha Base, this is James. James Wilmot. Come on, someone pick up, please."

At last, a response. "Holy Shit! James? I read you buddy, loud and clear. Where are you?"

James fought back tears of relief. "I'm right outside." He choked back emotion and laughed gently. "Boy is it good to hear your voice. Who am I talking to?"

"This is Toby, man. Where the hell have you been? We figured you bought it."

James laughed. "Oh yeah," he said facetiously, "why did you figure that?"

Toby was oblivious to his sarcasm. "Because Charlie showed up yesterday saying he saw you get shot!"

James was stunned into silence for a moment. His jubilation turned into ice in his veins. "Wait a second, Charlie is alive? He came back here?"

"Yeah, last night. Showed up in the buggy all shook up. What, you thought he was dead?"

"What the fuck, Toby? He didn't check on me? Try to help? Of course I thought he was dead! I figure you all

TWENTY-ONE

thought we were both dead, or else you would have come to get us!"

It was Toby's turn to be silent. "...James, shit, I don't know, man. Your radio was down, we weren't getting any readings from your suit. Charlie said you were dead."

"Fuck. Fuck it." James was too tired and too scared to care. "I'll talk to him later. Can you see me?"

In the control room, Toby's eyes went wide. "Oh, of course, of course...hang on man, let me get the lights up..."

The base's exterior floodlights all came on at once, stinging James's eyes. The beautiful panorama of sky he had been admiring disappeared, replaced only by the rocks right at his feet and a glowing orb in the distance, surrounded on all sides by darkness.

"Do you see me?"

Toby peered out into the now-illuminated night. "Yes! Yeah, I got you right there, approaching from the south-west! I can barely make you out, but I see you."

The console at Toby's right hand began beeping. "Hey, James, EVA comms console is starting to pick up your med feed...looks like your bio sensors are out of whack. How are you doing?"

"I've been better" James grunted as he continued his grinding walk toward the base.

"The readings I'm getting aren't looking too good, man. CO_2 is way up...did your suit computer take a shock or something? These things are usually pretty sturdy..."

"Yes, it took a shock." James grunted again in amusement. "Couple of em' as a matter of fact."

TWENTY-ONE — | 293 |

"Ok, good, cause otherwise I'd be worried. Your heartrate is pretty elevated for a guy walking at a normal pace. Coupled with the C02...James can you do me a favor and check your oxygen levels for me?"

"You got me. They're low."

"How low is low?"

"Tanks about dry."

The computer chose that moment to chime in with another warning.

"God damn it," thought James.

"Was that one percent I just heard?"

James answered breathlessly. "Yeah."

"Fuck." Toby spun around and hit the intercom to the life-support station. "Chris, you there?"

Chris answered quickly. "Yeah, go."

"I need you in the control room now."

"Toby, I'm not supposed to leave this room..."

"Don't argue, just get up here now! It's an emergency." Toby re-toggled the EVA comms switch. "Alright James, just keep her coming. You should have enough to get back here just fine. James, are you still with me?"

"Yeah. Tanks not dry yet. Plugging away in your direction."

Toby peered through the glass again. He could see James, more or less in the same position as before, a shadowy figure stumbling ever closer. Toby was pretty certain that James wouldn't make it to the base before he ran out of oxygen; at least not at his current rate of travel. He and Chris were going to have to go out there and get him.

TWENTY-ONE

Toby suddenly had an idea and spun toward the main console. He checked the status of the rovers docked outside. As long as they were in the perimeter of the base, he should be able to remotely activate one of them and guide it to James's location. James would be able to hop in and ride right home. Toby checked the first rover, only to find that it was down for maintenance. He checked Rovers two through four and got the same result. The buggy that James and Charlie had taken to the potential landing site had been nearly out of power by the time Charlie got back. It was still recharging. The other buggy was also inside the hanger, deactivated. Toby could only activate a vehicle from the control station if it was on and in idle mode, or else the receiving antenna wouldn't be available for remote contact. "God damn it!" Toby muttered to himself. "What are the fuckin' chances?"

Chris burst through the control room hatch, out of breath and heaving. "Hey man, what's going on?"

Toby pointed in James's direction. "That's James outside."

Chris looked confused. "What? Charlie said James was dead..."

"I know what Charlie said. But there he is."

"Are you sure? Are you sure it's not one of those...other people?"

Toby rolled his eyes. "Jesus, Chris. I've been locked in a can with this guy for months. You think I don't recognize his voice?"

"But Charlie said..."

"Fuck what Charlie said! He was wrong, ok? Or he lied."

"Ok, ok. But what does that mean?"

"I don't know, dude. But we don't have time right now. He's still about four hundred meters out and his suit just reported an 02 level of one percent."

"Did you try booting a rover?"

"Yeah, I already tried. They're all down for maintenance."

Chris looked incredulous. "All of them?"

"Yes, all of them."

"And no 02 reserves, right?"

"Dude, do you really think I would have called you up here if he had reserves?"

"Ok, ok, ok. Just let me think a second." Chris stood stock still with his hands raised at shoulder height, as if he was holding an invisible box. "What if we...no, no that won't work...what about the heavy equipment?"

"Already thought of it. He'll be dead by the time it gets rolling."

"Ok...what about..." Chris was interrupted by beeping from the console.

Toby leaned over the screen and read it. "Shit." He whipped around to the EVA comms station. "James, I just got a reading..."

"Yeah, I know. I heard it too. Tanks' dry."

"Ok, well, just keep heading our direction at a steady pace. Monitor your breathing, keep it even. You still have the air in your suit. That should give you..."

James interrupted. "Three minutes of useful consciousness. Five if you push it." James laughed again. "Believe it or not, this is my second time doing this today."

"Copy. Let's make sure it isn't your last. Keep it steady, keep it coming. We're coming to get you."

"Roger, Roger." He laughed again. "Although, for the record, I'd be fine if this *was* my last time nearly dying."

"Got it. Alright, I'm heading out there for you buddy, just hang on." Toby muted the mic and stood.

Chris looked bemused. "Is he going hypoxic, or does he just have a really great sense of humor?"

"Don't know. I'm going to assume hypoxia." Toby moved towards the door. "I'm going outside. Get on the mic and keep him awake. Try to minimize his talking, but get a response so we know he's conscious."

"Toby, by the time you get suited up…"

"I know, Chris! But I gotta' try." Toby began racing down the hallway, toward the west airlock.

Chris yelled after him. "Should we wake the others?"

"No point!" Toby yelled back. "By the time we get them up and explain, he'll be dead!"

...

James kept walking. The knowledge that he wasn't alone anymore was almost enough to distract him from the all-too-familiar numbness in his hands and feet; the general sense of malaise and unease associated with hypoxia. His body was so, so tired. He wasn't sure he had it in him to go through suffocating again. He shook that thought off. He had to keep walking – they were coming for him. He would be home soon.

...

Toby sprinted down the hall to the west airlock. He hated having to rush like this – EVAs were already dangerous enough without adding poor preparation into the mix – but a man's life was on the line. He just hoped he didn't get himself killed as well.

He rounded a corner too fast and tripped over his own feet, flying shoulder-first into the southern bulkhead, then bouncing from there to the floor. He picked himself up and kept running.

...

The ground in front of him had taken on some color now. James was firmly in the dome of light cast by the base. He smiled, very proud of himself.

He was dimly aware of someone talking to him. He had thought it was the suit computer, barking more warnings, but now he thought it might be a person. "Hello?" He asked. "Is someone...who's there?"

"James. This is Chris Marshall, from life-support. How you doing man? I've been calling your name for about a minute now."

"Oh." James was confused. I'm good, I'm fine. Just plugging away."

"How is your suit power?"

"Just...just plugging away."

"I asked about your suit power, James. What level is it?"

TWENTY-ONE

"Level? I'm good man, level's good. Just plugging away."

"James. I need you to read me the exact amount of power on your HUD."

James was irritated. Who was this fucking guy talking his ear off while he was trying to walk? "I'm good. Just plugging away."

...

Chris moved to the comms panel and opened the intercom to the west airlock. "Toby, you there?"

"Yeah, I'm here. What's up?"

"You better hurry, man. He's not doing so good. Going downhill fast."

Toby cursed inwardly and stepped into the second leg of his exosuit. "Roger."

...

James had closed about half of his remaining distance from the base. Despite the vague sense of sickness and air hunger coursing through his body, he felt relieved and happy. Almost giddy. As a result, he was taken quite by surprise when his legs fell out from under him. He hadn't tripped this time...they were just...done walking.

"No matter." He thought to himself. All he had to do was pick himself up and keep plugging away.

Unfortunately, getting himself off of the ground and back to standing had never been so complicated. He had to move this arm here and that arm there...then get his legs to move, and they just...weren't having it. He tried rolling his body back and forth so he could roll to the side and move his legs more easily, but that just made him think how much he must look like a turtle stuck on its back, and he started to laugh.

...

Toby was suited up. He stepped into the airlock with a spare tank in his arms and closed the door behind him. As the air was being sucked from the room, Chris called him on the suit's radio.

"Toby, you there?"

"I got you Chris, loud and clear. What's up?"

"He just fell down, brother. All I can hear over the radio is laughter."

"Fuck. Ok. In the airlock now. Headed out."

Chris chimed in again. "You better hurry, man. He's still a decent walk away."

"Who said anything about walking? I'm fucking running."

Toby opened the external hatch and stepped out onto the Martian landscape. He closed the hatch behind him. Toby hadn't been on too many EVAs during his time on Mars. It was easy to forget where you were when you stayed inside all the time. But now it was undeniable.

"Holy shit," he thought, I'm really on Mars." For a moment he stood in awe of the vast panorama of desolation and mystery before him. Then he started running.

TWENTY-ONE

Toby reached out to James on the comms channel. "James, are you there? I'm on my way to you now."

There was no response.

Toby could see that James wasn't moving. He ran faster.

Running in the exosuit felt strange. The reduced gravity made him quick despite the suit's weight and bulk, but the lightness and speed of his limbs made him clumsy – more likely to trip and fall. He felt like a puppeteer, guiding and directing a body he had control over but that wasn't his own.

Guessing by sight alone where a limb should land and where it should be directed to next, Toby kept running. His heart beating out of his chest, Toby skidded to a stop next to James. James was face up, unmoving.

"James! James, I'm here buddy!" Toby reached out and shook James to see if he could get a response. Nothing. He disconnected James's spent atmospheric tank and connected the spare he had brought. There was no sudden resuscitation. He activated the comms channel to Chris. "Chris, have the crash cart ready. West airlock."

Toby put his hands underneath James's arms and tried to lift him up. Even in the reduced gravity it was difficult. After a few unsuccessful attempts, Toby got on his knees and pulled the upper half of James's torso into his lap. Toby then rolled to his left, freed his right leg, planted his foot on the ground and tried to stand. The two men barely budged. Toby tried again, straining his muscles. This time their bodies moved upward. Toby slung James's limp right arm over his shoulder. Gripping a few inches of James's suit material with the fingers of his left hand, Toby began dragging James toward the safety of Alpha Base.

Chris's voice came over the radio, asking questions. Toby was too out of breath to respond. He trudged, one foot in front of the other, with James's lifeless body hanging next to him. James's feet left a trail in the thin layer of dust and sand covering the ground. Hardened clay was revealed underneath, itself a compacted version of the grains which covered it.

Toby lost track of how long the walk took. It couldn't have been too long, but every second counted. They had to revive James before he suffered brain damage or, worse, death.

In the last fifty meters to the airlock, Toby began seeing stars. His heart was trip hammering in his chest. His muscles were on fire. In the last ten meters Toby saw Chris's head, peering through the porthole of the exterior airlock door. Chris disappeared as quickly as he had arrived, racing inward to cycle the airlock.

Toby finally reached the door and collapsed onto it. He swung the door open, then threw James toward the raised doorway.

James's body landed half in-half out, his upper half past the threshold. Toby rushed up the few metal steps between the ground and the door, fell to his knees and grabbed James by the waist. In three quick pulls, Toby had him in the airlock. He got to his feet, kicked James clear, slammed and sealed the door, then collapsed in exhaustion. From the other side of the interior door, Chris hit the button to re-pressurize.

TWENTY-ONE

Toby lay on the floor and gasped for air while the airlock cycled. He looked over at James, who was face down and motionless. He hoped all that work hadn't been for nothing.

A chime sounded and the interior airlock door opened. Chris rushed in with the crash cart in tow. He fell to his knees and quickly rolled James over.

Toby watched as Chris went to work on James's faceplate, then lifted off his helmet. Silently, Chris began contorting his face and mouth. It took Toby a moment to realize he was shouting something. Toby lifted off his helmet and the world's noises came roaring back, in high definition.

"Help me take his suit off!" Chris yelled.

Toby moved to do so and took note of James's face. It was a stark shade of white, with a hint of blue.

"Hurry up." Said Chris. "I need access to his chest."

Toby realized Chris was going to defibrillate. "He doesn't have a heartbeat?"

"No pulse, no breathing." Chris replied.

"Where's the med team?"

"On the way! Suit!"

Working together, Toby and Chris removed James from his suit quickly. Inexplicably, it was filled with garbage, which made the removal difficult. James was still dressed in his EVA under suit. Toby noted a large, burned looking gash in one of James's legs.

Chris stood, whirled around and reached for the crash cart.

Toby grabbed the neckline of James's under suit, then tore it down to the waist. He made sure James's chest was exposed,

TWENTY-ONE — | 303 |

then began performing CPR. Toby was one round of compressions and breathing in when Chris returned with an oxygen mask in his right hand, two paddles in his left, and an epi-pen between his teeth.

Chris handed Toby the mask, then plunged the injector into James's thigh. "Get clear when I say!"

Toby heard the telltale whine of the paddles charging. A single tone sounded, indicating that the paddles -and James's heart - were ready.

Chris pushed Toby out of the way and held the paddles over James's chest. "Clear!"

James's body jumped as electricity coursed through it. The whine resumed as the paddles recharged.

"Get the mask on him!" Yelled Chris.

Toby leaned forward, held the mask firmly to James's face, and began pumping the oxygen bottle attached to it.

Chris leaned in to deliver another shock. "Clear!"

Again, James shook.

Toby delivered more oxygen and put his fingers to James's neck. "Pulse!" He cried. "I've got a steady pulse!"

Chris lowered the paddles, which had been charging. "Thank Christ."

A moment of silence passed between the three men. Toby and Chris sat watching James, shell-shocked. James, now breathing gently on his own, lay unconscious on the floor, color slowly returning to his cheeks.

Nurse Stone and Doctor Boss rushed in and began hurriedly assessing vitals.

TWENTY-ONE

Toby and Chris scooted out of the way and continued watching, unsure what to do next.

A noise caught their attention as the door to the hallway slid open. Lynette walked in. "Hey, guys, you mind telling me why the outside lights are on? I got up to pee, and..." She trailed off as she took in the scene before her. Her eyes widened as she comprehended James's half-clad, blood-soaked body. "Holy Fuck! This right here – this is why nobody wants second shift."

22

TWENTY-TWO

James groaned as his eyes fluttered open. Was he dead?

He looked around. He was in the infirmary. Across the room, the Doc was busying herself, seemingly reviewing his vitals.

Ira stood by his bedside. "Hey. Welcome back."

He smiled weakly. "Hey. Good to see you."

Ira grabbed his hand and squeezed hard, her eyes misty. "It's good to see you too."

The Doc walked to the other side of his bed. "Hey James," she said softly, "how are you feeling?"

James thought before answering. "Ok, I think. A little dizzy."

The Doc smiled. "That's our fault. Gave you something for your leg."

"Ah, I see," said James, "mighty nice of ya'."

"Can you sit up for me?" asked the Doc.

James did as he was told.

The Doc, excited to have a patient, let alone a high profile one, left nothing to chance. She broke out an old-fashioned stethoscope and manually listened to his heartbeat. "Strong and steady. You got lucky."

James smiled. "Glad to hear it. How long have I been out?"

"About a day," said Ira. She hesitated, then added, "A lot has changed that you should probably know about."

"Like what?"

Ira looked at the Doc. The Doc frowned, but didn't stop her. Ira continued. "With you incapacitated, base decision making fell to Steve. We held a big meeting. People are pretty pissed about what happened to you, but also worried. Blaine identified what he thinks is a second landing site. Bigger than the first. Charlie was able to convince Steve to round up a group of people to go there and...confront the threat."

James frowned and sat all the way up. "They rounded up a group of people to 'confront the threat'? Like a posse?"

Ira shrugged. "I guess you could call it that."

"Why the hell is anyone listening to Charlie? Charlie who left me to die?"

"Well, he didn't know that...apparently. He's the only other survivor of the attack. That gives him a certain...cache."

James stared at Ira blankly.

"We had to do something, James, they about killed you."

James held up a hand. "Wait...had? When is this group leaving?"

"They already left."

James half growled, half sighed in frustration. "God damn it. Get me unhooked." He swung his feet to the floor and began pulling off sensors.

"Hold on a second!" cried the Doc. "Where do you think you're going? Lay back down! You're obviously in no condition to go anywhere."

"Doc, I have to go. They're making a mistake."

"Like hell you do! Whatever you have to say can be said by someone else. You just came back from cardiac arrest and a day long coma. Strenuous activity is out of the question. Tell Ira what you have to say and she'll make sure the others get the message."

James didn't lie back down, but he stopped trying to get up. "Ira, how long ago did they leave?"

"Two hours ago. They went in rovers because of the distance. I think they said it was going to take four hours to get there."

James sighed in relief. There was still time. "Did they take...weapons with them?"

"Of course. They know the others are armed. Steve authorized use of the less lethals we keep for restraining people in crisis. And they improvised a few...I guess you could call them projectiles."

"Jesus Christ, Ira! Projectiles? You mean guns? They made guns in space?"

"I wouldn't go that far. These things are mostly made from warehouse spares. Nail guns and the like. They couldn't kill anyone unless you shot them point blank. It's for intimidation."

"Or to breach an exosuit."

"Maybe. But if they attack us, what are we supposed to do?"

TWENTY-TWO

"They aren't a threat, Ira. I saw it myself. I think they're refugees. Whatever is happening back home, I think they came here to get away from it. But they're ill-equipped. And the equipment they do have is largely homemade. I'm guessing they stole from us because they didn't have a choice and they knew we had spares."

Ira frowned. "Are you sure? We thought they were soldiers..."

"I'm sure. I took shelter in the wreckage of a craft they landed here. Evidence was everywhere."

"Even so," said Ira, "they tried to kill you."

James paused. "You're right. That's obviously a problem. As was stealing from us. But I don't know that the answer is to...go in there guns blazing."

Ira nodded. "I agree it makes sense that this is information the team should have. I'm going to get Blaine to pass this on. Be right back."

James watched her go and hung his head. He was still very dizzy. And his leg hurt.

"Lay down," said the Doc, in a kind but firm tone, "there's nothing you can do from here."

James sighed again and lay back, feeling defeated. He only hoped that Steve and his group would make the right decision, whatever that was. And that Blaine could warn them to go easy.

Fifteen minutes later, Ira returned. Her cheeks were flush, and she was breathing heavily. She had obviously run to the clinic. "I have some bad news," she said.

...

Despite the doctor's protests, James stood in the control room, listening to Blaine explain why they couldn't raise the group on the radio.

"It's the same thing that happened to you," said Blaine. "Between the current satellite position and the group's distance, we just can't reach them."

"When will we be able to?"

"Three hours, soonest. Which is after they're supposed to arrive. I'm sorry, James. I really am. Our comms systems just weren't designed to operate at these distances."

James shifted his weight to his unhurt leg and sighed. "I know. I know. Damn it."

"It won't be so bad," said Ira, "I'm sure of it. They'll keep a level head."

"For all they know, I'm in a coma," said James. "They're armed and angry enough to travel hours away from base. Doesn't sound very level-headed to me."

James turned back to Blaine. "How many people left with Steve and Charlie?"

"A lot," said Blaine. "They didn't want to risk being outnumbered. About twenty."

"Was Brad or Owen with them?"

"No," said Ira, "they both stayed."

James turned towards the door. "Take me to them."

Ira followed. "What exactly did you have in mind?

...

TWENTY-TWO

They were suited now, and outside, the four of them. James, Ira, Brad and Owen, lined up before the landing capsule.

James limped forward and placed his gloved hand on the capsule's exterior.

"You sure about this?" asked Brad.

James turned to face the others. "Can you think of a better way to close the distance in a hurry?"

Brad shook his head, his helmet following suit. "No. Doesn't make it a good idea, though."

James shrugged. "Maybe not. But it's the only one I've got. What'll it take for you to get it ready?"

Owen cleared his throat. "We'll have to recalculate the fuel to weight ratio, get it up in the launch cradle, then add fuel...at least an hour. Maybe two."

"We don't have two."

Owen shrugged. "As close to an hour as we can get, then. Probably an hour forty-five."

"How long will the transit time be?" asked James.

"I assume you're planning on going all the way to the second site, given the fast turnaround time?"

James nodded.

"About a minute then. Fifteen seconds up, thirty seconds of lateral movement, then freefall"

James raised his eyebrows in surprise. "Fast."

Owen smirked. "It's a rocket. You burn any longer and you won't be coming back down. Any idea how you're going to get it back here?"

James shook his head. "None whatsoever. But that's tomorrow's problem."

It was Brad's turn to smirk. "You hear that, Owen? I didn't know our name was 'tomorrow'. You realize, Mr. Wilmot, that we need both capsules present and in good working order to get everyone back to the *Vectio*?"

Brad's tone was lighthearted, but James responded seriously. "I know. And I'm sorry. I'm just trying to stop people from being killed."

"I know," said Brad, "I know."

A beat of silence passed, then Brad spoke again. "You'd better let us get to work. We'll call you when we're done. Be ready."

...

Ira helped James re-don his new exosuit. He groaned as he twisted his torso to put on the top half. Toby and Chris may have fractured a few of his ribs.

Ira frowned. "You shouldn't be going."

James put on a brave smile. "Probably not."

"Then why do it? Send me."

"I have to go myself. They need to see with their own eyes that I'm ok."

Ira finished fastening the latches between the top and bottom halves of the suit. "At least let me go with you."

James shook his head. "I don't want anyone else getting hurt. Besides, the boys calculated the fuel with only one person in mind. If you go, they'll have to re-do the math, and we don't have time. Not to mention the fact..."

Ira interrupted him with an embrace.

James didn't pull away.

After a time, Ira drew back and looked into his eyes. "Just don't die, ok? Swear?"

James smiled. "Swe...," he hesitated. "Don't worry. I won't."

...

James strapped himself in, the only person on board the capsule. His chair shook as the engines beneath him warmed up, ready to catapult him into the atmosphere.

Brad's voice came in over the airwaves. "Ok, quick up, quick down. Nothing to it. You ready?"

"As I'll ever be," replied James. "Let er' rip!"

Brad wasted no more time talking. Somewhere yards away, at a remote access console, he pushed the launch button.

The engines fired, full power. Their noise was deafening. The capsule broke free from its earthly bonds and sailed into the heavens. As before, when leaving Earth, James felt his body press back into his chair.

Almost as soon as they had started, the engines cut off, and James' body floated up from his seat.

Brad spoke again. "You're drifting now. We're gonna' let gravity do some of the work here."

"I noticed," said James, holding tight to his seat's harness.

"Your arc should set you right down over the target area. Parachutes will deploy once you lose a little altitude. Don't worry, you won't flip over in the meantime - the capsule is designed for this."

"I wasn't even thinking that, but thanks for the reassurance I guess."

"We should lose contact soon, but the sequence is already..." Brad's voice dissolved into static.

James listened to his own breathing as the capsule continued to drift. Soon enough, the capsule began its mad descent. Invisible forces shook the machine as it fell, filling the cabin with a rattling noise and James's heart with dread. Ignoring the queasy feeling in his stomach and the panic in his chest, he breathed deeply. "Almost there," he said aloud to himself, "almost there. You're gonna' make it. You got this."

The parachute deployment was nearly as loud as the launch, and twice as violent. The capsule's flight profile was erratic under such a light load. Gravity returned with a flourish, and the bile in his stomach was pushed down toward his feet, along with everything else in his body.

Blinking back the colored spots that had spontaneously formed before his eyes, James looked and listened for a hint of his craft's status. No lights blinked. No more rattling came from the walls. Even his stomach felt better. The capsule was floating down now, seemingly motionless again.

He fought impatience and tried to raise the convoy on the radio.

...

TWENTY-TWO

Steve watched as the capsule streaked across the sky, then deployed its parachutes to slow its descent. He knew from the outset that the deployment had been too late, and that something was wrong - it wobbled as it flew in a way he hadn't seen before.

He raised the other rovers on comms. "Anyone else seeing this?"

Charlie responded. "I see it! I see it! Are the invaders shooting at us?"

Steve frowned. "That didn't come from their direction. It came from the direction of the base..."

"Maybe they have another location we don't know about...shit, maybe they attacked the base!"

Steve's frown deepened. "Maybe, but we don't know that. Seems just as likely they're trying to get our attention...all we know is that somethings wrong...I think we need to call this off."

Charlie raised him on a private channel.

Steve told the others to standby, then switched over.

Charlie's voice was at fever pitch. "We can't turn back Steve! If we do, we may never get this chance again. They've seen us coming, now. We'll lose the element of surprise!"

"Charlie...something major is going on back at base. That was a full-blown suborbital launch. Those don't just happen. We need to turn back and find out what's going on."

"We can't do it, Steve! We're here now! See this through!"

"Charlie..."

TWENTY-TWO

"No! No, God Damn it! We didn't come all this way for nothing! There's no turning back now! Whatever happened back at base, it's even more important that we deal with this threat directly! These strangers are the cause of all of this. Deal with them, then everything rights itself."

Steve paused. He hated to admit it, but Charlie's rantings had a certain logic. If he was triaging threats based on severity and his ability to handle them, the interlopers were the clear winners. They were a bad, known threat that was already right in front of them. It would be a shame to turn back now, only to find out they'd missed their chance...

"All right, Charlie. We stay the course."

He broke the private link, reopened the public link and advised everyone to continue. Then he turned to his copilot. "Raise the pilot of that capsule. I want to know what the hell is going on."

...

James tried to raise the convoy again. Without direct line of sight between their suits the comms software couldn't connect automatically, and he had to guess which frequency the convoy was currently using. He cycled through all of their typical frequencies, but, again, there was no response. Finally, he tried going back to the first, main channel and opening an encrypted line. As soon as he did so, he was assaulted with a blast of static.

A voice in the static was struggling to make itself known. "...again...pilot...capsule...identify..."

TWENTY-TWO

James adjusted the radio's settings. "Say again, you are broken and unreadable. I do not copy. Say again please."

The voice spoke again, more clearly this time. "Pilot of...please identify..."

"Steve, is that you?"

"Affirmative, this is Steve! Pilot of...please identify yourself. James...that you?"

James smiled. "Yes! Yes, Steve, it's me! Its James!"

Steve sounded relieved. "Oh, thank God you're alright! What the hell are you doing out here?"

"Long story my friend! Listen, I have to..."

The encryption process caused a slight delay, and the two men spoke over each other.

"I think we..."

"...tell you something..."

"...say again?"

"...I have to tell you..."

"...I think we've got a delay here..."

James felt his blood pressure rise. "Switch to an open channel please Steve! Over!"

Steve's reply was hesitant. "...not sure we should. Not secure..."

"Ok, then, just listen..."

"...seems like we might have been alternating between the same open freqs, before, but missed each other. Encrypted is always on the same channel. Plus, it's secure. Over."

"Ok, fine. That's fine. Steve, listen to me – it's important that you understand: the visitors..."

TWENTY-TWO

The capsule's retrorockets fired hard, slowing his descent, cushioning his fall, and scaring him half to death. He landed on the ground with a spine-shattering shake. Then, all was calm.

He listened for Steve's voice, but heard nothing. The capsule had shut down upon landing, killing the radio.

He growled in frustration, then collected himself. At least he had arrived.

Double checking the integrity of his helmet seal, James climbed the ladder and opened the capsule door. It flew open as the small amount of air inside the cabin rushed out, ripping the latch from his hand.

Panicked, James withdrew to the ladder. "God damn it, God damn it!" he shouted, frantically inspecting his glove for tears. Finding none, he took a deep breath, held it, and listened for the telltale whistle of air escaping his suit. He heard only the beating of his own heart, rapid and incessant.

A few breaths later, he crept back toward the capsule opening. Peeking his head out, he surveyed his surroundings. To his left, the convoy of vehicles from Alpha Base was visible, a cloud of dust on the horizon, growing ever closer. To his right, the visitor's second landing site was also visible, although much further away than he had anticipated.

The second visitor craft was in better shape than the first. Under the right circumstances he could imagine it surviving another launch - although that was far from a sure thing. He could see areas where the inhabitants had attempted ad hoc repair work, including the installation of several pieces he thought might be EM shielding. The stolen generator was visible on the ground in front of the craft, where several wires fed from it back to the hull. "At least," he thought to himself, "they're putting the generator to good use."

He turned his head back to the convoy and tried to raise them with the less powerful transmitter in his suit. The only reply was a vague chirping garble that might have been words, but was largely indistinguishable from static. They were still too far away for a clear signal on the ground. He would have to try again once they were closer.

Swinging his leg over the side of the capsule opening, he climbed down the outside ladder and walked around the craft, surveying it for damage. The news wasn't good. While it could have been worse, his landing had been much harder than normal, and the bottom of the capsule was dented in places, with visible cracks in the outer composite layer spread throughout. He shook his head. "Damn," he said aloud, "so much for getting this back the easy way."

Completing his circumnavigation, he attempted to raise the convoy one more time, with the same result.

Sighing, with only a small grunt of pain, he turned and started walking quickly toward the visitor's craft, hoping against hope that he would get there first.

23

TWENTY-THREE

James kept walking, and the craft grew closer. He tried to raise the visitors on the radio a few times, alternating frequencies, but either he hadn't found the right one, or he was being ignored.

He turned to look at the convoy behind him. They, too, were closer - almost, he hoped, within comms range.

He placed his hand on his leg, where his wound was, and drew in a sharp breath. It hurt, and may have started bleeding again. Gathering himself, he resolved to keep walking. He was almost there...

Five minutes later and the craft was close enough to throw a rock at. He slowed his gait, wondering what his next move should be. Then, at last, an icon in his HUD indicated that he was being hailed. It was Steve. He faced the approaching convoy and opened the channel.

"Steve, listen to me - the visitors are not a threat. They are ref..."

James stopped speaking abruptly when an arrow planted itself in the dirt to his right. He spun around quickly to find

TWENTY-THREE

two suited figures taking cover amidst the debris in front of the craft, makeshift weapons raised.

A second arrow planted itself at his feet, and James stood, frozen, arms above his head. No words had been exchanged, but the message was clear. If he took one more step forward, he was dead.

Again, he scanned the airwaves desperately, looking for a channel through which he might communicate with the visitors, but found nothing. Unsure what to do next, he stood silently, arms raised, staring at his would-be assailants. They stared back, fear obvious in their body language, even though their actual faces were obscured by tinted visors.

James looked up at the craft itself, where he was surprised to discover small, low portholes with a clear view to the interior, similar to the first craft. Backlit figures were crowded around the portholes, looking out at him from inside. He couldn't make out much about them, save that they were numerous, and active. The bodies jockeyed for viewing position, pushing one another out of the way in a constant turnover.

His radio crackled. Steve again, clear this time.

"James! James, are you ok?"

"Hey Steve! Yes, I'm fine."

"We are headed to you as quickly as we can! Three minutes, tops! Just hold on!"

James tried to take a measured tone, speaking slowly and carefully, keeping his hands and body absolutely still. "No rush, Steve. Take your time. All good here."

"Bullshit you're all good! I can see you through the scope! They've got you held up!"

"Well, Steve, I think we're still good."

"How the fuck do you figure?"

James chuckled nervously. "What you need to understand, Steve, what I've been trying to tell you, is that these guys don't mean any harm. They're not dangerous. They're refugees."

Steve was incredulous. "James, they shot you. They're holding you at gunpoint now! Refugees or not, these guys are dangerous."

"I disagree. They're only trying to survive. I think they're desperate. They did what they did because they had to, and they shot me because they thought we were attacking them. Pretty sure they think that now. I need you guys to back off, so they stay calm, and I don't get shot again."

"James...I'm sorry, but we can't just turn around. These guys are a clear and present danger to the wellbeing of our staff and crew. We have to respond. If they make another move on you, I promise you, they will regret it. Two minutes!"

James tried to plead his case again, but there was no point. Steve had closed the channel.

James returned his attention to his assailants. They had looked on nervously during his exchange with Steve, but they hadn't taken any action. No doubt they could see that he was talking, since his faceplate was un-tinted, but they had made no effort to silence him, or to determine what he was saying. Instead, they had just watched, arms and fingers twitching, weapons raised.

He tried to take a step backwards now, but the two figures jumped at his first indication of movement. He froze in his tracks.

TWENTY-THREE

His eyes wandered back to the jostling figures in the portholes above. Their constant movement had slowed now, and the winning lookey-loos were firmly planted in the dead center of each porthole, with the others gathered behind. Unsure what else to do, he slowly waved his open hand.

To his surprise, one of the figures waved back.

James turned his attention back to the armed figures before him. He looked at them carefully. Their suits were ancient and bulky; not surprising given the state of the equipment he had seen before...but there was something else...something he couldn't quite put his finger on...

The suits seemed more than bulky. They seemed...ill fitting. He looked the assailants up and down. He realized for the first time that they were slightly below average height. Wasn't it odd to send two of your more diminutive people to confront a threat?

He looked again at the portholes. One of the onlookers had pushed their face right up against the glass, trying to get a better view, and James was finally able to get a good look at their features. They were small, delicate, cherubic...childlike.

"Oh my God," he said aloud to himself, "they're children. They're all children..."

Without thought to the jittery hands of the two guards, he pivoted quickly on his heel and began running toward the oncoming rovers. Luckily, the guards did not fire.

The rovers were mere yards away now, and closing fast. James could see the men behind the wheel of each vehicle, shoulders tense, poised for action. He opened a comm link to the entire convoy and waved his hands frantically over his head.

"Stop! All of you, stop! They're children! All of them! Fucking kids!"

There was no immediate response. James feared that things had come too far to be stopped by words. Time to use his secret weapon, and hope for the best.

...

James cleared his throat. "Attention, all. This is James Wilmot. I'm making this announcement because our team is about to make a mistake..."

He stopped talking and glanced at Ira and Blaine, who watched him attentively. Blaine nodded for him to continue. James made sure the intercom button was still depressed, then kept going.

"In a well-intentioned effort to ensure the safety of this base and the people in it, many of our colleagues have embarked on a dangerous mission to confront the unknown individuals in our area. Yes, the same people who recently attacked me. While this may seem like a good idea, I am here to tell you that it is absolutely not. After I was attacked, I spent one night sheltering in the wreck of a craft these people took to get here. I saw things there that strongly suggest they are refugees, not antagonists. I suspect that they are fleeing whatever crisis is unfolding on earth, not accomplices to it. I have attempted to pass this message on to the expedition directly, but they are too far away for radio contact. For that reason, I

TWENTY-THREE

have directed our Aerospace Propulsion team to prepare one of the transfer capsules for a sub-orbital flight. I will be taking that flight to the expedition's target location, in an attempt to interdict them before they can establish contact with our undocumented visitors."

James paused again, searching for the right words.

"I sincerely believe that these visitors are not a threat, and that even if they might be, we need more information before confronting them. I also believe that many of you who chose not to be a part of the expedition share my reservations. If you agree with me, and if you are close to one of the people who left, I urge you to contact me in the command module. I hope that your personal connection will be more effective at deterring potential violence than anything I can say. The flight itself is a risk, and a resource drain, so I'm not asking anyone else to come with me. But, if you have anything you'd like to express, I'd be happy to pass your message along. Out here."

He lifted his finger from the intercom button and waited.

Soon enough, there was a knock on the door. It was Kate Cooper, with Lewis Rowe in tow.

"Mr. Wilmot? James? We'd like to say something."

...

James began broadcasting the messages from the team members back at base.

"Freddie...this is Lewis. Listen man, I didn't say anything before you left, but this isn't a good look. We don't know who

these people are. We thought they killed Wilmot, but they didn't. He says we should slow down. Maybe listen to him."

"Freddie...this is Katie. Lewis thought I should say something...he says you've been trying to get to know me better this whole time and...I didn't realize. You're so quiet, and...well, anyways, I'd like to get to know you, too. You're a great guy. I think starting a fight with these strangers is going to get in the way of that. Please, just, take a minute, breathe. Make sure you're doing the right thing."

"Lucas, this is Carolyn. I know I said I thought you should go, but I've changed my mind. Wilmot is fine. Please come back to base."

"Andre, Cecilia here. You're a good man. I know you headed out there to keep everyone safe. Because that's who you are: a protector. But what if these people, these strangers, need protection too? I should have said something before you left. I'm sorry. Please come back."

"Jim, this is Owen. I know things have been difficult for you...up here and back home. I could have...should have...made it easier for you, not worse. I know you left partly because of what I said. I didn't mean it. Don't take it out on these people. Just come back. We'll talk."

"Jay, Alvin – this is Lynette. Get your asses back here! This was a stupid idea. I told you that before you left, and now look: Wilmot is fine. Don't be dumb, or I'll fight you."

Mark – this is Melvin. We're men of science. Starting fights – or even finishing them – is not what we came here to do. James thinks these people have peaceful intent, and I believe him. If he can think that even after they attacked him...well, we have to

TWENTY-THREE

give these visitors the benefit of the doubt. Return to base and let's reason together. Don't let your name be associated with something as foolish as the first war – or, God forbid, the first murder – on Mars."

Silence filled the airwaves after the messages ended.

The rovers came skidding to a halt.

The roof-born emergency hatch of the center-most rover opened, and a suited figure emerged, weapon in hand. It appeared similar to the ad hoc weapons of the children behind him, and James marveled that a common design for killing would be so readily apparent to so many. The figure exited all the way and crouched on the roof of the rover, sighting one of the child-guards and readying to fire. James' HUD automatically identified the shooter as Charlie Gibson.

James started screaming on the open channel. "Charlie! Charlie, goddamnit! No!"

What happened next took everyone by surprise, including James. Launching into a full sprint, James closed the remaining distance between himself and Charlie's rover, then leapt. He would like to have claimed that the maneuver was a complicated calculation; a sophisticated gambit accounting for the reduced gravity of Mars and the temperament of all belligerents. But it hadn't been. He was simply desperate.

As his feet left the ground, he felt the wound on his leg tear open, and the muscles in his core strain past their limits. Happily, though, the exertion paid off. He flew in one swift motion onto the nose of the rover, and from there onto the roof. He slammed full force into Charlie, taking the two of them over the side of the vehicle and toward the dirt below. Charlie's weapon went flying, and his body hit the ground, hard.

James landed on top of Charlie, then rolled off. Scrambling to his feet, James spun around and raised his fists, ready for a fight. Instead, he saw Charlie frantically pawing at the top corner of his visor, where a visible crack had appeared.

James lowered his fists and rushed to help. Grabbing Charlie's shoulders, James continued broadcasting on the group channel. "Suit breach! Visor crack! Get the door open and close the top hatch!"

The rover's main door flew open. Charlie climbed inside, then the door slammed shut. The top hatch closed, and the rover was pressurized again in seconds.

James barely had time to walk toward the front of the center rover, under the awestruck gaze of his staff and crew, before an irate Charlie filled the airwaves with his voice.

"What the fuck are you doing, Wilmot? You almost got me killed!"

James moved to where he could see Charlie through the front window of the rover, where he was furiously shouting into the driver's side radio console.

"I'm sorry, Charlie, I didn't mean to..."

"You motherfucker! I'm here to save you! You should be court fucking marshalled!"

James held his hands up, beseeching calm. "Charlie, calm down, I wasn't trying to hurt you. I'm trying to get you to see reason!"

"What reason?"

TWENTY-THREE

James pointed in the direction of the craft. "These people! These people are kids! Children! I saw it myself. They're on the run. Scared. They aren't here to hurt anyone."

Charlie fumed. "Bull shit! They shot you! They stole life support equipment! They shouldn't even be here!"

Steve piped up. "He's right, James, they've put us all in danger."

"I know, I know! By the way, Charlie, thanks for the help with that! Appreciate you checking on me before running back to safety!"

James took a breath and angled his body so that he was facing Charlie and Steve's rovers equally. "You're both right. They did wrong."

"Well then what the hell are we waiting for?" screamed Charlie.

"Because," said James, "they're kids! It doesn't matter what they did. They're kids. Scared, desperate kids. Who did what they had to to stay alive. They don't deserve a vigilante posse ready to kill them, or leave them without the tools to survive. They need help."

"They're still wrong," said Charlie.

"And killing these kids is right?" asked James.

"We don't have to kill them," said Steve. We can just take back what's ours."

"That's the same as killing them, Steve. We have to help them. Nothing else matters. They're kids."

A silence filled the airwaves as the group considered James's words.

James turned back toward the craft, where the child guards were still present, stock still and more scared looking than ever. He walked slowly toward them; arms once again raised above his head. When he got within ten feet, the closest guard poked his weapon forward into the air and took a step backward, as if to say "close enough." James stopped where he was.

Steve's voice crackled in over the radio. "James, what are you doing?"

"Communicating," said James, as he crouched down to the ground.

The guards watched warily but did not move.

James lowered one hand, finger pointed, toward the sand at his feet.

At this, the guards twitched, but did not loose their arrows.

The sand was sparse in this area, but there was enough of it to write with. James made four figures on the ground: three numbers and a dot. It was a radio frequency, currently unused. Once he was finished writing, James stood and tuned his radio to the frequency in question. Then, he waited.

The guards took a moment to understand what he had written. Then, one of them slowly backed into the airlock of the craft, while the remaining guard took position in front of it.

Before long, a crackling sound filled his helmet, and a soft voice said hello in an accent he couldn't quite place. James smiled and cleared his throat.

24

TWENTY-FOUR

The next few weeks were a blur. First, the refugees had been brought back to Alpha Base and given lodgings. There were twenty-three of them in total, drastically increasing the population of the base overnight. Some prior residents of the base, especially those who had already found a partner, abandoned all pretense of singlehood, vacated their rooms and doubled up with their partners. The now empty rooms were given to the older refugees, who benefited from a modicum more privacy than their younger peers. This gesture was mostly ceremonial, of course, as there was little of the older ones that the younger ones hadn't already seen. Still, the older ones seemed to appreciate it.

The younger ones were set up on cots in the rec area. The refugees' ages spanned from four to seventeen, and the younger ones seemed ok as long as they were together, and as long as one of the teens watched over them as they slept. The teens, five in number, took turns doing so, one night each, every five days. What would have been a massive inconvenience to your average teen was greeted as a revelation

TWENTY-FOUR — | 331 |

by these five. Their conditions now were so much improved from those of the past year, it was hard to imagine an arrangement they would have rejected.

Of the twenty-three children present, two spoke English. Between those two, and liberal use of translation programs stored on the base's intranet, James and the crew were able to piece together what had happened to bring them here.

Evidently, Earth had experienced some kind of calamity. The details on this calamity were sparse, but the children all agreed that the trouble had been worldwide, that there had been much fighting, and that food was hard to come by at the time they left. James estimated that whatever it was must have started shortly after the current crew's original departure on the *Vectio*, then escalated from there. NASA must have made the decision not to share any details about the crisis with them, to avoid distraction from the mission over something they could do nothing about. They must have also censored their private communications with family to this end, which angered James more than he could say.

Alternatively, NASA - and their families - hadn't realized the seriousness of whatever was going on until it was too late. Suddenly, the recent dearth of messages from back home made more sense, and James was both relieved to have an explanation and deeply worried for their loved ones.

The refugees were the children of middle-to-upper-class professionals with access to space technology. In short, people like the Base's crew. Observing that the battle for continuity was lost, they had sought to copy the actions of the corporate and political elite, who had already fled to the safety of underground bunkers and off-world habitats.

Space travel was more accessible than ever now, but the resources required were still formidable. It had been all they could manage to scrounge together enough material for two ships. Predictably, when it was time for boarding, children were prioritized. A handful of adults - most infirm - accompanied the children as chaperones, but, when food supplies ran low, they went without. The last of them had died shortly after the first ship's crash landing, the wreckage of which James had seen up close.

No stasis pods had been found prior to their departure, so none of the refugees spent any time on ice during their journey. Instead, they had been awake, malnourished and living on top of each other, for the better part of a year. To describe their journey as hellish would have been too generous. Naturally, upon their arrival they were half-crazed, alone, and desperate.

In an impressive display of ingenuity and tenacity, the older kids stepped up as leaders, stabilized the wreck and saved the bulk of the children. Shortly thereafter, they had rightly assessed that the first ship was no longer habitable. Using a single, antiquated rover, they led a caravan to the second ship, which, by then, had successfully landed. For the few that made it to the second ship, as well as its original inhabitants, fortifying their last remaining habitat was a matter of life and death. Unsure of who to trust, stealing from Alpha Base was an easy decision - one that James thought most people in their shoes would have made.

TWENTY-FOUR

Shooting James had been an accident. On a mission to retrieve a few of the first craft's unused oxygen tanks – the same tanks that had later been pivotal in saving James' life – James and Charlie had shown up, and the kids on the mission had panicked. One nervous twitch, one slip of the finger, and their already precarious situation had spun into crisis.

Knowing what had happened - or at least part of what had happened - was a start, but it still left James and the crew with the question of what to do next. The *Vectio* was still on its way; about three weeks out. That was enough time to decide who among them, if anyone, would make the trek back home. In another week the incoming crew would awaken, and then they could join the discussion.

Steven had considered sending the emergency signal that would awaken them early, but had decided against it. After all, what would the extra time accomplish except burning through more of the ship's resources? Better to let the ship crew sleep until the citizens of the base had something resembling a plan to share.

Speaking of resources, James and the base crew knew that their existing supplies would not be enough, long term. They now had twenty-three new mouths to feed, with more on the way. The food shipment coming with the new crew would help, but the base was definitely beyond its design capacity in terms of every non-renewable resource: food, water, clothing, sundries, and so on. Renewables, too, would become stressed over time, as the machines providing water, cleaning the air, and powering the station would have to work harder and would proceed to burn through parts quicker.

TWENTY-FOUR

To combat all of this, James had established a strict rationing schedule. He had also doubled the number of saplings they planted in the greenhouse, which had, thankfully, been designed with room to spare. James thought that it was that feature - the general overengineering of the base - which may end up being their saving grace. More of everything than was actually needed during normal operations would hopefully translate into just enough, now. But only time would tell.

...

James was leaving the office module, heading back to his room, when he ran into Olive - literally. James would have been surprised to see the reclusive artist under any circumstances, let alone right behind the door as he was leaving for the day.

Olive stood stock still, eyes on the floor, the fringe of his hair flowing down from his forehead.

James stood in the doorway, unsure what to do next. "Olive...hey! What can I do for you?"

Olive looked up hesitantly, making furtive eye-contact before returning his gaze to the floor. "I wanted to show you something. Would you follow me please?"

Without waiting for an answer, the artist spun on his heel and made a beeline for the sleeping quarters.

James let out a deep breath and followed. He wasn't sure what to expect in Olive's room, being that the man was so odd. To his surprise, the room was tidy and unremarkable.

TWENTY-FOUR

Olive picked up a pair of AR specs from his bedside table and put them on. "Put yours on please."

James did as he was told, taking his specs out of his pocket.

"I've been working on a picture since we arrived," said Olive. "I've gone through a number of versions. Most of them were scrapped. But not this one. I finished it. I finished it because of you."

With that, Olive flicked his wrist and filled the room with a three-dimensional image from his personal data library. The image was of his own design. It was beautiful.

James was in awe. "You...you made this?"

Olive nodded. "Yes. You were the inspiration. Thank you."

James studied the image as it hung in the air before him, rotating in a slow circle. It depicted the rec area, on the night of the winter party. The whole crew was represented: some drinking at the bar, others talking in the lounge, still others gathered around the central screen, cheering. It was a beautiful memory of an eventful night. However, it was also more.

What stood out to James was the inclusion of the rescued children - scattered about, participating in their own ways; talking and laughing with the others. The picture was life in action - as it should have been, even if not as it was.

Olive gently cleared his throat. "I wanted my subject to reflect our reason for being here...what I found that justifies this place. It took me some time to find it."

James smiled. "Me too, Olive. Me too."

...

TWENTY-FOUR

The *Vectio*, it turned out, was empty. Whatever had happened on Earth had occurred before the new crew had time to board. The bad news, of course, was that resupply hadn't made it aboard either. The good news was that Alpha Base now had fewer mouths to try and feed.

In the end, eight people volunteered to board the remaining capsule and fly to the *Vectio*. Each did it for their own reasons.

For James, it was his family.

For Ira, it was James.

For Brad, it was Ira.

For Steve, it was love.

For Jim and Owen, it was Brad, and each other.

For Lynette it was a promise, and for Alvin it was Lynette.

The returnees held their reasons before themselves, like beacons. Bright lights which represented the things they held most dear. Nothing else could have compelled them to board that craft, away from safety and into the unknown.

Before leaving, James spoke privately with Blaine.

"We'll send word to you as soon as we can."

Blaine nodded. "I know you will."

"Do you think you'll be ok here?"

Blaine shrugged. "We'll have to be." He extended his hand. "Be safe out there. And if you don't find anything, hurry home."

James smiled wryly. It was odd to think of it, but Blaine was right. This was home. He took Blaine's hand.

That shake, and those words, echoed in James's mind as the engines roared, thrusting the eight toward the stars.

ACKNOWLEDGEMENTS

This novel would not have been possible without the support of the following people, and I would like to offer my earnest thanks...

To James Stewart, for being an inspiration by fulfilling your own dreams, and for the excellent publishing advice.

To Mariah Bassler, for putting up with me in general, for sharing your experiences "in the biz" and for agreeing to preview the work.

To Joe Jakubowski, for your detailed critique and helpful insights – the book would rhyme so much more without you.

To Shannon Switzer, for your enthusiastic support and awesome stickers.

To Lauren Stuart, for taking time you didn't have and spending it on me.

To Declan Giles, for being my very first reviewer.

To Layla Giles, for giving me so many opportunities to write.

And, finally, to Jill Giles, for giving me everything, listening to me drone, keeping me on task, and, most of all, for believing in me.

From the bottom of my heart, I thank you all.